THE HAIGHT

BOOK ONE IN
THE HAIGHT MYSTERY SERIES
BY PETER MOREIRA

The Haight by Peter Moreira

Cover by Xiaodan Jiang

This edition published in 2018

Poplar Press an imprint of

Pike and Powder Publishing Group LLC
17 Paddock Dr.
Lawrence Township, NJ 08648

This edition publishing in 2017
Copyright © Peter Moreira
ISBN 978-0-998059-34-1
LCN 2018942991

Bibliographical References and Index
1. Fiction. 2.Mystery. 3. Crime

Pike and Powder Publishing Group LLC All rights reserved
For more information on Pike and Powder Publishing Group, LLC,
visit us at www.PikeandPowder.com

twitter: @pike_powder
facebook: @PikeandPowder

CONTENTS

It looked as if a night of dark intent
Was coming, and not only a night, an age.

– Robert Frost
Once by the Pacific

Tuesday, May 28, 1968

PROLOGUE

His lips had turned blue by the time she heard the birds singing in the ash tree outside the window. She wondered if he'd like the shade. Blue was so prominent in his paintings – deep blue skies, or a lurid blue light that bathed his figures. As she slumped in a corner with her guitar across her lap, she realized he was a study in blue. Paint-smeared blue jeans, blue-tinted lips, blue veins mapping his left forearm. His blue eyes stared at the high blue ceiling edged with molded plaster. The only exception was the tiny sphere of blood where the needle had dropped from his arm.

Jasmine had spent most of the night sitting on the ledge outside John's window, playing her Guild six-string and singing while he painted. She liked to sing alone, and he liked her music, so she often sang outside his room. She'd been tripping, lost in the bizarre landscape she'd created in her mind. Throughout the night, she'd climbed in and out the window to rap or see who'd come by to view his painting. At one point, she noticed something as she sang the first verse of "Mercury Sea":

> For twenty-six seasons now, they have found me
> Skipping red stones in a mercury sea.
> They hid by mauve bushes and keenly observed
> My thrill-struck euphoria as the rocks swerved

Just as she entered the instrumental after the verse, she heard something strange. It was a sort of wooden creaking sound, a diminishing rattle. It sounded perfect – the wooden rattle adding rhythm to her acoustic guitar. She was sure John had made the sound. She hoped he would repeat it. Maybe they could record that cool sound together on her next album. But at the end of the next verse, he was silent.

Soon she was consumed by the blaze of swirling colors in the ash tree that choreographed her song. She continued playing and singing, glancing occasionally into the room where John lay.

When she felt herself coming down, she climbed through the window and sat in the corner, playing guitar and wondering if John would make the rattling sound again. All that happened was the sky brightened and the birds began to sing. Dawn was breaking, so she played music that melded with the timbre of the birds' chirping. She'd always loved daybreak. Even the best sunset ends in blackness, but every sunrise means rebirth and creation. She hummed a melody to suggest the beauty of daybreak. She strummed a chord and heard a voice tinged with a black accent.

"Hey Jasmine."

Looking through the crack in the door, she saw Raven staggering down the hall. Raven opened the door and slouched against the jamb, flattening her afro against the white wood. "Hey John."

Jasmine nodded and kept strumming her guitar.

"John," said Raven. "John."

She stepped into the room and shook him. "John!" Raven checked his wrist, and slapped his face. "Someone come help me!" she screamed. A burly man with shoulder-length hair ran into the room, and crouched beside Raven.

Jasmine put her guitar down and pushed herself away from John. She began to scream. Something horrible had happened to John. Her shrieks pierced the morning stillness over Haight-Ashbury.

Friday, May 31, 1968

CHAPTER 1

As he stepped from his unmarked 1966 Monaco, Lieutenant Jimmy Spracklin gazed up Haight Street and thought something was strange. A few clusters of hippies were chatting beneath the two- and three-story storefronts. A few sat on blankets. Others were walking along, their bellbottom jeans flapping with each step. He checked them all out in an instant and only one looked anything like Marie. It was a girl in a purple and lime afghan who was talking to a skinny boy in a ragged T-shirt. Spracklin studied the girl. It wasn't Marie. He'd scanned and rejected all the kids within a couple of blocks. And that's what was odd. Even on a sunny spring day, there were so few hippies he could size them all up in a few seconds.

"This place feel different to you?" he asked.

"What you mean, different?" Ed Burwell grunted as he pushed himself out of the car. He looked around, his muscular shoulders swiveling with his big head. Then he checked his new J.C. Penney suit, making sure it hadn't gotten wrinkled during the car ride. The shirt still had the creases from the packaging. They were sure signs of a recent promotion from uniforms to the Bureau of Inspectors.

"Dunno. Just . . ." Spracklin stopped to check out a few more kids who'd wandered on to the street. "It just seems, I guess, emptier than last year."

"You were here last year?"

"Yeah."

Spracklin began to walk toward Masonic Avenue. "Wouldn't have thought anyone from homicide was needed here," said Burwell. He walked after the Lieutenant. "I mean, the losers around here are a pain in the ass but they're not violent."

Spracklin waited by a poster shop on the corner of Masonic, and glanced up the street once more as he mopped his brow. It was warm enough that he wanted to remove his beige suit jacket, but he was wearing a shoulder holster with his Smith and Wesson .357. "It just seems empty," he said.

"These bums never get up till noon."

"Place was a fucking circus all the time last year. Now it's empty. Think it could be the King killing?"

"Last summer," said Burwell as he looked around, "Martin Luther King, LBJ, the Pope and the Queen of fucking England could have all assassinated each other, these turds wouldn't have noticed."

Spracklin didn't laugh. He felt his lips tighten. His new partner had made clear all morning he didn't want to return to Haight Street. He'd talked all the way from the Hall of Justice about how he'd hated Haight-Ashbury during his three years in Patrol at Park Station. Fair enough. No patrol officer liked Haight-Ashbury. But now he was making jokes about Martin Luther King's assassination. Spracklin couldn't joke about Dr. King. Seven weeks after the killing, he still felt numb at the loss of King himself, sickened by the fallout and exhausted by the extra work. In the fury that followed King's assassination on April 4, the San Francisco Police Department had needed its most senior – and its most diplomatic – officers to make sure nothing ignited the type of riots that erupted in Oakland and Washington. Spracklin was known for his calm demeanor and was neither Irish nor Italian, the two groups of cops known to be hard-asses. He had been overseeing the Inspectors while working with the Chief's office on community relations. Hunter's Point and Fillmore were still powder kegs. King's killer was still at large.

Spracklin looked at Burwell. He needed to explain to him that he was in the Bureau of Inspectors now. His job was to engage these people so they could help to find a killer, not antagonize them.

"Your jacket's too tight." Spracklin said.

Burwell shrugged. "The guy who sold me the suit said it was my size."

"Your weapon's bulging." Spracklin touched his own jacket and asked: "Can you see my sidearm?" Burwell shook his head. "When you buy your next suit, keep the pants but get them to swap the jacket so it's a size larger. It hides a shoulder holster better." Down Haight Street, a couple of kids burst into gales of laughter. "We need kids to talk to us. They don't talk if they're constantly looking at the bulge in your jacket."

Spracklin began to climb up Masonic Avenue, past the wooden houses set shoulder to shoulder. As the head of the Bureau of Inspectors, the SFPD's prestigious homicide department, Spracklin always took new inspectors under his wing. So he'd invited Burwell to work with him on his first week and was realizing how much the guy had to learn. Spracklin was going to make sure he learned it quickly, even if it did mean working again in the notorious Haight-Ashbury neighborhood.

In the previous two years, the intersection of Haight and Ashbury streets had become ground zero for the global cult of the new drug lysergic acid diethylamide, or LSD. An estimated hundred-thousand of hippies had poured in from around the world for the Summer of Love in 1967. They crammed into run-down Victorian homes, parading about in multicolored clothes, plastering the walls with bright posters with swirling letters, preaching free-love. The Haight had been featured in *Time* and *Life* and on all the TV networks. The messiahs, author Ken Kesey and chemistry professor Timothy Leary, were folk heroes. Local rock 'n' roll bands like the Grateful Dead and Jefferson Airplane sold records around the world. Patrol at Park Station spent all their time booking narcotics charges, fielding questions about under-aged runaways and getting hassled by hippies.

"Your step-daughter," said Burwell, stopping in his tracks.

"Huh?"

Burwell smiled and wagged a finger. "I remembered, your step-daughter's a flower child?"

"My daughter," Spracklin corrected him. "I was up here looking for her, yeah."

"I heard it was your step-daughter."

Spracklin slowed down, almost stopping. "I adopted her when my wife and I married. She's my daughter."

They were now within view of 1340 Masonic. Three hippies had gathered on the step, listening to a blonde girl play guitar. The house was a hybrid of Queen Anne and Stick-Eastlake styles and its white paint was peeling. Someone had started to paint the spindlework on the gables orange, but the job was only half done. The kids studied the cops as they approached.

"I know that place," said Burwell, nodding at the house. "Belongs to a guy called Andy Fox, an older guy who sells acid. Word on the street is he's moving into heroin."

Spracklin continued walking.

"You might want to bring Vice in," said Burwell.

"This is a homicide investigation." Spracklin wanted to appear casual in the hopes the kids would relax. "I'll do the talking," he said.

"We gonna take all of 'em in?"

"I don't plan to take any of them in," Spracklin said quietly, as they approached the hippies. "We have no information and the vic died three days ago. We need them to talk to us."

He paused by the step and listened to the girl's song.

> *The rugged, roguish boys*
> *Run with Satin's Earthly flock*
> *It's just a whiff of mischief*
> *And it's only two o'clock*

Beside her, a husky boy with sandy hair stared down at his bare feet. Two other women leaned against the railing. One was a strapping black woman with a broad afro and hoop earrings; the other was an overweight white girl who wore a blue and gold kaftan.

> *And Jesus wore Old Glory*
> *When He came to claim his soul*
> *In faded stripes and fraying stars*
> *He pondered boyhood's toll*
> *This mischief is the stuff of life*
> *The reason to draw breath*
> *Without it life is pointless*
> *He found it and found death*

The girl wound down the song and continued to pluck at the guitar, staring at no particular point on the horizon.

"Lovely song," said Spracklin.

"Thanks."

"You write it?"

She nodded. "I write all my songs. About one a week." Her voice was flat. She repeated a riff, trying to perfect it. "Even if a week only had, like, four days, I think I'd still turn out one a week. And then I'm always rewriting old stuff. A song is never finished. It's a living thing as long as the songwriter's alive."

"Do you have…"

"What do you want?" said the heavy white girl.

Raising his voice just enough to be heard above the guitar, Spracklin said, "I'm Lieutenant Jimmy Spracklin, head of the Bureau of Inspectors. We have some questions about John Blakely."

The singer seemed content with the riff she was perfecting and moved on to a second line.

"Dude's dead," said the boy.

"I know. And I'm sorry about your loss, but we're looking into his death."

"He OD-ed."

"There were some issues that raised questions," Spracklin said. "We'd just like to have a look around his room."

The singer was having trouble. She repeated the same riffs over and over again.

Spracklin gave a smile as he said: "Of course, we'll need to ask some questions, talk to some of you. I'd really like to talk to a young woman known as Seamstress, if any of you know her."

The black woman laughed. "Are you telling me that you pigs can look into John's OD but no one's looking for Dr. King's killer yet?"

Spracklin nodded. He had just spent the last week dealing with similar questions. This might be his chance to engage these kids. "Well Miss . . ."

"Just answer the question."

"I'm with the SFPD and responsible only for homicides in San Francisco. But I can tell you, if there was anything I could do to bring in Dr. King's killers, I'd be on it. Twenty-four hours a day."

"What sort of questions?" the boy blurted out. "The cat bought it three days ago. What questions have popped up all of a sudden?"

Spracklin nodded again. He was glad they were questioning him. Conversations brought out evidence. "We just got the autopsy this morning. We noticed a few puzzling things."

"What sort of things?"

"Don't be an idiot, Soldier Boy," the large girl spat at the muscular guy. "The pig just wants to search the house for dope. Bet he has a warrant already."

The husky boy swiveled and glared at the woman. "My name is Derek and I want to know what he finds puzzling."

"Soldier Boy suits you. And now you're falling into line and saluting the authorities just as they kick our door open." She turned to Spracklin. "So where's your fucking warrant?"

"I was hoping I wouldn't need one."

"If you don't have a warrant, then fuck off outa here," hissed the black girl. "We're in mourning and want some privacy."

"Maybe the guy's trying to help, Raven."

Derek, the soldier, obviously wants to cooperate, Spracklin thought. *Raven must be the black woman's nick-name.*

"I've been here three years and never saw no pig helping any hippie," said the fat girl. "John Blakely overdosed. Period."

Everyone waited for Derek to respond but he just looked at his feet again.

"I understand," Spracklin said, "that everyone's upset, but there were some elements of John's death that aren't in keeping with a heroin overdose —"

"Tell us what wasn't in keeping," Derek said, making eye contact.

"Jesus, you're a putz," the fat girl screamed.

Derek stood and Spracklin realized he was even more muscular than he'd appeared sitting down. "Our friend is dead, Gloria," he yelled. "A great artist's gone. And you don't even care." He shoved past the police officers and headed down the hill.

Gloria turned to Spracklin. "No warrant, no entry."

She took Derek's place on the step beside the guitar player.

Spracklin nodded and motioned to Burwell. As they walked down toward Haight Street, the guitar music resumed.

"You can't let them talk to you like that," muttered Burwell.

"I want to talk to Derek," Spracklin said.

"Christ, Jimmy, it's probably a suicide. We should bring in Vice."

"Head back to the office and fill out an affidavit for a search warrant for 1340 Masonic. The whole building." Before Burwell could answer, Spracklin was striding down Haight Street trying to catch Derek.

CHAPTER 2

Andy Fox recognized the fat cop he saw with his tenants. The cop had been at Park Station and was now wearing a shiny suit that still had the creases in it. He'd got a promotion. But Fox didn't know the lean guy doing the talking.

Fox and his partner Jethro stopped by the house on Masonic a few times a week. But today they saw the cops outside the house, so they drove past and parked a block away. Their van was so noticeable nowadays. The Econoline's exterior was Day-Glo paisley, a swirling masterpiece that Fox and Jethro had painted themselves. It had blended nicely into Haight-Ashbury a year earlier, when everything and everyone was decked out in fluorescent colors. But it might be time for a new paint job.

Fox made sure the cops were gone before he approached the house. He knew the grey streaks in his shoulder-length red hair and Jethro's size also made them highly visible. Once he was convinced it was clear, he crossed the street to Jasmine, Gloria and Raven.

"What's happening?"

The girls wheeled around. Gloria said, "Andy."

"Yeah, hi. What they want?"

Jasmine stopped playing her guitar. "They *said* they're looking into John's death," said Gloria. "They want to see his room."

"Narcs?"

"Homicide. A guy called Spracklin did the talking. I said they weren't getting in without a warrant."

Fox knew they were nervous. Talking to cops was against his rules. He could sense Jethro's imposing size beside him. Jethro made people uneasy. Fox let his tenants fidget as he thought about the cops, who were likely using John's death as an excuse to snoop around.

"Soldier Boy wanted to let them in, Andy," Gloria said. "But I told them to fuck off."

Fox raised a hand. "Here's what I want you to do, Gloria," he said. He spoke to her because he knew she liked to think she was the leader. He often gave her low level tasks to organize. "Get everyone together to clean the house. One-hundred percent clean." He paused to make sure she understood he meant to get rid of all drugs. "They're coming back with a search warrant. We'll let them search, knowing they won't find anything."

Raven and Gloria nodded.

"I need to talk to Reg. Seen him?"

"Jack Magee's," said Raven. "Looking for an installation site."

It made sense. Reg – a guy who Fox did trust with important work – was a poster artist who liked painting murals. Jack Magee was beatnik who'd opened a boarding house in his place on Oak Street. Reg must be offering to decorate Magee's rooms. He would catch up with Reg at Jack's. The only thing that bothered him now was Derek. Why had the cops followed him?

"So what did Derek say to the pigs?" he asked.

"Nothing," said Raven. "He just asked them about Blakely."

"So you don't think he's gassing with them now."

"You know Soldier Boy wouldn't do that," she said.

Raven was answering too quickly. She was loyal – he liked that about her but he hoped she was loyal to the right people. She was obviously lying, and that meant Derek was talking to the cops.

CHAPTER 3

Spracklin followed Derek past a bunch of freaks listening to a girl playing "Johnnie B. Goode" on a bassoon. The Lieutenant had a feeling Derek knew he was there. The guy was an outcast. He probably wanted to talk. Just after Central Avenue, the soldier started to climb a dirt path on Buena Vista, a hilltop park east of Haight-Ashbury, just far enough from Masonic that they could talk. The thick body lumbered up the path, the heavy arms swinging with each step. Derek was barefoot but moved effortlessly over the rocky terrain. Spracklin pushed himself to keep up.

At the top, Derek turned to survey the street below. Spracklin stopped and they studied each other. Spracklin knew enough not to hurry the boy. The Lieutenant was good at talking to people, and especially good with soldiers. Derek sat on a park bench with his hands in his pockets and stared out over the miles of wooden houses.

Spracklin could just hear the bassoon from the foot of the hill as he took a seat beside the boy. He took a pack of Chesterfields from his pocket. He offered one to Derek. The young soldier didn't respond, so Spracklin lit his own and took a short drag.

"Don't smoke?" he asked. Derek continued to look out at the roofs of the Victorian houses that extended to Golden Gate Park, now brilliant with the new leaves of spring. The spires and dome of St. Ignatius added an air of grace to the hazy horizon.

"It's weird hearing that instrument – what is it? A bassoon? On Haight Street?" Spracklin said. The sound of the bassoon filled the gap in the conversation. "When I think of music on the Haight, I remember –" He paused, as if he'd forgotten something. "I recall walking past a house on Page last summer and I heard a song, that guy with the scratchy voice." He snapped his fingers, struggling to remember the singer's name. "Forget his name, but the song went, 'The circus is in town.' It seemed to describe Haight-Ash—"

"Dylan's 'Desolation Row.'"

"Huh?"

"Dylan. The singer's Bob Dylan. Song's 'Desolation Row.'"

17

Spracklin paused. "Don't think so. Anyway –"

"I'm telling you it's 'Desolation Row.'"

"I don't think so. But you've got to know it. You heard it everywhere you went last summer."

"Yeah. 'Desolation Row.'"

"You were here last summer, weren't you?"

"Naw. You heard them back at the house." Derek gestured with his head toward Masonic. "I was in Nam. Killing babies and eating corpses."

Spracklin removed the cigarette from his mouth and turned to the soldier. "They really tell you that shit?"

Derek nodded. "Some do. Only some cats, but they say it every second of every day."

The Lieutenant shook his head. "Can't imagine that. We were heroes when we came home from Europe."

"You cats had it easy."

Spracklin was about to say something but he caught himself. *The Second World War was easy.*

"Easy may be an exaggeration."

"You weren't ridiculed for fighting for your country."

Spracklin nodded for a moment. "It's one aspect, isn't it?" He leaned back and put an arm on the back of the bench. "But on November 18, 1944, when my buddy Al Howard was shot through the eye right beside me, he was just as dead as your friends are."

The tune on the bassoon had changed. It was something by the Beatles now – "Yesterday". Spracklin kind of liked it.

Spracklin kept talking – he had to get this guy to open up. "I still fantasize that I shot the guy who killed Al later in the day. Maybe I did. I don't know." Spracklin took a drag on his cigarette and asked: "How many close friends did you lose?"

Derek shrugged.

"Well then, who was the closest?"

"Mike Allison. Went through boot camp with him."

"Can you picture his face now?"

After a moment of thought, Derek said, "Sometimes."

"I know that feeling," Spracklin said. "For years, I tried to picture Al's face. I'd check a photo all the time. For some reason I couldn't picture him, not really.

My memory edited it."

"Mike bought it in January. Tet Offensive. We were due to ship out a month later. We thought we were safe in Saigon, but Charlie iced him."

Spracklin whistled and shook his head. "That Tet Offensive. I thought we were winning that war until Tet."

"I could have told you different."

"I'm sure you could have. You from San Francisco?"

Derek shook his head. "Boston."

"Kennedy country," Spracklin said with a nod. "I've been telling people Bobby will end this war."

"Just like his brother did?"

Spracklin let it pass. "So what brought you here?"

"In Nam, I read about the Haight. Summer of Love and all. Wanted to experience it. Thought about the American Psychedelic Circus in Boston but that was too close to home. So I chose the Haight. Thought I'd get my head together here."

"Interesting spot."

"Yeah. I was hoping I could move into 710 Ashbury, but you don't just move in there." He gave a little laugh, suggesting Spracklin should know what he was talking about.

"Seven-ten Ashbury?"

"The Dead, man. It's where the Grateful Dead live. I'm not even a musician. I ended up at 1340 Masonic. Commune for visual artists." Spracklin knew of the Grateful Dead, but only because he had heard that Bobby Kennedy attended a party with them a year earlier.

"But it wasn't what you were expecting."

Derek took his hands out of his pockets and rubbed his eyes. He rested his forearms on his thighs and looked at Spracklin. "Shit man, some of it is." He looked away. "Cool vibe, you know? You hang out with Jerry Garcia, Michael McClure, John Blakely, Chet Helms – cats you read about in *Rolling Stone*. But –"

"But . . ."

"People come, people go on the Haight. The guys who've been here a few years are tight. Hard to break in." He looked toward Oakland and added, "I thought I'd fit in as an artist, a potter." Spracklin waited for him to finish, but the boy just stared into space.

Spracklin felt sadness cloud his throat. Here was another lost kid. These hippies thought they were free and cool, but they were just a bunch of lost children.

"You're a potter?"

"Yeah." Derek smiled, admitting he didn't fit the image. "My sister taught me. Always loved it."

"You have a kiln?"

"I got an oven."

"That hot enough to really cook the clay?"

"Hey man, they just have to last till someone buys 'em." He started to laugh. "Like The Mantis used to say, art is not eternal, man." They both laughed.

"The who?"

"The Mantis. Friend of John's, big guy, played college football. He had these tattoos – everyone knew him for this tattoo of a praying mantis that John did on his shoulder."

"What's his real name?"

"Dunno. We just called him The Mantis."

"You're speaking in the past tense."

"Yeah, he split a few weeks ago. Good enough for him. Never liked the prick."

Spracklin leaned back. He'd let the boy talk for a while.

"He was the kinda cat, like. . . Okay, so he didn't do anything artistic. But he was funny and, I guess, articulate. Thought he was a philosopher, like, but he'd just bust your balls. He saw me firing my pots in the oven, and Mantis says to me, 'Hey Soldier Boy, why don't you just napalm 'em?' You know? Right in front of everyone. Nasty. Most of the cats I hang with, they're cool that I was in Nam. But The Mantis used it as a weapon. Him and Gloria."

"Was he nasty to John?"

"No, man. John was too cool. Everyone respected John 'cause he was so talented, right?"

"Tell me about John."

"Great artist. Always painting. Nice guy – let me work odd jobs for him, like making frames."

"Were you there the night he died?"

"All I know is Raven – the black chick – came in the other night late, four in the morning, and found him lying on the floor. Jasmine, the guitar player, was in the room, playing guitar. She was tripping, I heard."

"Did John have enemies?"

"No."

"Everyone liked him?" asked Spracklin. He reached into his breast pocket as Derek nodded his head and took out a color snapshot. He handed it to Derek.

"You know her?"

Derek studied the photo, and Spracklin thought he saw a hint of recognition cross the boy's face. "Seamstress," Derek said. Spracklin tried to hide his astonishment. "Yeah, you notice her because of her jean jacket with the tree on it." This guy who'd only been in the city a few months knew Marie. Spracklin remained casual but his heart was racing. The fact Derek recognized her jacket, the one she'd embroidered a willow tree on, proved it was her. His daughter was in town.

"Is she a suspect in John's death?"

"She's someone we'd like to speak to. Do you know her?

"I've seen her around." He handed the photo back to Spracklin.

"Where?"

"I think it was at Free Street. You know Free Street? Local craftsmen bartering their stuff on Haight Street on Sunday mornings. I hang out there myself, selling my pottery. You have to barter them for shit you don't want, but I hope tourists will pay cash now that summer's here."

Spracklin had to force himself to appear casual as he pocketed the photo. Marie was back in San Francisco. "Did John Blakely sell stuff on Free Street?"

"Naw. He just had his own show at a gallery in North Beach." He sat up and looked at Spracklin. "What happened to him anyway?"

Spracklin had already decided how much information he would release.

"All we know is two people brought John into the clinic at about 5 a.m. Tuesday morning and he was pronounced dead there. It was assumed a heroin overdose."

"Assumed?"

"We got the autopsy back this morning. His heroin had been cut with silver cyanide. There was a vial in his pocket and we tested it as well. It was confirmed – heroin and cyanide. It was either a suicide or he was murdered. We have to get into his room to see if we can find any evidence that John handled the poison himself."

"Fucking hell," Derek groaned. He grabbed his head and leaned forward. He held the pose then came up, as if for air. He stood. "I came home to get away from that sort of shit."

"Let's talk . . . " Spracklin was going to continue but Derek was already stumbling

21

down the hill. The Lieutenant could have gone after him, but he let him go. He had a lot to go on, and would ask more questions once he had a search warrant for 1340 Masonic Avenue.

CHAPTER 4

While Burwell finished the affidavit, Spracklin pushed through a few administrative tasks until there were only three sheets of paper on his desk. He'd opened a window so a moist spring breeze and the sound of traffic flowed into the glass-walled office. He studied the two pink phone messages that the receptionist – a ditz who spent all day painting her fingernails different colors – had left on his desk. Her lime-green nail polish had smudged on one of the slips. Spracklin's wife had phoned at 9:45 and again at 10:27. He checked his Timex and saw it was almost 11:30. She'd be expecting him to call soon. He placed the slips to one side.

The final document was a typed memo from Tom Jackson, a cadet who had just graduated from University of San Francisco. Spracklin was impressed with the guy. He had asked Jackson that morning to dig up background on John Blakely and the poison that killed him, and the cadet had prepared a brief already.

Lieutenant:

I was able to learn that John Eliot Blakely was the son of Proffessor Elliot and the late Iris (McMahon) Blakely. His mother died in 1963 of cancer – a photostat of her obit from the Cronicle is attached.

Merciful Jesus, thought Spracklin. He made a mental note to talk to the university grad about sloppy spelling.

Elliot Blakely is a professor of literature at Stanford and the author of several books, including Aristotle's Heartbreak. According to Whos Who, John Blakely is the second of three children. I checked with the registrar at Stanford and John Blakely attended the university for two years studying fine arts and leaving without a degree in May 1965.

Prof. Eliot's secretary told me he is visiting his son Geff today in Pacific Heights. I called and made an apointment for you to talk to him at 0300 today. I can call and cancel if that time doesn't suit you.

I checked with my cousin Max who works at the Cronicle, and there files shows that an artist called John Blakely recently had an exhibition at a gallery in North Beach called Tableaux and Trinkets. I'm not sure if it's the same John Blakely, but I can look into it further if you like.

I investigated silver cyannide, as you requested. It's an industrial compound commonly used in silver plating. It would be used in fine houseware, jewellery and among academic chemists. It's use is restricted to industrial uses and buyers have to establish their using it for a commercial purpose.

I've attached the Cronicle review and the extract from Whos Who. I also retrieved Blakely's effects from the morgue. Let me know if you want me to look anything further.

Jackson

Spracklin nodded his head and withdrew a blank file from his credenza. He rifled through his middle drawer to get a label, and stopped when he glimpsed a favorite snapshot. It was a blurred black and white he'd shot six years earlier in Washington, when he was working for the Attorney General. He had been seconded by the SFPD to the Justice Department early in the Kennedy administration to work on the human rights file, and had grown close to Robert Kennedy. The date, July 62, appeared in black type in the margin. A grinning Bobby Kennedy was seated by his desk in his shirtsleeves, his left arm wrapped around Marie, then 11. She was leaning into the AG's hug, a child utterly swept away by the Kennedy charisma. Spracklin always smiled when he saw the photo, always proud of his daughter's poise and charmed by Kennedy's warmth. He placed the photo beside the two pink message slips.

He wrote on a label "JOHN BLAKELY, 68-0528-M-021"and as he stuck it on the file he saw Ed Burwell walking toward his office with a typed affidavit in triplicate. Spracklin had a bad feeling about what might be coming. He placed the file over the photo. "Busy?"

"Door's always open, Ed."

"Got something big."

"Good, good," said Spracklin. "Just starting the file on the Blakely case. You should have a look at it today."

Burwell glanced at the file, and ignored his boss's suggestion. He thrust the application for the search warrant at Spracklin. "Take a look at this."

Spracklin studied the top sheet of the application. It was actually pretty clean. Burwell had spelled Masonic with a double S. But they could correct that and have the judge initial it.

"This is nice work, Ed. We'll have to fix –"

"I've double-checked with the City Assessor. Fox definitely owns the place."

"We're investigating a homicide."

"But Fox was one of the three top guys producing acid on the Haight last summer. Now he's importing heroin from the Far East. I just talked to my buddy Hal Edwards back at Park Station. Fox hangs around the Haight because he likes the image. But he's getting too big for the Haight. Moving into Fillmore, maybe Oakland. This is our chance to investigate."

Spracklin studied Burwell. He wondered if he should reassign the Sergeant. That might be hasty as Burwell knew the turf around Haight-Ashbury.

"You know him?""

"We brought him in on an assault charge in February," said Burwell. He pulled a chair close to Spracklin's desk and sat down. He spoke with an eagerness that worried Spracklin. "One of Fox's runners – I forget his name – had three stab wounds to his abdomen. He wouldn't talk. We dragged Fox in but he lawyered up. Turns out Fox was the lead suspect in another knifing in San Diego last fall. We gotta tell Merrill Flanagan about this."

Spracklin peeled the cellophane off a new pack of cigarettes. "This guy didn't kill John Blakely."

"I think John Blakely killed John Blakely, but I wouldn't rule out Fox," said Burwell.

Spracklin tore at the carton and shook out a cigarette. "Everything you've told me says Fox likes a knife. He maims. Blakely was poisoned – the weapon of cowards. Blakely's murderer didn't want to be there when he died."

Burwell thought about what Spracklin was saying. "Yeah but," he fumbled for the right words. "Shouldn't we tell Flanagan?" Burwell wanted to bring in the head of vice.

Spracklin tossed the package across the desk to Burwell. "We're judged in this bureau by one thing: how many killers we convict. We tell Flanagan about this, he raids the house tomorrow. And probably finds nothing. My guess is that any drugs that were in the house were cleaned out the second we left this morning. And we lose the cooperation of those kids. Completely. Or they just take off."

"They aren't cooperating now."

"One has. Others will." Spracklin lit his cigarette and drew the relaxing smoke into his lungs. "Right now, you and I have to go get a judge to grant us a search warrant."

Spracklin's phone buzzed, and the square button showing his local lit up. He thought Burwell would take it as a cue to leave, but the Sergeant remained in his seat. "So we're going to ignore this drug dealer?"

Spracklin removed the receiver from its cradle. "We're going to catch Blakeley's killer. Fix the spelling on Masonic. I know a judge who'll sign it." He pushed the blinking button. "Spracklin."

"Lieutenant, your wife's on the line."

"Put her on," he said. He nodded at the door. The Sergeant lifted his haunches out of the seat and left the room.

"Hi Val," he said. "Everything okay? I was just about to call."

"Hi Sprack," she said. After four years in California, Valerie still bore her Texan accent proudly, so "Hi" sounded more like "Hah." The weakness of her voice told him she was having a bad day. There had been fewer bad days through the spring. She was no less obsessed with finding Marie than before. But July 17 would be Marie's seventeenth birthday, and Valerie had fallen back into her gloom as the day approached. "I've been. . ." She was trying to say something, and changed her mind. "So how's your day been, Loo-tenant?"

She hadn't called three times to see how his day was going. "All right. We got a new case, an artist, and we're just getting started with it. And how's your day, Honey?"

"Oh, it's – You know."

"I'll know if you tell me."

Outside, an ambulance zoomed along the freeway with the siren blaring. "I don't know about this cake. I know it's a little thing. But I don't know about – Jimmy, what if the worst *has* happened?"

The Spracklins didn't know how to celebrate the birthday of a missing girl who they hadn't heard from in half a year. Their two younger sons couldn't understand the point of a party without the birthday girl. Both sets of grandparents said she didn't deserve a party. But Valerie and Spracklin wanted to honor their daughter with a family dinner. They wanted a cake with seventeen candles. Spracklin thought it might help his wife in the recovery from her breakdown. But Valerie had been wondering about the propriety of – though she never used the words – holding a birthday party for a girl who could be dead.

"We don't know what's happened."

"She wouldn't go six months without calling or writing. At least to me."

Spracklin closed his eyes. Why had Val added those last four words? They had been through this so many times and still she was diminishing his relationship with Marie. He couldn't let this spiral into another fight. Not while he was at work.

"She's a kid, Val. She's angry and mixed up and rebellious."

"But there's been no sign of her – in – six – months."

He had to end this calmly and get back to the Haight. He stood and, stretching out the long phone cord, walked to the door and closed it.

"Listen, Val. Honey. I was going to discuss this later, but this case I got today is up on the Haight."

"It's not Marie."

"No, no. But one witness I interviewed said The Seamstress is back in town." He let it set in. "Val, it's vague information, but it could be credible. I'm not telling you to get excited. I'm telling you so you understand there's reason for hope."

"Oh Jimmy," she whispered. "Could it be true?"

"It could be. We'll have to see. Meantime, I have to get a search warrant from a judge."

"You're going back up to the Haight district."

"I'll be there for the next few days. I'll look for her."

He spent a few more minutes encouraging his wife to be neither too optimistic nor too pessimistic. He encouraged her to plan on baking the cake. He told Valerie he loved her and hung up and picked up Jackson's report again. He glanced at the attachments, noting Dr. Blakely's academic career at Amherst and Stanford. Then he read the photocopy of the Chronicle's April 23 review of John Blakely's exhibition. The photo showed the artist standing in front of a painting. Though the quality of the photocopy was poor, Spracklin could just make out that the painting depicted the stem of a rose with three thorns. No blossom. It was called "Rose". He skimmed the review.

> *Blakely paints with the refined, controlled brushwork of a Japanese master and the howling passion of a Fauvist. His medium is oil, his subject the most basic experience of life, and not just human life, all life.*
>
> *As evinced by his "Carrion Dessert", he is fascinated by the process of dying, the gradual erosion of healthy tissue and organisms, the malfunction of organs and the end of life's energy. "Carrion Dessert", measuring 62 by 48 inches, depicts a dead butterfly on its back, four legs limp, two pointing heavenward. Surrounding this central figure are a battalion of busy ants carving off and carrying away its magnificent wings, painted as if they were the panels of a celebratory diptych. In the background, crocuses spring from ashen ground. The work is twinned with another called "Clarion Desert", a picture of a geranium that's left to die in an arid pot.*
>
> *Death is not denouement for Blakely but the crescendo, the climax in grand comedy. Death is the fertilizer of all new life.*

Spracklin tucked Jackson's papers into the file. *Death is fertilizer*, he thought. *Maybe the kid did kill himself.* Spracklin took his silver lighter from his pocket and caressed the shiny metal. When he was lost in thought, he often ran his thumb over the arms of the Military Police engraved in the silver. He looked at it and read the motto, "Of the Troops, for the Troops." He grabbed his jacket and went to get Burwell and the affidavit.

27

CHAPTER 5

The house on Masonic had to be completely clean when the cops came back with their search warrant. And Reg had to get his stash right out of the Haight, so Fox was counting on Reg being at Magee's.

Reg had made a name for himself creating vibrant posters with swirling letters announcing rock shows or festivals. Now he was graduating to murals. He'd painted much of 1340 Masonic, so he was looking for rooms in other buildings, like Jack Magee's townhouse on Oak Street.

Jethro pulled up beside a townhouse facing the narrow strip of parkland that constituted the Panhandle. The window frames, the doors, the brick foundation – they'd all been painted red years ago. They found the two hippies rapping round back, near the entry to the cellar.

"The ceiling is perfect," Fox heard Reg say in his soft voice. Reg liked low ceilings because he wasn't tall enough to paint high ones. "Completely perfect."

Fox smiled. He could tell what had happened. Reg had come along and suggested Magee's rooms could use some color. He'd told Magee about his ambition to paint murals around the Haight and prodded until Magee suggested the cellar. Reg was persuasive. It made him a good salesman. When The Mantis had disappeared a few weeks earlier, Fox needed someone to lead the dealers. Reg didn't have The Mantis' leadership abilities, but he sold a lot. It wasn't a perfect arrangement, but it was working for the time being.

"Reg," said Fox as he came up to the two men. "What's happening, man?"

"Andy," Reg said. "I was – I'm looking for an installation site." The artist nodded into the open entryway to the cellar. "I'm thinking, like, 'bout Beatles' lyrics wrapped around the room and spiraling into the center of the ceiling." He squatted and looked into the darkness, then up at Fox. "Dig?" There was a dullness in his eyes that Fox didn't like. He was wearing a jean jacket on a warm day – usually a sign someone was hiding needle tracks.

"Sounds like a plan, dude," said Fox. "And you're the cat to pull it off." Turning to Magee, he said, "You seen Reg's posters?" Magee shook his head. "They're outa sight. Pure magic." Fox had found the way to reach Reg was to validate him as an artist.

Encouraged, Reg spent the next few minutes describing his vision for the mural. Fox interrupted. "There's nothing you can do here right now," Fox told him. "You've got to make plans, design the ceiling, right?" Reg understood, and he said goodbye to Magee, who looked surprised that Reg was suddenly leaving.

Fox slipped his arm around Reg's shoulder and walked him out of the alleyway. As they reached the sidewalk, he said, "I've heard there were some guys in suits hanging around the house, asking questions. You got to make yourself scarce for a day or two."

Reg glanced back at Jethro, who, as usual, was pacing behind them. "Okay," Reg said. "I'll get the stuff and head over to Oakland for the night."

"Get the – the stuff isn't on you?"

"I was coming out to do work. I hid it before I split."

Fox paused, and his arm dropped from Reg's shoulder. Reg had left the stuff in the house. Fox couldn't believe it. He was about to tell Reg to go get it, but he knew that would show a lack of discipline. Fox never gave direct orders to anyone but Jethro, and Jethro would know how to handle it.

Fox turned and nodded to Jethro, then walked away. From the passenger seat of the van, he watched Reg nod at everything Jethro said. Fox knew he had to find someone to replace The Mantis, and that person clearly wasn't Reg MacIntosh. Reg was stoned and had left his stash at the house. Fox wondered about Raven. She was smart. Her sales were good. People respected her. But there was something gnawing at him about Raven. He recalled how she had rushed to the soldier's defense. He had to think about whether to give her more responsibility.

CHAPTER 6

Ed Burwell's swearing drowned out Dean Martin on the radio as the Sergeant dropped the car into first and inched up the hill on Haight Street in Fillmore. The day had grown hot – too hot for this stop-and-go traffic. Spracklin looked out at the vanilla tenements on Steiner Street and saw someone had spray-painted "I still have a dream!" on one building. Beside it, someone had painted the raised fist of the Black Panthers next to a poster protesting plans to relocate families to the Western Addition – the cornerstone of an urban renewal plan cooked up by some hare-brain in City Hall. It had ripped the guts out of what had been a great neighborhood, where people of all races owned their own homes and the streets had been alive with jazz clubs and cafes. Now there were vacant lots and crumbling buildings.

"Aching to get back in there?" asked Burwell.

"Into Fillmore?" asked Spracklin. "Nope. I'd rather be going to Haight-Ashbury." The black neighborhood was still too volatile, and Spracklin was relieved to have taken an assignment in the Haight. Up ahead, a truck finally made a left turn, and the Monaco made better headway. "You have a problem with that?" asked Spracklin.

"No," Burwell said, braking again for a car in front of them. "Just surprised. I heard you live to nail Bogdan Polgar."

"Who?" asked Tom Jackson. The muscular cadet in a blue uniform and black-rimmed glasses had been silent in the back seat since they'd left the Hall of Justice. But he perked up at the mention of a criminal Spracklin was after.

"Bogdan Polgar," said Burwell. "A Russian hood. Runs a gang in Fillmore."

"Polish," said Spracklin.

"Thought he was Russian."

"Some say Hungarian, some say Russian. I'm told the only language he knows other than English is Polish. I'm pretty sure he's Polish."

The traffic started to clear and Burwell accelerated up the hill. Over his shoulder, the Sergeant told the Cadet: "Whatever he is, he put a contract out on a couple of his hoods last year and the case is still open. Legend has it the Lieutenant's been burning for a year to clear those two murders."

Spracklin nodded his head. "I cleared ten murder cases in '67," he said. "I have three open and two of them were Polgar's."

He wanted to tell the cadet about the cases, but they were now pulling up outside 1340 Masonic. None of the kids was outside the house. On the porch, the three policemen found the front door wide open with a hand-written sign saying, "We're Open – C'mon In". By force of habit, Spracklin held the search warrant in front of him as they walked into the hallway. They could hear an acoustic guitar upstairs. Spracklin called hello but no one answered.

As they grew accustomed to the darkness, they began to make out the posters taped to the crimson walls. There were row after row of concert flyers with bold, swirling letters. They showed freaks in marching band uniforms, like the Beatles on the Sergeant Pepper's album cover. Women in hipsters and tank tops. A pirate ship sailing past Alcatraz.

"Blakely?" asked Spracklin as he studied a poster featuring a Sphynx sitting on the Bay Bridge.

"This one's signed," said Jackson. He stood by the stairs, carrying the briefcase containing Spracklin's evidence kit. "I think it's by someone called, called Reg Mac-something."

Spracklin called out again, but they only heard the acoustic guitar. He began up the staircase, with the others following. At the first floor, they wandered down the hall toward the music. In an empty room, they found Jasmine sitting cross-legged under a window, lost in a song.

> *So I said Hey Hey to the crimson dusk*
> *With a weekend eve delight*
> *We'll paint our toenails tangerine*
> *And tap dance through the night*

Spracklin held up a hand and the girl stopped playing the guitar. "Where are your housemates?"

She shrugged. "They eighty-sixed." Spracklin quelled an instinct to frown. He was sick of the hip talk. She could have just said they'd left. "You're the cops, right?"

"Yeah."

"Gloria said to tell you that's John's room. Across the hall."

She began playing the song again, and Spracklin nodded to Jackson, telling him to keep an eye on the girl. He didn't want her slipping out. Just as he had downstairs, Spracklin paused to take in John Blakely's room. The walls were painted to look like a clearing in a forest of bonsai trees sheared into geometric shapes – cubes, spheres, pyramids, cones. Three banners – one red, one yellow, one blue – were blowing through the forest. A covered easel stood in one corner, and a mattress covered with clothes and sleeping bag were across from it. A warm breeze blew in an open window.

Spracklin couldn't help but be hypnotized by Blakely's work. Derek had called him a great artist, and he was realizing the dead kid burst with imagination and talent. "Ed, we're looking for anything indicating murder or suicide," he said. "But above all else, look for some sort of packaging for silver cyanide. If Blakely had the packaging, we can rule it a suicide."

The other two were still studying the walls as Spracklin began to examine the easel. He made sure there was nothing noteworthy about the sheet covering it, then lifted it off. Beneath it was an oil painting of dead flowers drooping out of a vase. The top half of canvas was empty. It wasn't blank, but there was a grey emptiness where blooming flowers should have been. The details of the flowers and vase were perfect.

"This guy was talented," said Jackson.

"You're watching the girl, right?" Spracklin said over the sound of the guitar. He had noticed a jean jacket hanging on a nail on the back of the easel. He walked around the easel. "So Blakely covered this painting of the dead flowers before stopping to shoot heroin on Tuesday morning." He studied the jacket. "If we assume no one's disturbed the painting, then no one's seen the jacket." He removed a pair of tweezers from his breast pocket and tapped them against the pockets of the jacket. There seemed to be something in one. He unbuttoned the pocket and used the tweezers to extract a piece of orange paper. He unfolded it to find a note handwritten with a ballpoint pen.

> *there's a night of eternal blackness, endless in both time and space and whatever other dimension Man may discover. All of which of course is impossible as black does not exist in nature. That's where I'm at. That's what I'm exploring.*
>
> *Yours with respect.*
> *John.*

"Suicide note," said Burwell.

Spracklin read the note again, then looked up at the jacket hanging on the back of the easel. He shook his head.

"Admit it, Jimmy. This proves it's a suicide."

"If this is a suicide note, why did he hide it?"

"It was in his coat pocket."

"A suicide note is your message to the world. No one hides them. And I doubt he'd write something so cryptic."

"He knew someone would search his pockets."

Spracklin took a cellophane bag from the briefcase and placed the note in it. He made sure both pockets of the jean jacket were empty. In the closet, he found old clothes stacked three feet deep with sandals and running shoes on top. A few old sports coats and a Nehru jacket hung from hangers. Stacked on the top shelf were a few books and shoeboxes full of paints and inks, brushes and pencils. A few syringes were stained with green, yellow and black ink. Spracklin used his handkerchief to pick them up and drop them in a plastic envelope. They were probably used for tattoos, but he wanted to examine them more closely.

Under the clothes, he found two cartons full of papers – some sketches, written notes. The hand-written pages were each a different color. Spracklin dragged them out of the closet, and checked the closet once more to make sure there was nothing else of interest. He asked Jackson to bring the girl in, and flipped through the papers.

Holding her Guild guitar by its neck, Jasmine shuffled into the room. She wore faded hipster jeans. Her white T-shirt bore a silk-screened design that read: "HEIR TO AN AMEBA." She sat on the edge of the mattress and looked up at the Lieutenant.

"You wanna rap?"

"I want to ask you a few questions about the night that John Blakely died." He shook a cigarette out of the package, and offered one to Burwell. "Where were you that night?"

"On the roof." Spracklin raised an eyebrow. Was she going to be difficult? "The ledge. I sit out there and play."

Spracklin lit the cigarettes, pocketed his lighter, leaned out the window and saw the ledge facing into the bank of leaves.

"I don't like being looked at." She drew her knees up and wrapped her arms around her legs. "John told me that wasn't cool. He said I should play for all the cats I could. Every cat in town, he'd say. I play sometimes in public, like I'm jammin' Saturday at Vague Dimensions. But I like playing alone. It's my trip."

"So you were sitting out on the ledge. All night?"

"I came in sometimes. My hands got cold." She smiled.

"And what was John Blakely doing?"

"Painting. The dude was always painting." Jasmine looked out the window. "He was, like, always fussing over every detail. Yeah. Reg liked to tell John he wasted his artistic expression worrying about detail. But I always thought detail defined his worldview."

34

The girl could be articulate when she wanted to. "Reg?"

"Reg. Yeah, he does posters."

"He did the posters in the hall downstairs."

She nodded. "He can't dig John's details. It was, you know, like part of their rivalry." Jasmine shrugged. Spracklin could hear someone running down the hall on the main floor.

"Was it a friendly rivalry?"

"Dunno. John could be, oh, you know."

"I know what you mean but I can't quite put it into words."

"Yeah, yeah, I dig." She thought for a moment. "Impatient, quick-tempered, irritable," she finally said. "Some people thought he was stuck up."

"Blakely was that way with you?"

"No ... He was pushy with me. Insistent. But he could be nasty to Reg."

"Insistent?"

She paused and thought. "He was, like, always getting me to pose. He liked to touch my skin. To get the texture. Said Rodin always touched his models."

"Clothed?"

"Sometimes."

Spracklin heard an indistinct sound. He wasn't sure where it came from, but he had a feeling about this house he didn't like. "Tommy, take that stuff down to the car," he said, nodding to the cartons of papers and tattooing equipment. "Make sure you protect the evidence."

As Jackson walked down the hall, Spracklin returned to Jasmine. "You were singing for him the night he died."

"Yeah, 'Whiff of Mischief' and 'Crystal Dawn.' I think. He dug those tunes."

"Did you see him inject heroin?"

She hesitated. "No."

"Do you know who gave him the heroin?" She shook her head. Spracklin heard distinct footsteps in the hall. He walked to the door to see who was there. "When did you know he was dead?" He thought he saw someone duck into a room down the hallway.

"In the morning. Just before dawn. After Jesus took his soul. I think Raven came in." Her voice was drifting now in a hypnotic monotone. Spracklin wasn't paying attention. Whoever was down the hall was acting strangely. He heard drawers opening and closing. He stepped into the hall as a young man, medium build

35

with long hair came out of the room. The guy clutched something under his T-shirt, which was smeared with multi-colored paint splashes.

"Hang on there," called Spracklin. The hippie glanced at him then began to run.

The Lieutenant sprang after him, down the hall and into another room. Spracklin found the guy trying to climb out a window. He was about to jump into the back yard when Spracklin grabbed him by the shoulders. He pulled the guy in, surprised by how little resistance he offered. The kid crashed on to the floor. A white package flew from under his shirt. Spracklin stood in front of the hippie, blocking him from going either to the door or the window. The guy scrambled to his feet and brought something from his pocket. He squeezed it and a knife blade flicked open.

"You don't want to do that, Reg," said Spracklin. The boy's eyes widened at the sound of his name. Spracklin had guessed correctly. "Listen Reg, put the knife down. You'll only make things worse."

Reg lunged at him, blade flashing, trying to force the cop out of his way. Spracklin dodged and held his position. He just had to calm the guy down and it would end peacefully.

"Put the knife down, son. Let's talk this –"

Spracklin didn't even know Burwell was in the room. All the Lieutenant saw was a blur to his left. With one movement, the Sergeant stepped past the blade, grabbed the boy's forearm with his left hand and drove his right into the kid's jaw. Reg hit the floor with a thud. The knife went sliding into a far corner. Spracklin took his handkerchief from his pocket and picked up the white package. They didn't need to open it to know what it was.

CHAPTER 7

Driving around the Haight reminded Fox of how much the scene had changed, and it made him more nervous about the 1962 Econoline. He and Jethro had painted the van in spring 1966, when acid was still legal, and the Day-Glo paisley paint-job attracted freaks looking for acid. They could drive through the Haight selling tabs and the cops couldn't do anything. Even after the California legislature outlawed LSD in October 1966, the van was just part of the Haight-Ashbury scene. Everything was decked out in wild colors, and Fox's van blended in. Now he was always nervous cruising through Haight-Ashbury. The van was too conspicuous. He should paint the van but he had to admit he'd grown fond of the psychedelic pattern. Fox felt some relief as Jethro drove the Econoline to Japantown to leave it in an alley for a while.

"Could you believe Reg?" Fox said as they pulled out on to Haight Street. "Leaving the stuff at the house."

A couple of freaks outside the Victorian Café – a guy who looked like George Harrison and his chick in a full-length flowery skirt – spotted the van and started pointing. New arrivals. The people who'd been around for a while knew the van and were cool about it. Jethro was about to turn north on Stayman, but Fox stopped him.

"Let's just check out Masonic," he said. The quickest route would have been to turn left, but that would have taken them by the Park Police Station. Jethro always avoided that stretch of road. He turned right and planned to double back to the house on Masonic.

"Did Reg seem high to you?" Fox asked as Jethro pulled up to a red light. There was a cop standing on the corner in his shirtsleeves, his six-cornered cap pushed back on his head.

"Jean jacket on a hot day."

"Exactly." Their main sales guy was now mainlining and had to hide his tracks. The Mantis had got hooked before he vanished. Reg was becoming like The Mantis but without his smarts and muscle. "We need to get a new 'Mantis' – one that's clean." The van crossed Haight Street again. "His brains. His muscle. Not his habits."

37

Fox was sick of working with junkies. It was the first rule of the business – if you use, you don't sell, and if you sell, you don't use. Fox knew he needed someone smart, even if they didn't bring muscle to the deal.

"Why do they have to have The Mantis' muscle?" Jethro asked.

Fox thought about it. In their line of work, they needed muscle, but they had strong people in their group – Jethro, Derek, a few others. He had his knife. They had a pistol in a clip under the glove compartment. And they were forming partnerships with people with lots of muscle.

"We don't need more muscle, do we?" he said.

Jethro took that as a compliment. He nodded and pulled into a parking spot on Waller, knowing Fox would want to approach the house on foot.

"Chicks?" asked Fox. He was looking for a response but Jethro had already stepped out of the van and was heading toward Masonic.

CHAPTER 8

Spracklin and Burwell lit their cigarettes as they watched the black-and-white carrying Reginald MacIntosh drive off for the Hall of Justice. Jackson was looking through the carton of papers in the trunk of the Monaco. Spracklin ran his thumb over the engraving on his lighter, and wondered what he should say to Burwell. Burwell was acting like he'd saved the Lieutenant, but Spracklin knew he'd had everything in hand. Reg was too weak to be a threat, even with a knife.

"Well?" said Burwell.

"Well what?" countered Spracklin.

"Let's finish the job. We have a warrant to search the place."

Spracklin released a jet of cigarette smoke. "We have a warrant to investigate a homicide."

"It was a suicide, Jimmy."

"My title is Lieutenant." He spoke evenly. "I head the Bureau of Inspectors, which had a clear rate last year of 68 percent, and all but two of those cases resulted in convictions. We're the best in the country, and this is your first fucking day on the job. Don't tell me I don't know a homicide."

"I'm just saying we got a warrant. We should search the place."

"Sure," said Spracklin. "Search for narcotics on a homicide warrant. It's what Hobbes and Estevan would have done, right?" He was sure Burwell understood what he meant. Peter Hobbes and Manuel Estevan were Phoenix detectives who hauled in a rapist called Ernest Miranda in 1963 and got a confession without informing Miranda of his rights. Three years later, the Supreme Court ruled that Miranda's rights had been violated. Miranda walked, and every cop in the country was shackled with the inability to interrogate suspects, once they were charged, unless they'd been read their Miranda rights. No one wanted to be the next Hobbes and Estevan – a cop who's just a bit too eager to crack a case and sets back law enforcement across the nation.

Spracklin dropped the butt on to the sidewalk and ground it out with his foot. He checked his watch. They had about an hour to get to Pacific Heights to talk

39

to Blakely's family. He joined Jackson in looking through the carton of papers, which now sat in the trunk next to the evidence kit.

Jackson was looking at a series of drawings. They were studies of hippies. All were lying down. Most had their eyes closed, though some stared out at some spot above them. The shading was heavy, giving a morbid look to the sketches. That made Spracklin think the subjects were dead rather than asleep. All the studies had been signed, "Blakely". Below some was an odd notation: "HACC 3/17/68", "HACC 12/28/67" or "HACC 4/4/68". Spracklin pondered "HACC" for a moment. *Something-Something Community College? Hash and Canadian Club?*

Burwell came up and studied the cellophane bag with the note in it. Spracklin could tell he wanted to find something that would prove it was a suicide note. *Good luck*, thought Spracklin.

The Lieutenant began to rifle through the other papers. In the lower layers, there were reams of colored paper, which Blakely had obviously used as letterhead. It looked like Blakely always wrote his letters on different colored sheets of fluorescent note paper. His archive was a rainbow of brightly colored sheets.

"The guy was an artist, right?" said Burwell. "It's not such a longshot that he would write a suicide note like this."

"Why'd he hide it then?"

Burwell had to think about this. Spracklin took out a sheet of yellow paper with smudged print left by carbon paper. It was to an agent in New York. Spracklin read it while Burwell stood and tried to adjust the evidence to fit his theory. The letter read:

> *Dec. 15, 1967*
>
> *Dear Mr. Policy,*
>
> *Many thanks for your proposals, which I received today. I like the idea of a New York exhibition coinciding with an East Coast Trips Festival. But please understand that I will not exhibit with Reg MacIntosh. Simply put, it's not in my interest to be linked with such a slapdash dabbler in crafts.*
>
> *You'll appreciate I would like this kept between ourselves. . .*

"Listen," said Burwell. "The guy wanted to kill himself. He didn't want anyone talking him out of it, so he put the suicide note in a jacket pocket."

Spracklin shuffled through about thirty multicolored envelopes at the bottom of the box. He could feel the muscles in his temples ache as his jaws tightened – his sure sign that anger was building. He tried to focus on the letters. Each was addressed in Blakely's handwriting. Most were addressed to a Julia Blakely, at the Ashram of Eternal Benevolence in Lucknow, India. Spracklin wondered whether this was a sister, a cousin, a mother. A sister possibly – the *Who's Who* listing for Eliot Blakely mentioned three children. Wife? Could Blakely have been married? He glanced at a few envelopes and saw the postmarks were dated 1967 to early 1968. The others were addressed to Professor Eliot Blakely, the boy's father. All had been returned unopened.

"He knew someone would check the pockets of his jean jacket, right?"

"His family members were returning his letters," said Spracklin to Jackson. "What do you think it means?"

"It might be why he killed himself," said Burwell.

Spracklin opened one of the letters to Eliot, in a purple envelope. He pulled out two sheets of matching purple paper. One thing he noticed – each letter was a different color of paper, but if there were two or three pages, all the pages were the same color and matched the envelope. The writing looked erratic, especially when he considered the controlled hand with which Blakely had painted. It opened, "Dear Daddy" and told of his recent experiments in art and his success in convincing the owner of a gallery to host an exhibition of his work.

> *I'm working diligently and developing a style I believe will set me apart from the pack. My exhibition sold out in two days, and I'm painting day and night to get more material for another show. Gilbert Osmond himself would be agog at the quality and quantity of my work. My only wish is that you, Daddy, had been able to come to S.F. and see the exhibition. I hope you'll see the next one – at the opening.*
>
> *You'd be so revered – all the artists I know would want you there. If I don't hear from you I'll still be looking for you. Mummy would want you to at very least [unreadable word] me.*

Spracklin frowned, touched and saddened by the artist's obviously futile attempts to win his father's approval. Another family was in agony because the generations clashed. He moved his jaw from side to side to ease the tension.

"Why won't you even consider a suicide?" Burwell interrupted his thoughts. "We could be in there busting more dealers, maybe even Fox."

"This boy, this artist, was murdered," Spracklin said, feeling his temper rise. "His family had been torn apart by this hippie thing – the drugs, the music, the whole fucking Haight-Ashbury scene. Then he was killed." He realized he was screaming at Burwell but he didn't care. "There's no evidence of suicide, no packaging or anything, suggesting he bought cyanide. I'm not even sure he would have known how to get it. It's an industrial product. It's restricted. He could have just OD-ed on heroin if he wanted to kill himself. And I'm disgusted that someone in my bureau is dismissing the case. You have a responsibility to this young man and his family to find his killer." Spracklin paused, trying to regain his composure. "You might be in the wrong division," he added.

Spracklin realized that Burwell and Jackson were staring at him in astonishment. He returned to the letters, opening one addressed to this Julia woman and read further pleas for a reunion. It was written on October 14, 1967, on three sheets of lime green paper.

> *Look Julia, you don't have to live with us or even come home but at least open the lines of communication a bit. Let us know where you are and whether you're well. Jeff says dad's worried sick about you and at least wants to know that you're all right...*

Spracklin frowned again, touched by the letter-writer's pain. He knew what a fracture in the family felt like. It seemed Julia was a sister. Spracklin was sure Jeff was another brother – the one who owned the house where he was meeting the professor. He checked his watch again, handed the carton to Jackson and told him to go through the papers back at the Hall of Justice.

"I want a report on it by the end of the day. I have to go meet Blakely's family." He looked at Burwell to see if the Sergeant was joining him. Burwell paused, then walked to the driver's seat.

CHAPTER 9

The house was silent when Fox and Jethro finally stepped inside. The pigs had taken forever to leave. Now the house seemed empty – Reg was long gone. Fox heard someone move in the parlor in the back. Gloria and Jasmine were sitting on the beat-up sofa.

"Where's Reg?"

They said nothing. Fox knew what that meant.

"Did they get his stuff?"

Gloria looked at the far wall as she spoke. "They were questioning Jasmine when Reg got back. They were in John's room, right next to Reg's. They got him and his stuff."

Fox nodded and tried to control himself. He could feel his rage beginning to bubble, hot and wild in his chest. He breathed deep, subdued it. He had to keep a clear head and react to his own advantage. "Gloria," he said. "How clean is this house now?"

"One-hundred percent."

"A hundred percent?"

"Yup."

"Okay. Round everyone up. I want a meeting tonight."

CHAPTER 10

Spracklin turned on the radio to catch the 3 o'clock news and break the silence in the car. The lead story was the Democratic Primary heating up in California. Senator Eugene McCarthy had won the primary in Oregon a few days earlier – the first loss by a Kennedy in 26 elections.

"Oregon is only sending 35 of the 2,600 delegates to the convention, but the stakes are far higher in Tuesday's poll in California," said the reporter. "There will be 174 delegates from California in Chicago." California was the key, Spracklin knew. With wins assured in New York and Massachusetts, a win in California would all but guarantee Bobby the Democratic nomination.

"I hear you're a Kennedy man," said Burwell.

"I used to work for him."

"Loved his battle against Hoffa."

Spracklin looked over to the Sergeant, who wanted to chat now. "All the shit that's going on now – the war, the hippies, civil rights marches," Spracklin said. "If anyone can sort it out, Bobby can." As the car pulled past Geary Avenue, the news report discussed Major League Baseball expanding into San Diego and Montreal the next year. The surroundings became more gentrified. The youthful decay of Haight Street seemed light years away. The lawns were bigger, the houses better kept. Children played on their driveways.

"So who did it if it was a murder?" Burwell asked. "Those hippies back at the house?"

"Dunno, Ed." Spracklin knew he had to share information with him. "It was a poisoning. So the perp could have given Blakely the poison and then left. This guy called Mantis – don't know the real name – he was Blakely's friend and he's disappeared."

"Sounds suspicious," said Burwell.

"It's a transient population. Who knows?"

The question hung in the air as Burwell steered the car down a street full of huge houses built by people who'd made money in the Gold Rush. The window frames were painted many colors and the lawns perfectly tended. Spracklin pointed to one house that had been divided into flats.

The oak door was opened by a man who seemed to straddle generations – close shaven, but his brown hair covered his ears. His pressed black suit trousers had wide bottoms. He carried more belly and jowls than a man his age should have. He shook hands firmly and introduced himself: "Jeff Blakely."

Inside, the apartment had no color, only white walls, white rugs, white ceiling. Black-and-white photographs of bag-ladies and boxers adorned the hall. In the all-white kitchen, a woman in a yellow mini-skirt and a beehive hair-do was at the table, leafing through a glossy magazine. Jeff's wife, Spracklin assumed. They could see into the bleached living room, lit with spotlights on tracks on the ceiling. In one chair, looking out the window, sat a brooding form – likely Eliot Blakely, professor of English at Stanford University.

Spracklin offered his condolences to Jeff Blakely and nodded toward the older man. "Your father," he whispered. "How's he doing?"

Jeff shrugged. "All right."

"And you?"

"It's difficult. I was in London when it happened – I work for Bank of America and we have a credit card deal with Barclays. I came back as soon as I heard." He went silent. "I thought I could help out. Help settle John's affairs. But he had no affairs – no bank account, no possessions, no estate." He was silent again. It was a hazard in homicide. People mourn in silence, and there's no information in silence. Spracklin had to keep them talking. He glanced again toward the old man. "Have you had the funeral yet?"

"Memorial service Saturday morning. Then John's being interred Saturday afternoon in a private ceremony, next to my mother in Carmel."

"Just family?"

"Just family. Except my sister, Julia. She's traveling in India. We haven't been able to contact her."

A sound came from the living room. "Jeffrey," the man cried. "Is it the police?" The deep voice had a New England accent that sounded almost English. They strode into the living room to find Eliot Blakely, a heavy-built man weakened by grief. He was probably fifty-five to sixty years old, with a crop of thick salt-and-pepper hair and a fleshy face. He wore the type of perfect tweed jacket that professors are so good at finding.

"Dr. Blakely," Spracklin said after he'd introduced himself and taken a seat. He could feel his mind sharpen as he plotted the difficult task of gaining information from the recently bereaved. "I wish we were meeting under happier circumstances. I've been studying your son's art, and he strikes me as a young man of exceptional talent."

The old man looked toward Spracklin, not quite meeting his eye. "Talent, yes. It's a shame the way he squandered it – with those dreadful punks he was living with."

Spracklin leaned forward, his elbows on his knees. "Did you know them?"

"I know their kind. I teach." The professor studied Spracklin. When he spoke his words were slow and deliberate. "You should see, Lieutenant, you should see what I see each day," he said, using the British pronunciation of lieutenant, LEFFtenant. "I witness depravity and desolation at every turn. And where? In the depths of a war-torn Hell? On Skid Row? No, in one of the finest universities in the world."

"Sir, I know what you mean—."

"I stood in my office and watched students, young men and women to whom I taught Chaucer and Dante, applaud while arsonists set Wallace Sterling's office alight. They tried to burn down the office of the president of Stanford University. They said it was to protest the war – as if the war would stop because one of the world's great schools was vandalized. Now they've claimed my son."

Spracklin nodded. He'd also been outraged when students at Stanford set the President's office on fire during a sit-in. Getting the mourning father to talk wouldn't be the problem. It would be getting coherent information out of him.

"And we parents are helpless to prevent our children from falling under the spell of Haight-Ashbury," said Spracklin, partly as a ploy, partly in genuine outrage. "I know I was."

The professor's eyebrow cocked. "You have a son there?"

"Daughter. The last time I saw her, she was on Haight Street. That was in November."

The professor nodded, looked calmer, knowing he wasn't the only parent suffering through the Sixties.

"Professor Blakely," said Spracklin. "I'd like to talk about your son. Tell me about him."

Blakely paused before answering. "He was a forthright lad, determined." There was a steely quality to his voice that showed a resolve to say nothing uncomplimentary about his dead son. "He worked hard at the things he considered important. He was forever painting and sketching. He had some talent, as you say."

The old man's eyes watered and he dropped his face and cried into his hands as he blurted something inaudible.

"I beg your pardon, sir?"

"He could be difficult at times. I suppose all youth can, especially in this day and age."

"Was he depressed?"

"I hadn't seen him in months."

"Do you have a photograph of him?"

The old man motioned to his eldest son. The banker walked to a book shelf and returned with a color photo of a young man with brown hair to his shoulders. He had a touch of acne, and an air of shyness. Spracklin tried to picture this boy trying to persuade Jasmine to sing nude and found it difficult.

"Do you know if he had any enemies?"

The professor shifted in his chair. "I know nothing about the primordial oafs he lived with. The only person I know for sure had a vendetta against John and my family was a childhood friend called Rupert Hill."

"Go on."

"I liked Hill as a boy. He was articulate, intelligent. Came from good stock. My daughter Julia always liked him. When Rupert and John went to Stanford, Hill began to experiment with drugs." He leaned forward in his chair, his eyes gleaming. "He gave them to John and then to my daughter. She was seventeen."

The professor was obviously trying to shock him. Spracklin waited a moment, as if he were taking on the gravity of the information. "It's a terrible thing you've endured, but why does this make Rupert Hill your son's enemy?"

Blakely leaned back in the chair. "I couldn't get the police interested in Rupert's crimes. But the university was another matter. I convinced a disciplinary board that this man had been selling drugs on campus. They searched his room and found marijuana seeds. He was expelled. Rupert's an ambitious lad and he blames both John and me for his expulsion." He paused for a moment. "He certainly hates me, but I believe he also held John responsible for what happened."

"Do you think he had it in him to kill John?"

The father threw up his hands. "With these drugs in them, who knows what young people are capable of? But John told Jeffrey recently that Hill had been trying to contact him, trying to get together."

"And your daughter?"

"She's traveling. In India."

"And how did your daughter's decision to travel affect your relationship with John?"

The man's voice broke as he answered. "I told him to leave our house." Spracklin gave the father a moment to compose himself. "He introduced my daughter to Hill. He wasn't living by the rules of the household and we fell out. He moved to Haight Street. And yes, Lieutenant, I blame myself for sending John out to live in that jungle." A tear began to flow down his cheek. "Ever since I got that call on Wednesday – "

"What call?"

"From one of his housemates. A girl, um – "

"Gloria?"

"No." He tried to remember the name. "A bird."

"Raven?"

"That's it. Yes. At least one of them had the decency to let the family know what had happened."

Raven hadn't mentioned that she'd contacted the family. Maybe she didn't want to say it in front of the other hippies. Spracklin jotted a few notes down in his pad as the phone began to ring. The blonde with the bee-hive rose to answer it.

"Did John ever mention someone who called himself The Mantis?"

Blakely thought for a moment and shook his head. Spracklin was about to ask about the others when the girl came into the room.

"Lieutenant Spracklin," she said. "Phone."

Spracklin picked up the white telephone. "Jim-meeee," said the voice, drawing out the final syllable in a show of friendly familiarity. It was Merrill Flanagan, head of the vice squad. Spracklin had expected him to call but was surprised it was so quick.

"How did you track me down here, Merrill?"

"Your receptionist."

"Whatever it is, can't it wait?"

"We had the stuff tested, Jim. It's heroin. It's been cut with something, probably icing sugar. But it's 280 grams – a big bust. We're getting a warrant now. We're raiding the place."

"Can't you wait a day? We've got a homicide, barely started the investigation."

"This is too big. As soon as the judge gives us the warrant, we're in there. It's Fox."

Spracklin looked back into the living room where the professor was sitting uncomfortably with Burwell. He knew Flanagan would go in with or without his blessing. Spracklin had to use it to his advantage.

"I can't approve it."

"I don't need your approval."

"I'll fight this, Merrill. You've got to understand what the Bureau of Inspectors is going through. Even in our understaffed position, our clear rate last year was — "

"Look Jimmy, you can still investigate. It might not be as collegial as you like, but you can still investigate." Spracklin knew what the raid would mean. It would be a shitstorm. The hippies would scatter. But Spracklin knew he couldn't prevent Flanagan from raiding the house. "I'll back you in the budget meeting," said the head of the vice squad.

Flanagan knew Spracklin was after another three inspectors and an executive assistant. And Spracklin also knew the dynamic of the Blakely case was changing in ways he couldn't prevent. He'd use it to build a better department. "Promise?"

"You missed the meeting today. Brendon's pushing hard for Patrol and he has Hawkings' ear, but I'll help you out. But we have to go into that house on Masonic today."

Flanagan knew full well that Spracklin's greatest worry with the administration of his bureau at the moment was that all the funding increases would go to Mark Brendon's Patrol division. The nightly news reports showing rioting in Oakland had created fear among middle class voters, and Brendon was using it in his campaign to get more uniforms on the street. Chief Bud Hawkings was buying the argument. Spracklin could use Merrill Flanagan's support in the budget meetings, and they knew there was nothing Spracklin could do to stop Flanagan from raiding the house. If the head of the vice squad wanted to move on the house, he could move with or without Spracklin's permission. This call was simply a courtesy.

"When do you expect to go in?"

"We're just typing up the affidavit."

Spracklin checked his watch. It was 4:15. He asked Flanagan to call him at home once the warrant was approved. He'd join the raid and bring Burwell with him. He hung up and quickly called the Homicide department. He got hold of Jackson. He asked the cadet to find Rupert Hill's address and to contact Stanford for confirmation the boy had been expelled. Then he went to make his farewells to the bereaved father.

CHAPTER 11

Andy Fox watched Derek the Soldier work on his handmade potter's wheel in the basement of 1340 Masonic. His massive hands, covered with watery clay, pulled up the walls of a curvy vase. He was oblivious to Fox, Jethro and their mounting rage.

Fox admired Derek's competence. He knew some people thought Derek was stupid because he moved and spoke slowly. But Fox sensed Derek was just ponderous, cautious. Derek had depth. Reg, on the other hand, was stupid. He had proved that today. What was perplexing was that Fox couldn't get through to Derek. Fox took pride in his ability to understand what made individuals tick, and to use that knowledge to his advantage. He searched for the unique element in each person that would win his or her trust. Derek was a craftsman, and Fox had shown an interest in his craft. The guy had not responded. Fox asked Derek about the war. No answer. Now the drug dealer was ready to try a different tack. He was about to challenge Derek's courage as a soldier. Reg had just lost Fox's stash of heroin, and Fox felt like testing someone's toughness. It might as well be Derek.

"What you making, Derek?" Fox asked.

Derek jumped, his thumb slipping and making a dent in his pot.

"Andy," he said. "I was focused on my vase. Didn't see you."

Fox and Jethro studied the ruined vase, slumping into shapelessness as it spun around. Fox looked over at the shelf and saw a half-dozen pots that were still drying. They were various shades of grey. Another dozen were white. Derek had baked them.

"So how many of these you knock out a day?"

"I can throw about four an hour. The slow part is firing 'em."

"You don't paint them?"

"I'd need a kiln to glaze them."

"Expensive?"

"Four-hundred bucks used."

"What did the cops want?"

Derek shrugged. He seemed calm. It pissed Fox off. "They said they were looking into John's death."

Fox squatted beside him. The soldier's broad forearms, wet clay dripping from them, rested on his upper legs. "I know that," said Fox. "What I want to know is what you talked about when you met Spanking or whatever his name is."

"Spracklin," Derek said. "Spracklin." Jethro took up a position behind the soldier. "He followed me up Buena Vista. He had some questions about Blakely. I told him about John. That's all. Don't matter. Dude's dead."

"What was he like, this Spracklin guy?"

"Like how?"

"Ballbreaker? Threaten you? Pretend to be friends? If a pig has your number, you gotta study him."

"He was, I don't know. Nice guy. A former soldier. I thought he was straight."

"Now this is important, Derek. Did he act like he was investigating a murder? Or was he just—"

"Oh yeah," Derek said. "He said someone cut John's stash with poison, cyanide, I think. He has a suspect." Fox was surprised, and tried to hide it. "Yeah, he was asking about some chick called Seamstress. Has a photo of her and everything."

Fox remembered The Seamstress. She was a pretty brunette who did wall hangings and sewing. Elegant. He hadn't seen her in months.

"I heard she just got back from the East Coast," said Derek. "She knew some cats in this very house, right?"

"Did you tell him about her?"

"Said I knew of her." Derek glanced back at Jethro. "Then I figured I shouldn't say too much, so I didn't tell him where she was."

"Where is she?"

"She's hanging out at Vague Dimensions." Fox nodded. A German businessman had opened the club, hoping it would be the next Fillmore. There was an old catwalk leading to the lighting booth above its stage. Fox sometimes crashed there when he needed a place to sleep. "She's doing odd jobs in the office. I saw her when I was down there Wednesday. All I told the cop was she was hanging out at Free Street."

"Except everyone knows you don't talk to cops at all," Fox said. Derek didn't flinch. Maybe Nam killed something in him, thought Fox. He sometime wondered if he'd enjoy Nam. The government would pay him to do a lot of what he did on the Haight.

As Jethro reached around and bent Derek's arms behind his back, Fox whispered: "I want you to take this like a soldier. No screaming." He pulled the knife out of his pocket. The blade flicked open.

"Gonna cut my toe off?" Derek asked, as Jethro lashed his wrists with a length of rope.

"No," said Fox. "It makes it hard to walk. That's bad. Especially with people who owe me money. It affects their earning potential."

"I don't owe you bread, man."

Fox scraped away the muddy liquid on Derek's lower arm, revealing the needle tracks. "But you would, Derek." He poked the scars with the knife. "If you couldn't work, you'd still need what I have, and you'd owe me real soon."

"I'm not an addict." Derek said. Jethro placed his arms around the soldier and squeezed. Fox studied Derek's eyes for some sign of fear, but the soldier just kept staring back at him.

"What concerns me isn't your addiction but your decision to talk to the cops." Jethro tightened his grip – he liked to pit his strength against a guy writhing in agony. Fox had never seen even a panic-stricken man that could overpower Jethro. He considered cutting off all Derek's heroin tracks but the guy might bleed to death. "You have to realize no one can talk to the pigs." Fox wondered what it would take to scare the guy. He was intrigued by Derek's stoicism. At least Derek was tense now, and the shoulder muscles bulged as he strained at the cords.

"I don't want you to yell," Fox said. He stared into the soldier's eyes. They were showing hatred, not fear. He placed the knife on Derek's shoulder, just at the top of the bulge. Derek clenched his teeth but did not scream. He had a soldier's mentality and an artist's sensitivity – a fascinating man, thought Fox. With his left hand, he pinched the point of the blade and used both hands to bring the knife down so it peeled off a thick layer of shoulder muscle. He moved to one side to avoid the gushing blood. Derek kept his mouth closed, and his muffled cries filled the room.

Fox inspected the slab of skin and muscle on the blade. Jethro still grasped Derek and the blood began to stain the big man's left sleeve. "Quiet," Fox said. Derek continued to keep his mouth closed as he moaned through his nose. "Quiet. You're a soldier. You've learned to accept pain." Fox tossed the slab of flesh into the spinning vase and a few drops of blood flew from it as it rotated. Derek got control of himself. His breath came in gasps but he was no longer trying to scream. "Jethro's going to let go of you. You're going to show us you can control your pain."

Derek was grimacing with agony, but he remained stoic. "Now what you should know is that we'll make sure you're supplied. The cops busted Reg today and we lost a lot of shit, but not all of it. You'll be okay. But no one talks to the pigs."

The blood was pouring from Derek's shoulder. Jethro slowly let go of him, untied the chord and stood again. Derek's right hand shot up and covered the wound. Blood seeped between his fingers. Fox thought he was going to spit abuse at him but he just glared at his attacker. Fox walked over to the shelf, grabbed some paper towel and wiped off the blade.

"Go dress your wound," he said. "Jethro and I are staying here for dinner. We need to talk to everyone and want you there." He picked the slab of skin and muscle from the ruined vase, wrapped it in the paper towel and slid it into his pocket.

CHAPTER 12

Johnny Walker Black Label always helped Jimmy Spracklin transition from the stresses of work to the stresses of family. By the second glass, just floating the ice, he'd begun to relax into an evening on the floral couch with Valerie and the boys. Watching Get Smart, he had to simultaneously finish off his paperwork and keep the peace between the boys. Eight-year-old John-John, born the same year as President Kennedy's son, was exaggerating his laughter at all the jokes on Get Smart, knowing it annoyed Sam, two years his senior. The little brother knew Sam couldn't belt him while his parents were in the room.

"John-John, son, it would help if you laughed a little more quietly," Spracklin said without looking up from his notebook.

"But it's so funny."

"We've all heard him say 'Sorry about that, Chief,' before. Just tone it down a bit."

"You boys behave yourselves," said Valerie, her voice tense. "Or you won't be going to see Monkey World this weekend."

"It's Planet of the Apes, Mom," said Sam. "And Dad promised."

To his left, Valerie fidgeted, uncrossing and crossing her legs. They were all used to him working at home during week nights. He didn't like the inspectors to see him filling out reports at work because it made him look like a bureaucrat. Monday to Friday he signed reports while watching TV with the family. He took Saturday off and on Sunday he polished his wingtips and cleaned his handgun. He'd already signed a stack of administrative papers for the Bureau of Inspectors, and skimmed a report on a modernization of the evidence repository. Now he was going over his notes from the Blakely case.

"All you need to do is mention to them there's been a report she's been sighted," Valerie said.

"I'll mention it."

"Can you make sure it's included in the briefing? Before each patrol shift?"

Spracklin tried to be patient with his wife because he understood how Marie's disappearance had worn her out. She had barely aged through the first fifteen

55

years he had known her. She'd been youthful in widowhood, through the birth of four healthy children, and with the worries that hound the wives of all policemen. But ten months of not knowing where her daughter was had aged her. She now seemed hollowed out.

Born Valerie Palin, she was a slight woman with sandy brown hair, and her nervous energy had maintained her thin figure. She'd been a widow two years when Jimmy Spracklin met her in San Antonio in 1953. Her first husband, George Mercer, had survived the Bataan Death March and a Japanese POW camp, but had come home a broken man. He had been unable to work, barely able to function. In 1951, he drove his Chevy pickup into an oak tree on a winding road, killing not only himself but also his and Val's three-year-old son. Valerie and one-year-old Marie were alone, finding strength only in their family, their church and each other. She took a job as a receptionist at the local police academy, where she met a visiting sergeant, James Spracklin from San Francisco. He fell in love with the sprightly Texan and her studious little girl. He married the mother and adopted the girl. He loved Marie as deeply as he later did the two boys he and Valerie produced together.

"I said I'd mention it, Val," he said. Her hair had greyed so quickly, and her eyes were wrinkled with worry. It still surprised him. "We want to do what's most effective."

"But what's most effective?"

He put a hand on her knee. "It's almost July, Honey. I told you what it was like last year." In July and August 1967, the police department had received about one-thousand missing juvenile reports each week. The department was inundated by pleading calls from parents across the U.S., even Canada and England, searching for lost minors. The Spracklins did not want their requests lost in the babble of all the calls.

They had realized the human cost of the swarm of kids on Haight-Ashbury on August 23, the day Marie didn't come home from a trip to the mall with some friends. They spent the day patrolling the neighborhood looking for Marie, who had turned sixteen a month earlier. The hours of worry soon gave way to days of panic then months of misery. The panic was horrendous – Val's crying, her praying, their sleepless nights, the expectation they would be called to the morgue to identify her at any time. The officials tried to empathize, but they had been desensitized by the number of families in similar straits. Yes, the Spracklins had told them, they had been fighting more often with Marie lately. Yes, she had been drawn to the hippie culture. Yes, Valerie admitted, she knew the girl had smoked pot – information she'd withheld from her husband. They were hopeful when they'd heard that one of the neighborhood teens saw Marie in Haight-Ashbury. It led to the evenings in late summer and fall when Spracklin would cruise through Haight-Ashbury in search of Marie. He found her once, brought her home, and she was gone again two days later. Now he had to convince his wife he could find the girl again.

"Now look Honey, in the next few days I'm going to be spending time in the Haight – maybe even tonight if Flanagan gets his search warrant. I'll look for her. You know I will."

"But Jimmy, you get so very busy," Val said. Sam glanced back at his mother, his glance asking if she had to speak so loud. "You've got this case, and the Bureau to run. And the meeting with Bobby. And I don't know—"

"What meeting with Bobby?" He didn't have to ask for a last name. If they mentioned a Bobby, it meant Kennedy.

She stopped mid-sentence and gave him a puzzled look. "I told you about Jack Herbert's call."

"No, you didn't."

"I thought I did. The note's on your desk. Jack called this afternoon and said Senator Kennedy's getting together with old friends in the Bay area. They want to know if you can make it."

Spracklin took a sip of his drink and felt the burning liquid slide down his throat.

"Is something wrong, Jimmy?"

"Well, I'm a bit surprised you didn't mention it. I mean, Bobby's the guy who may give me a job in Washington."

"But things change. Marie might be back in the Bay Area."

"We agreed: if I can get Bud Hawking's job I'll take it. If I don't get it we'll see what the opportunities are like in Washington." For years, they'd both been planning on him becoming police chief when the current chief retired. He was now one of a few internal candidates, and the commission could always choose someone outside. So when Bobby Kennedy announced he would seek the Democratic nomination, they realized they had another option: they might join the second Kennedy administration in Washington. It would be a chance to move away from the house where they'd experienced so much misery.

"But that was before Marie was seen here."

"We have a vague report."

"But there's a chance she's here. And if there's a chance, we couldn't go to Washington." He wanted to be angry with his wife, but couldn't. He knew what the last ten months had done to her – the yearning to see her daughter again, just to see her. He knew how she jumped every time the phone rang, hoping it was Marie and dreading bad news. He knew she contacted the Haight-Ashbury

Switchboard, a community group that connected parents with runaways, vainly leaving a message for Marie. He understood the physical pain in the gut she suffered from worrying. He felt it himself. "She's my daughter, Jimmy."

The tears were beginning to well in her eyes.

"She's my daughter too."

They gazed into each other's faces, neither daring to say what they were thinking. Val didn't say Marie was her biological child and that was different than an adopted daughter. Spracklin couldn't say he knew she blamed him for Marie's disappearance and for allegedly preferring the two boys. Those words always led to a fight.

The silence was broken by the phone ringing. Spracklin strode to the kitchen, careful not to slip on the freshly waxed floor. Valerie had consumed herself in housework since Marie left, trying to distract herself from the enduring crisis. The black and white checks of the kitchen floor, like the rest of the house, glistened – space age shiny, space age tough, as the ad said.

He lifted the black receiver from the cradle and said hello.

"Good news or bad news?" asked a gruff voice. It was Merrill Flanagan.

"Gimme the bad news."

"It only applies to daylight hours." Spracklin understood immediately. The good news was they got the search warrant. But the judge had placed a restriction on it – they could only go into the house during day time. They'd found a quarter pound of heroin in the place and the judge was protecting the hippies' civil rights. Typical, he thought.

"What judge did you get?"

"Hamlin"

"Ooooh! So when are you going in?"

"O-six-hundred. Sharp."

"See you then."

Spracklin hung up and thought for a moment. He called Burwell and Jackson to tell them to be at 1340 Masonic at 5:30 the next morning. Neither complained that it was a Saturday morning. The television show had ended and Spracklin could hear Valerie herding the boys upstairs. He returned to the family room and picked up his notes on the foolscap pad. He studied what he'd written during Get Smart. He tried again to make sense of it.

Reg MacIntosh	*Artist – Rivalry?*
Derek ???	*Teased about being soldier*
Jasmine (Real name?)	*Pressured into sex?*

Rupert Hill	Vendetta against family.
Gloria ???	Loud mouth (harmless?)
Raven (Real name?)	Don't know enough yet. Withheld info.
Andy Fox Drug dealer	Did Blakely owe him money?
The Mantis ?????????	

He reread it several more times. Then he wrote two more words at the bottom of the sheet: "Silver Cyanide". *Why silver cyanide?* He had double-checked with the pathologist and confirmed that it was indeed silver cyanide, not another poison. As Spracklin studied his list of suspects, he saw none that would have access to silver cyanide. He needed information.

He walked to his office and took out a small notebook from the desk drawer. He dialed a number from the back page, ready to hang up if the wrong person answered, but he heard the familiar voice.

"Is this Jerry's Pizza?" Spracklin asked. It was the password he always used.

"It's all right. I'm alone. Hang on." Spracklin waited while Mel Byatt turned down the TV.

"How you doing, Mel?"

"Squeezed for time, my man. What's your passion?"

Mel had been the driver in a liquor store robbery that went bad in 1957, and Spracklin had arrested and convicted him. One of the assailants had panicked and begun shooting, killing a customer. Mel had pleaded guilty to being an accessory to a capital crime, and served twenty-eight months at San Quentin. He'd found religion in prison. When he got out, he returned to his parents' flat on Eddy Street. He worked odd hours in an auto shop and spent most of his time organizing a program for troubled youth with the Salvation Army. When he ran into Spracklin in the street, the Lieutenant had expected the ex-con to threaten him. Instead Mel shook his hand and thanked him for setting him on the path to salvation. Since then Spracklin had used Mel for information on the street in the area around Fillmore. Mel had even supplied information on Bogdan Polgar. If Polgar had known, Mel would have been killed. But Mel was always nonchalant about sharing what he knew with the detective.

"How's your man?" asked Spracklin, referring to Polgar.

"Nothin' new to relay to you."

"I need dope on Andy Fox."

"Word is he's moving our way." Our way meant he was moving into the Fillmore.

"That's what I hear. What do you know?"

"Bogdan wanted to avoid bloodshed, God bless him. It could have been ugly, man, really ugly. So the word is they drew a line at Grove Street. Fox don't go north of it and Bogdan don't go South. And Bogdan helped him out." Spracklin nodded. They had divided the Fillmore neighborhood, which meant Polgar had given up turf.

"What do you mean helped him out?"

"Bogdan bank-rolled him."

"How much?"

"Dunno. Bogdan hasn't shown me his books and it would be, um, impudent to ask." He laughed. Spracklin laughed as well, just loud enough that Mel could hear him.

"But it's enough money that you know about it?" he asked.

"Bogdan has let a few people know what the situation is." Maybe this did make sense. If Polgar was making money off his loans to Fox, maybe he could make money without having his guys actually selling in some areas.

"What can you tell me about Fox?"

"Nasty reputation. I don't know particulars but no one wants to get on the bad side of him."

"Thank you, Mel. I owe you."

"No, Sir, I owe you."

Spracklin hung up the phone and thought about what he'd learned. He put on his shoulder holster and a windbreaker over it. He wandered into the family room and turned the channel to Channel 4. He checked every night in case there was something new on the King case. Nothing but shots of Russian tanks rolling through Prague. He couldn't believe it. They still hadn't caught King's killer after seven weeks.

"They're in bed," said Valerie, as she entered the room. "Was that Merrill Flanagan?"

"Yeah."

"And the raid?"

"Ready to go. We're going in at midnight." He checked his watch. "You know, if I head down now, I could do a patrol and look for Marie before we go in."

He knew his wife would buy into that. He also knew he would have several hours to investigate the Blakely case before Merrill Flanagan raided the house and muddied the waters.

Val came up to him, wrapped her arms around his waist, and held him tight. "Well, you be careful out there, Loo-tenant Spracklin."

"I'm always careful."

"Keep that gun in its holster."

"I'm a crack shot, Honey. Everyone knows it."

She stepped back, held him at arms-length and smiled. "I clean the toilets in this house, Loo-tenant. I know what your aim's like." They both laughed. "That's why I said be careful."

He pulled her to him, stroked her hair and kissed her, thankful that he occasionally still caught glimpses of the woman he'd married.

CHAPTER 13

Once night fell, Haight-Ashbury tried to recapture the atmosphere of the Summer of Love. Spracklin's patrol took him past scattered groups of hippies in tie-dyed shirts, fluorescent pants, Joe Cocker shirts and floppy felt hats. But there was no sign of Marie. It had been so long since he'd seen her, he started to wonder if he'd still recognize his daughter. The thought made his gut swirl with anxiety. After searching for an hour, he wandered to Masonic, wondering if he'd have more success investigating the Blakely case.

He stood in the shadow of an Econoline van painted with paisley designs, and gazed at the house. He needed to talk to Raven – she'd been the first to arrive at the death scene after Jasmine. She might prove cooperative if he showed he knew she'd contacted Blakely's family. He also wanted Gloria to open up – she seemed to be one of the ringleaders.

He squeezed through a narrow alleyway and found himself in the back yard. The far window was open, and he could hear a guitar. Crouching in the shadows, he crept closer.

He stopped beneath a blackened window. Candlelight was flickering against the high ceiling. Jasmine was sitting on a sofa. Before her on a coffee table, half a dozen homemade candles dripped wax down the sides of the empty wine bottles that held them. Jasmine was strumming and singing. She did not seem well coordinated and her voice was weaker than before.

> *In back a rusty pickup on a dusty mountain road*
> *Hurtling t'ward a blues show in a clearing in a wood*

The lyrics held him for a moment. Jasmine had struck him as a burned-out acid head. But she produced these lyrics. It seemed impossible. *Could a woman who seemed to barely speak really write such lines?* Jasmine realized the guitar was running ahead of her singing. She paused, studied the words in a notebook, got her timing right and started the next verse.

> *Sunset turning mauve mirrored on a lake below*
> *You sat up on a tailgate and Timmy held you so*
> *Your fates were chained together, arm on shoulder, on the fly*
> *Two swaying, solid silhouettes before the purple sky.*

"That's lovely, dear," said a woman's voice, surprising him. Spracklin couldn't see who it was. He fought the urge to stand and possibly give himself away. Jasmine jotted something – he assumed her lyrics – down in a notebook beside her.

"I needed, you know, something different," said Jasmine.

"I know you did."

Spracklin was sure the other woman was Gloria, but she sounded pleasant.

"It's like, too much 'Whiff of Mischief'," said Jasmine. "You know. I had that song in my head all week. Like it lived there. I needed to write something new." She put the guitar down and rested her head in her hands. "It's a bummer week," she said.

Spracklin saw Gloria rise from the floor and sit down beside Jasmine. Gloria held the girl while she wept.

"We were awful to him," Jasmine said. She wiped her wet cheeks with her hand.

"He crossed the line."

"But he's gone now."

"That doesn't mean he was right."

Other people drifted into the room. The only one Spracklin recognized was Derek, who was acting strange. He seemed withdrawn, sitting by himself in a far corner. Maybe that wasn't surprising—he must feel like an alien in the house. A girl with long red hair sat down next to Jasmine. A large blond guy slouched near the door, glancing occasionally at Derek. And one thin red-headed man, who looked like he was in his thirties, took control of the gathering.

"We have to get a few things straight," he said.

"Jesus, Andy," said Gloria. "Let poor Jasmine catch her breath."

Andy. This was Andy Fox. Spracklin studied the man, taking note of Fox's measured tone and command of the room.

Gloria tried to insist they let Jasmine have a few moments, but he calmly explained they had to talk now.

"Jasmine will be worse off if we don't clear this up," the red-haired girl told Gloria. It was as if Fox had scripted the line for her, and Fox nodded his head. There was something glistening on the side of the red-head's nose, and Spracklin realized it was a stud. Jasmine sat up, signaling to Gloria that she was all right.

Fox looked slowly around the room, fixing his gaze on each of them. "The cops will be coming back, maybe tonight. This place will be spic n span."

"It's clean already," Gloria said. "You don't have to tell us this."

"We all have to be pulling in the same direction," the red-haired girl with the nose stud told Gloria.

Fox nodded. "What we have to do is get the pigs to search the place, and when they find nothing they have to leave."

He was about to say something else but Gloria cut him off. "This is how you get us to all pull in the same direction?" She gestured to Derek. It seemed she was now the champion of the boy she'd ridiculed that morning. Derek flinched. He was sweating and looked pale.

"Gloria, you as a leader in the house should know that there are rules. We all have to follow the rules."

"One of the rules is no maiming anyone," she said.

"Could I speak to you alone please, Gloria?" Fox said calmly. She rose as Spracklin looked again at Derek. The soldier was wearing a cutoff pair of sweat pants and a red sweatshirt and he was trembling slightly. Spracklin assumed he was an addict and needed a hit, but there was something more than that. The sweatshirt was bulky on the left upper arm. Gloria had mentioned a maiming.

Spracklin was beginning to put it together when the light flicked on in the window to his right. All of a sudden, Spracklin found himself standing in the light. He dropped down into the weeds, but was still exposed. He saw Fox and Gloria step into the room beside him. Heart thumping, he crawled past the window and crouched by a door, which he assumed led to the basement.

But light still shone on him. He had to get out of it. He took a Shell charge card from his wallet and inserted it in the crack of the basement door. Feeling for the bolt, he pressed the card against it and gently shook the door. After two or three attempts, it slid open and he was in the basement. He edged the door shut, making sure it didn't lock.

Now, standing in pitch blackness, he heard footfalls and voices overhead as his nose filled with the dampness of the basement. He fished his lighter from his pocket and lit it. Basements in these houses had once been the servants' quarters, and this one was now derelict – just a narrow corridor with planked walls. Spracklin took a few paces and looked into the closest room. There was a shelf lined with white and grey pots, an oven and a potter's wheel. It was Derek's pottery shop. The wheel and area around it were splattered with wet clay. Then, just as the lighter became too hot to hold, he thought he saw something else in the clay. He waited a moment for the lighter to cool, then lit it again and walked toward the wheel. There was a puddle of blood near the potter's wheel and different shoe prints in the muck. Spracklin touched a finger to the blood and put it to his mouth. Yes, the unmistakable iron taste of blood.

Closing the cap of the lighter, he stood in the complete blackness and thought about what he'd witnessed. Fox had tortured Derek, but Derek was still here.

What power did Fox have over them? It had to be more than the drugs. He'd just seen how Fox dominated everyone in the room – all except Gloria.

Feeling his way along a wall, Spracklin stepped out into the corridor again then felt his way across the hall. The mumbled voices grew louder as he stepped into a black room. He could hear them through a vent in the ceiling.

"It's just like The Mantis," said Gloria.

"He's gone now. He's not the issue."

Spracklin flicked the lighter on again and surveyed the room. There was sawdust all over the floor, and a pile of it by a workbench in the far corner. Stacked against the wall, he saw lengths of wood, and a few empty frames. This must have been the place where Blakely made his frames. There was a stack of boxes and an old freezer against the far wall. Spracklin moved to the side of the freezer, which was right below the vent. He listened closely. Fox was telling Gloria to calm down, that they all needed to work together to get through the next week. Then his voice dropped and he asked some question. Spracklin couldn't hear the whole thing but discerned the word "Seamstress". He strained to listen.

"The cops were asking about her?" asked Gloria.

"It's what Derek says."

There was a pause and Gloria said, "Well, you know he liked women. I mean, he used her, and she felt dumped. But I couldn't see her poisoning him."

Fox continued talking, but the only thing Spracklin could hear was the tone of Fox's voice. He was trying to calm Gloria. Spracklin had to get closer to the vent to hear the whole discussion. He placed a foot on the freezer and pushed up. He felt his foot slide from under him. Water must have condensed on the surface. Unable to save himself, he tumbled to his left, smashed into some of the frames and fell. A huge mound of sawdust softened his landing, but he knew his crashing around could be heard upstairs.

"What the fuck was that?" Fox said. As Spracklin found his feet and stood, he heard heavy footsteps above him.

"Pigs," said a woman's voice.

"Basement."

Fox again. "I'll go down. You take the backdoor." Spracklin assumed he was talking to the blond giant.

Spracklin didn't know which way the door was. He'd dropped his lighter. He reached inside his jacket and took out his handgun. He heard the door to the main floor open and someone flicked a light on by the stairs. The door was to his right.

He took up a position by the door of the storeroom and waited. He took the safety off his revolver. It would blow his cover, ruin his case but he had to defend himself. As the voices of Gloria and Fox filled the basement, he braced his body and stepped behind the door. They were coming down the stairs.

That's when he felt the thud on the back of his neck, and pain and numbness shot down his spine. He struggled to turn around but could only feel his body collapse.

Saturday, June 1, 1968

CHAPTER 14

In the blackness, Spracklin made out yellow dots circling the edge of his vision. He was aware only of the darkness, of the pain in his head and several joints, and the absurdity of gravity. His feet were not on the ground. He was dizzy, but he felt like he was floating horizontally, held in place by two heavy objects.

He squirmed and felt himself slip to the left. As he gained consciousness, he realized he was suspended in mid-air. He was wedged into a space above the floor. He breathed with difficulty and was aware of pain in his shoulder and hip where he was pinned against a stud in the rotten wall. He breathed, wiggled, and something shifted. He fell to the dank floor.

Fox, he thought. *Where is Fox?* Fox had been coming down the steps, with the big blond guy. He remembered nothing after that. Maybe one of Fox's guys had come up behind him and knocked him out. Now they were holding him, trapping him against a wall with some sort of large crate. He couldn't tell what was pressing against his body.

He could see nothing but blackness, and realized he couldn't hear anything either. He was aware only of the musty smell, the dank taste in his mouth and the all-encompassing dark.

He wiggled some more and realized he was resting on a dirty cement floor layered with sawdust. The object beside him shifted. Slowly, he bent at the waist, and the heavy object moved. He inched his way backward until he had enough room to stand.

Painfully, he stood in the expanse of darkness and rubbed his throbbing head. He assumed he was in the basement of 1340 Masonic, but he had no way of being sure. It certainly smelled the same. Fox must have caught him and locked him in one of the rooms. No one on the police force knew where he was.

He thought back to what had happened before he blacked out. He swatted his left side and felt that his handgun was missing. He'd had a lighter with him, but it was gone as well. His wallet was there, and his badge inside it. He tried to think back. He'd drawn the gun before Fox had come down to the basement.

Steadying himself, he put out his arm and felt along the floor. Possibly Fox had left booby-traps throughout the room for him to stumble into in the dark.

His arm hit something. It was a smooth, warm, vibrating surface. It was at a right angle to the smooth surface that had pinned him against the wall. The freezer. It was the lid of the freezer he had tried to climb on to. Fighting off his headache, he thought of the position of the freezer against the wall and tried to get his bearings, creating a map in his mind.

He edged in the dark toward the door, and found it open. *Maybe they're not holding me hostage. Maybe stuffing me behind the freezer was a prank.*

He crouched and swept his hand through the dirt, covering the area where he thought his gun should have fallen. As he stretched his arm into the void, he prayed there were no rats. He found his revolver on the third sweep. He ejected the cylinder. He could feel the bullets. It was fully loaded. He stood and thought about what was in the room.

A freezer. A freezer might have a light inside. *Was that a good idea?* He knew the vent was above him and the light would shine through the cracks, but he could hear no one upstairs.

He walked to the freezer, found it with his hands and lifted the lid a crack. A wafer of orange light cut through the basement. The door was ajar. Nothing dangerous was on the floor.

Pulling back his coat sleeve, he checked his Timex. Ten to two. He had four hours until Flanagan raided the place. He was about to shut the lid, when he looked into the freezer and saw its contents. He slammed the lid shut and jumped back.

He hoped he hadn't yelled, but couldn't be sure. He listened. No one was stirring upstairs. He tried to calm himself. His fear was ridiculous. The thing could not harm him. But in his dizziness and pain, he struggled to remain rational. He'd seen scores of dead bodies, sat in on autopsies, killed Germans. He lifted the lid again and looked into the frozen interior. He studied it, then left the freezer top open. He found his lighter by the sawed off stumps of wood.

Spracklin lowered the lid of the freezer and lit the lighter. He quickly left the basement by the back door and headed to his car to get his evidence kit. He might as well investigate the crime scene while he had time. Five minutes later he was back in the basement with the brief case that contained his gear – his fingerprinting kit, evidence bags, camera, flashbulbs and flashlight. He opened the freezer lid and looked at the dismembered body. It was a thin male, probably in his twenties. The head, forearms and one foot were missing. The only distinguishing feature Spracklin could make out through the coating of frost was a tattoo of a praying mantis on the shoulder. He now had two murders to work.

CHAPTER 15

By the time sunlight shone through the filthy windows, Spracklin had finished examining the crime scene and was putting away his gear. He'd found no useful finger prints on the freezer – the surface had been wiped down and the only full print he found was his own. He'd taken time to examine the cadaver itself and found the limbs and waist bent so it would fit in the freezer. He could find no damage to the joints, so the body was likely placed in the freezer before rigor mortis set in, within three or four hours of death. He'd searched under the body for the missing head and extremities, but there was nothing. The arms had been cut off at the elbow. The neck was coated with a dusting of frost but it looked like a clean cut – likely performed with a broad blade, an axe or machete. He found no blood around the wound.

He heard a door crash open above him, followed by the stomping of police boots moving through the house. He checked his watch. Six-zero-two. He heard policemen rousing the hippies and telling them to get down on the floor. Still feeling the effects of being knocked out, he walked up the stairs and stepped into the dreary kitchen with its black and red linoleum tiles. He waved to a uniformed officer, and stepped aside as a patrolman came in with a detection dog. Ignoring Spracklin, the Alsatian began to sniff the open doors of the cupboards.

In the room where Fox had addressed his tenants, Spracklin noticed something he had missed in the candle light the previous evening. The walls were covered with a huge mural of tangled raccoons. The artist had used glow-in-the-dark paint in the whites of their eyes, so the eyes seemed to shine within their black masks in the dawn light. The thud of a body against the floor above snapped Spracklin's attention back to the job at hand.

He followed the back stairs up to an orange hallway on the second floor where Ed Burwell and Merrill Flanagan were standing by a hairy, half-naked man, who was lying on the ground in handcuffs. Blood poured from his nose. Two uniformed officers were dragging another man from his bedroom. A curly-haired girl wrapped in a bed sheet stood weeping in a corner. Spracklin nodded to Flanagan and Burwell.

"Fox?" he asked.

"No sign of him," Flanagan said in his slow droll. He was about two years away from retirement and looked it – bald, double chin, grey walrus moustache. He would always be known on the force as the cop who, in 1956, arrested the poet Lawrence Ferlinghetti on obscenity charges for publishing Allen Ginsberg's poem, *Howl*. Spracklin at the time didn't consider the poem pornographic so much as prophetic. Sure enough, Ferlinghetti won the case and Ginsberg's vision of America had proven accurate. Flanagan was an easy-going fellow, and Spracklin liked him.

"Narcotics?"

"None yet," he said above the sound of a distant scream. "We just got here."

Spracklin nodded. "Fox last night told all his troops he wanted the place clean. They had almost eighteen hours after I arrested that Reg guy."

Burwell and Flanagan both eyed him. "How do you know this?"

"I was outside. I heard." The screaming upstairs intensified. "I have two murders to investigate so I came –"

"One murder," said Burwell. "If that."

The noise was aggravating Spracklin's headache. "Two murders. There's a dismembered body in a freezer in the basement."

They continued to look at him, and finally Burwell said, "I thought we were partners on this case."

Spracklin just looked at the ceiling. "You spend all day arguing against a case instead of working on it, and you don't get the call." He stepped over the bleeding hippie on the floor and said, "I need to talk to Gloria, Jasmine and Raven." As he started up the stairs, he added, "I think I know where one of them is"

"Get the fuck out of here," he heard Gloria scream as he walked up the last flight of stairs. There was an edge of frustration and panic in her voice. Spracklin stopped beside Tom Jackson, who was standing in a doorway looking at Gloria. She sat naked on a bed with red linen. Her cheeks glistened with tears. The walls of the room were covered with a mural of wolverines similar to the raccoons downstairs. The only flaw in the work was a single hole in the plaster by the window.

"I said get the fuck out."

"Miss," said Jackson, "you'll have to calm down, get dressed and –"

"Fuck off and leave."

Spracklin said, "Shut up, Gloria. Put your clothes on."

"You said you were just looking into John's death." She glared at Spracklin with hatred. "You fucking liar."

"We were and are. Reg MacIntosh's pack of heroin changed things." He stared at the sketches on the wall.

"Liar," she hissed.

He took her wallet from her dresser and tossed it to her. "Wrap yourself in that sheet and show me your ID."

"You have nothing on me."

But her voice was losing its edge. She wrapped the sheet around her shoulders, took her driver's license from the wallet and handed it to him. "Gloria Vanhusen," he read. "From British Columbia." She shifted uneasily on the bed. "Have a green card?" She shook her head. "Papers of any sort?" Again she shook her head.

"I need to talk to Jasmine and Raven," he said. "And anyone else who knew John Blakely well."

"They're not here."

"Where are they?" She shrugged. "Which is Jasmine's room?"

She shrugged again and the Alsatian and its handler wandered into the room. Gloria stared at the dog and said, "Main floor." She clutched the sheet tighter. "It's the one painted like a coral reef." The dog sniffed near the bed, then moved to the hole in the wall and began to bark. Spracklin looked at the girl then stepped toward the hole. "No," she yelled and she lunged at the hole to stop him. As he resisted her, a large triangle of the wolverine mural broke off. "You asshole," she screamed, clutching the sheet to herself again. "John drew that."

A cloud of plaster dust was drifting from the wall. Spracklin reached inside the hole and pulled out a plastic bag of dried green leaves. He assumed it was marijuana.

"Go on, get some clothes on," he said, "before we ship you back to Canada." He turned and saw Burwell standing at the door. "Sergeant, let her get dressed and book her on a violation of P.C. 11530. I'll interview her downtown."

"What about the other murder?"

"You wanted to arrest hippies. So book her."

Spracklin grabbed Jackson as he left the room. Behind him he heard the drone of Miranda rights being read. "You have the right to remain silent —"

"Do you really expect me to exercise my right to remain silent, arsehole?"

"Shut up and listen . . . "

Jasmine's room on the ground floor was dark because the window had been blocked off. When Spracklin flicked the light switch, the only thing that came on was a black light, setting off the room's fluorescent decorations. It had been painted to look like a coral reef with aquamarine walls. Schools of fish loomed in orange, red and blue Day-Glo paint on the walls and hung on mobiles from the ceiling. Streams of cardboard bubbles flowed from their mouths, and each bubble was a peace sign. Plaster reefs came out from the wall to form a desk and little chair and the headboard of a bed in the corner. Spracklin realized the work hadn't been done by Blakely, it was too sloppy.

"We're going to search every corner of this room," he told Jackson. "I want papers, letters, syringes, anything to do with heroin or cyanide. Rip the plaster away from the window – we're going to need light."

Jackson moved slowly, as if reluctant to destroy the installation, so Spracklin found a loose edge, and pulled. A stream of light poured in from a window. "We're here to find a killer, Tom."

They began to rifle through the shelves and drawers. In the third drawer of the blue dresser, Spracklin found a stack of letters and a notebook. The first letter was from Philadelphia and addressed to Eleanor Jones. "Ha," Spracklin laughed.

"Sir?"

"Jasmine's real name is Eleanor Jones."

The hand-written letter was from Kenneth Jones, a partner of Burnaby & Co., a Philadelphia accounting firm. He signed the letter Daddy. It told of family news and said Eleanor's mother would love a letter from her.

> *April 23 was hard on her since it was the first anniversary of Paul's death.*
> *We visited his grave. We had a granite headstone made over in East Forest and*
> *it looked fine under the tree with the daffodils starting to come up around it. I*
> *wanted to put Lieutenant Paul Randall Jones on it but your mother wanted the*
> *'Lieutenant' left off. Visiting the grave was difficult for her. Jane and Elizabeth*
> *helped her. There was a sense of relief by the end of the day. The first anniversary*
> *was over.*

Spracklin scanned other letters, in which Eleanor's father implored her to return to Princeton. There were scraps of paper with loose verses, most with lines scratched out and rewritten. At the bottom of the stack was the worn orange cardboard binder. A label was written in green and red crayon:

JASMINE'S SECRET SONGBOOK.
DO NOT DECIPHER.

It contained the lyrics to her songs, about forty, Spracklin estimated. He flipped through them and stopped at one called "Ode to a Failed Artist." It seemed to be a poem for a friend with limited talent. All his friends wanted to applaud him to compensate for his shortcomings. Jasmine had lengthened the chorus after the final verse to read:

When our cultural commander
Skewers you with candor
Says your works will be forgotten,
Your canvas faded, rotten
And he murders you with mirrors
And his artist's psycho-terrors
'Cause you cannot help but seeing
Iron limits of your being
And a smile is just a smile.

When he looked up, Spracklin saw Burwell standing at the door.

"She's booked," Burwell said. He gave a weary grin. "I don't mind taking on the hippies with knives but don't ask me to deal with her again."

Spracklin showed him his own tired smile. "I figured you were the man for the job."

"So what's this about a new body?"

"Decapitated body in a freezer downstairs. The only identifying feature is a tattoo of a praying mantis on the shoulder."

Burwell nodded slowly. "So what's the plan now?"

Spracklin told Jackson to keep searching and led Burwell to the basement door. "We're going to work the two cases. I've done the crime scene in the basement, and we'll get an autopsy done on the victim today." He grabbed the papers and began to leave.

"It's Saturday."

"I know."

"You won't get an autopsy back till Thursday – Wednesday at the earliest."

Spracklin stopped at the door and turned around. "I'll get it done today. Blakely and the headless John Doe were killed by different people. We've got a couple of killers on the loose in Haight-Ashbury. I want the autopsy today."

CHAPTER 16

"The raid simply took longer than we expected, Honey," Spracklin said into the payphone receiver. "I've been searching the scene and then we had to interview people." At the far end of the lunch counter, Ed Burwell was tucking into his biscuit and gravy. Spracklin had finished his black coffee and toast. "You know, the hippies who live at the house."

"Jimmy, this is narcotics," she said. "Can't you just do the homicide stuff?"

Spracklin had to walk a fine line. If he told her about the interconnected deaths on Haight-Ashbury, she'd grow more frantic knowing her daughter was adrift among murderers. If he didn't tell the full story, she wouldn't understand why he was devoting so much time to it. "It's all related to my case, Val. It gave me a chance to do a thorough investigation of the victim's home."

Again there was silence, until finally she said, "I've been up all night, Jimmy. I've been worrying. My daughter is back on the Haight."

He turned away from Burwell and faced the wall. In a calm voice he said: "That's why I've worked so hard, so tirelessly, trying to get her and bring her home. I'm still doing that and always will. Now I'm going to hang up because I have work to do, including looking for Marie."

He put a finger on the cradle of the payphone. He knew the only way to end this would be to bring Marie home, and even then it would be a short-term solution. Marie would be age of majority in a year and she could do what she liked. Val hadn't thought it through. Sometimes he wondered if the fact he had thought it through was a sign he didn't love Marie enough. Maybe it was a sure sign of love if you drove yourself crazy with worry rather rationally working to find someone.

Spracklin glanced over to Burwell and signaled that he had to make one last call. Checking his notebook, he plugged another dime into the silver payphone and dialed. The phone was answered on the second ring.

"Ernie? Jimmy Spracklin."

"Lieutenant. Sir. How are you?"

"Just fine, Ernie. I hate to bother you on a Saturday, but I need a favor." He paused but Swanson didn't respond. "I just found a dismembered body in a freezer on Haight Street. Long story. It ties in with the artist who had cyanide in his heroin. Can you do an autopsy today?"

"Today?"

"I know, Ernie, I know I'm asking a lot of you, but it's important that we have an examination immediately."

Swanson sighed. "Of course, I'll be at it by eleven."

Spracklin thanked him, said he'd remember this and put down the phone. "Ernie Swanson," he said to Burwell. "He'll be on the autopsy by eleven." He clapped Burwell on the shoulder. "Let's go."

Burwell was silent as they drove into Fillmore. Spracklin knew he was trying to figure out how the Lieutenant had cut through the bureaucracy to get the autopsy done so quickly. Ernie Swanson was the deputy medical examiner, and Spracklin knew he wanted to be chief medical examiner. Spracklin also knew – he could just tell – that Swanson believed that he, Spracklin, would be the Chief of Police within a year. Spracklin had learned that if he needed something done quickly in the CME's office, ask Ernie to do it. He thought Burwell would figure it out, but as they walked up to Rupert Hill's apartment in a Fillmore tenement Burwell was silent. There was no sign he had clued in.

Hill's apartment had a glossy poster taped on the door showing Latin American farmers. The two detectives knocked and stared at it.

Support the people of
Venezuela in the
March Against
American Petro-Imperialism

San Francisco City Hall
Noon
July 19, 1968

Spracklin knocked again and a man inside yelled, "It's open." They stepped inside and found the bachelor apartment tidy except for the stacks of papers on every surface. The walls were covered in glossy photos of Jerry Rubin and Abby Hoffman and posters protesting the war or raising money for voter registration drives. There were three black-and-white photos of the rally at City Hall after Martin Luther King was shot. Spracklin bent over to see if he could find himself in the crowds. Then he noticed a poster for a hairy guy running for student council at Berkeley. It promised action on educational funding for minorities, opposition to Fascist regimes in Taiwan and South Africa, and leadership in confronting the reactionary conservatives in Washington. Beneath it read: *Vote for Action! Vote for Rupert Hill!*

The bathroom door opened and Hill walked out, his frizzy hair bouncing as he walked. His moustache hid his mouth. His beard hung over his T-shirt, which bore an American flag with the red stripes running, as if they were dripping blood.

"Can I help you gentlemen?"

"My name is Lieutenant James Spracklin." He badged the hippie. "This is Sergeant Ed Burwell. We have a few questions about John Blakely."

Hill introduced himself and shook their hands. "I'll help in any way I can," he said. "Would you like coffee?"

"I see you're active in student politics," Spracklin said when they were sitting with their mugs of instant coffee.

"I've been elected secretary of the Student Council at Berkeley."

"Any interest in wider politics? State or national?"

"I attend Berkeley, Lieutenant," the hippie said. "All politics for us are national, if not global." Spracklin gave him a sour look. "But to answer your question, I'm the secretary of the McCarthy committee at Berkeley."

"Kennedy would be more effective in ending the war."

"He was a member of the cabinet that got us into the war. His brother supported the Diem regime, brought in the evil McNamara. You have to remember one thing: their foolish imperialist invasion of the Bay of Pigs brought on the October Missile Crisis. No individual in history took humanity closer to the brink of extinction than John Kennedy, and he did so with his brother's support."

The two policemen sipped their coffees. Spracklin said, "Well you know, Rupert, we're here to discuss John, not politics."

"Was it suicide?"

"Difficult to say. You think it's a possibility?"

Hill shook his head and let out a sigh. "I don't know. I don't really know him anymore. He's changed. I've changed."

"When did you last see him?"

"It was well over a month ago, maybe more. In late sixty-six we both started hanging around Haight-Ashbury. It was an adventure, a different world. Soon we moved up there, sleeping on people's floors. But we began going our separate ways. I started hanging out with the Merry Pranksters."

"That was the group led by Ken Kesey?" asked Spracklin, referring to the author famed for his experiments with LSD.

"Yeah, that's right. But John was more interested in painting so he moved into that house with all the painters and craft artists."

"And you stayed with the Pranksters?"

"No. I couldn't. They were politically so nebulous." He laughed. "The only guy I met up there with even the vaguest activist outlook was a guy called Zepto Hategerm from Louisiana who was starting up a Committee to Clone Howard Cosell." He sighed and laughed. "I suppose they are right that we need demonstrations to promote positivism. I think the Trips Festivals or the Human Be-In – at least at the conceptual stage – progressed along that path but – "

"What happened to you and the Pranksters?" Spracklin said.

"I left and came back to school."

"To Berkeley."

"Yeah."

"Not to Stanford, where you and John had gone before."

"I felt there was a greater commitment – yes, a greater commitment to effective political leadership at Berkeley."

The Lieutenant leaned forward. "And your expulsion from Stanford for drugs had nothing to do with it?"

"I was never expelled from Stanford. It's just that my social conscience . . .'"

Hill stopped as Spracklin held up the photocopy of the Stanford expulsion order that he had got from Jackson.

"Rupert, we're policemen investigating a murder," he said. "If you lie to us, the charge is perverting the course of justice. The penalty is prison, not a bad write-up in *The Daily Cal*." He took a sip of coffee. "So let's start again. When did you last see John Blakely?"

"A month ago. He called me, suggested we bury the hatchet and get together. So I went up to their house on Masonic."

"How'd it go?"

"It was weird. Really weird. I went into this room with raccoons all over the wall. Their eyes glowed. John's painting a canvas in one corner – a study of different flowers' roots. He was intrigued that roses had uglier roots than dandelions. Other freaks were hanging out, watching him paint. This one guy – he was pretty stoned – was talking all the time, like he was the philosopher. Big guy. No shirt. You could see heroin tracks and tattoos on his arms."

"Tattoo of a praying mantis?"

"That's right, the guy walks with a limp."

"A limp?"

80

"Couldn't miss it. He went to get an ashtray and he was limping badly. Anyway, he was worshipping John almost. He philosophized about the Darwinist need for artists, that society needs them. If we were in a cave a hundred-thousand years ago, we'd have to make sure John survived because he created beauty and made our lives worth the struggle. Then he started insulting the others around him. There was another artist there—"

"Reg?"

"I think so. This Mantis guy turns to Reg and said if they were cave men they'd murder him and use his bones for jewelry because his art was garbage. And he told this loud, fat girl that they'd probably eat her because she consumed twice her body weight in food each day." Hill shrugged. "I have better things to do than listen to people degrade each other. After a while I left."

"What did John do all this time?"

"He, well, he just kept painting."

"So you didn't really talk."

"I asked him if he'd heard from his sister. He just kept painting and said, 'You, of all people, should know she's in India.'"

"What did he mean by that?"

"I realize I'm prejudicing myself here, but I am a slave to the truth."

"Go on."

"John and I used to smoke pot and we gave some to Julie. Then, Jesus Christ, she just changed from the girl next door to this . . ." He threw his hands up in the air. "This acid head. She would string these beads out of seashells, sell them to buy acid. One day her father found the sinsemilla she'd been growing among his sunflowers.

Hill exhaled and looked to the heavens. "Dr. Blakely went nuts. He kicked John out of the house and had me kicked out of Stanford."

"And when was this?"

"Just before the end of the school year two years ago. John left just before exams and moved up to Haight Street. I'd see him around but we never spoke anymore. And I don't think he spoke to his Dad."

"And you never called him after leaving the house a few weeks ago?"

"No."

"Eliot Blakely said you'd been calling him."

"Simply not so. John called me."

Spracklin nodded. Hill checked his watch and said he had to go – he was taking in a Big Brother and the Holding Company concert on the Panhandle that afternoon. Spracklin pretended to understand what that meant. He nodded his head as he took one of the student election fliers that had Hill's contact details. The hippie walked them to the door and shook their hands. They thanked him and left.

"Well," said Spracklin as they strolled past the cream-colored tenements toward the car. "What do you think?"

"I think he's a liar."

"I know he's a liar. But is he a murderer?" Burwell shrugged. "Pretty weak motive for murder."

"Revenge?"

"For what? The guy's moved on with his life, big man on campus. I don't buy it."

"He has political ambitions. Being kicked out of Stanford could hurt him." They crossed the street and stopped by the car.

"Weak motive," said Burwell.

Spracklin turned to the Sergeant. "Most murders have weak motives. Adultery's a weak motive for murder, but it happens."

Spracklin then noticed an envelope pinned under a windshield wiper. There was no name on it. He opened it and found a folded sheet of typewriter paper, and an object fell out. Spracklin picked it up from the ground and studied it. It looked like a slab of human skin, with muscle still attached to it. It was still moist and left a bloody residue on the paper. Someone had written five words on the paper in black marker: "I WANT MY HORSE BACK". Spracklin looked at five black guys gathered on a stoop nearby, drinking sodas. They looked right back at him.

"They didn't do it," said Burwell.

"How you figure that?"

"It was Fox. Horse means heroin. Fox is the only guy whose horse we have. I think he's telling us he's pissed off."

Fox wants his heroin back. Spracklin turned to the guys on the step again. "White guy did this, right?" he called to them and watched their responses. Four were perfectly still but one gave a slight nod before he could stop himself.

"So Fox's following us," he said to Burwell.

"Him or his people. I'd bet he's got some toady tailing us."

Spracklin scanned the street but saw no one that looked like a hippie tail. He looked back at the sheet of paper. "Does he really think we're going to give him his heroin back?"

Burwell shrugged again. "So in the envelope – was that human flesh?"

"Skin and muscle, I think," Spracklin said. He pointed to grey flecks on one side of the gross object in his hand. "I think we'll find those splatter marks are bits of clay."

"Clay?"

"Derek is a potter. I think Fox cut him in the pottery room in the basement of the house. The blood was still wet when I got there last night so it couldn't have been our friend in the freezer. I think we're dealing with a madman."

He looked around the street again. He unlocked the car and put the letter and skin sample on the dashboard. He turned and said to Burwell, "Follow me."

"Where we goin'?"

"To learn about a madman from a psychopath."

CHAPTER 17

Andy Fox knew he could not control the current situation if he could not control himself. Some problems could be overcome by losing his temper. This wasn't one of them. He needed to think clearly. Gloria, that stupid bitch, was busted with a dime bag, even though she had promised him the house was one-hundred-percent clean. Reg got busted with a half-pound of horse. The house was toxic. The Soldier couldn't be trusted. The Mantis, Blakely: both gone. Fox was in debt and under-manned and he needed to keep this Spracklin guy off guard while he rebuilt his organization. A little threat was a start.

As he strolled down Clayton Street, he tried to think things through. He would have stuff in a few days. By that time, customers would be crazy for it. The price would rise. What he needed was just two or three people he could trust.

He stopped at Oak Street and studied the Vague Dimensions, a vanilla building with large windows that had been a community center before it became a music hall. Inside, he found three kids doing sound checks on the stage below murals of cartoon farm animals playing horns. Fox crossed the floor, and looked in the office.

The girl at the desk had dark hair falling to her shoulders. She sat erect, her green eyes focused on the work before her. She was almost finished macraméing a wide belt from white twine. Her thin hands maneuvered dozens of bundles of white string, each held together with an elastic band, into a series of interconnected square knots.

Fox knocked lightly and she glanced up.

"Sorry," she said. The green eyes studied him. She couldn't have been more than twenty. "Have you been waiting there long?"

"Just long enough to be fascinated with what you're doing. A belt?"

"A wide belt, for jeans." Her face softened into a smile. "It was supposed to be for a thirty-four-inch waist, but I ran out of string." She laughed. "I had a customer for it but it's too small for him. Looks like I'll be swapping it at Free Street."

"Free Street? What a waste, man."

"You don't like bartering?"

"Your work's too good. Get some bread for it. Learn about the world of commerce, baby. You'll never get what you need by bartering."

She grinned and resumed tying knots in her belt. He watched and noticed the diamond-shaped design she'd worked into the fabric. "How much you want for it?"

She thought for a moment, her hands tying knots all the while. "Twelve bucks."

Fox let out a whistle. "That's steep."

She tugged to tighten a few knots. "That leather belt you've got is hurtin', man. Too old, too big." He looked down. The belt stuck out beyond the peace sign buckle and flopped over.

"Nice buckle but the leather is showing its age," she said. "Tell you what I'll do – I'll take the buckle off and put it on the new rope belt. Give me the old belt, I can use it for something. And I'll charge you ten dollars. You'll never get a deal like that in a store."

She tied up the end of the strings into fine knots. "Eight," he said.

She continued to finish off the belt without looking up. He unbuckled his belt and slid it through the belt holes. He threw it on the desk and said, "Fine, ten."

She examined the leather belt, took a pair of needle nose pliers from the desk and began to remove the rivets holding the buckle in place.

"I came here looking for Tony and I'll leave with a belt," said Fox.

"It's not finished yet."

"But it's perfect," he said, throwing ten dollars on the desk. "The only way I could get something this cool is to buy it before it's finished." She smiled. "Do you just do belts?"

She shook her head. "Clothes, mainly. Embroidery, patches on jeans." She grimaced as she tried to pry the rivets out. "My passion is wall hangings or complicated embroideries, like that jacket."

She nodded to a jean jacket folded over a chair. Fox picked it up. On the back, she had embroidered the black silhouette of a willow tree, its branches spreading into the neck flap and shoulders. The needlework was fine, and the thread was bold against the faded denim.

Fox believed the first steps in reaching artists involved complimenting their work and buying something. "You said you were looking for Tony," she said. "He split. Is there something I can help with?" She looked like a teenager, but had poise beyond her years.

"I just wanted to talk to him about booking acts. I have some friends who are interested in playing here."

"Who should I say called?"

"Just tell him it was Andy. I think he knows me. And you are . . . "

"The Seamstress," she said. "Just The Seamstress."

"Cool name," he said. He folded the jacket. But instead of replacing it on the chair, he sat down and laid the jean jacket across his lap. He would get her real name and find out about her. She liked money. She was smart. And for some reason the cops wanted to talk to her about Blakely's death. If she had anything to do with it, he thought, this chick was cool and unfazed. She'd be great to work with.

CHAPTER 18

Spracklin walked quickly, and Burwell tried to keep up. Unshaven and rumpled, Spracklin knew he looked half crazed. He was past caring. He turned up a back street, and they heard the sound of a group of black female singers emerging from a transistor radio above them. They breezed past a well-dressed black man in his thirties before he could get in their way. Burwell followed the Lieutenant into a storefront. The faded paint on the window read

FILLMORE LAUNDRY

Three women on the plastic chairs stopped the conversations they were yelling above the whir of the driers and looked at the white men. A burly guy in sunglasses and a pork pie hat held up a hand as Spracklin reached the back of the room.

"Tell Bogdan I want to see him."

"He's busy."

"Make him unbusy." The bodyguard sized him up behind the sunglasses. "I said I want to see him."

The door opened a crack. Someone peeked out, then said, "Spracklin." In a second, the door opened. The conversations resumed in the laundry room as the two policemen entered a paneled room with a desk in the middle and a bar at one side. Three black men sat in plastic chairs they'd brought in from the laundromat. Behind the desk, a hefty white guy pushing forty years and two-hundred-and-forty pounds was slouched into a leather chair. His grey sideburns and a cardigan gave him a grandfatherly appearance. A younger white man stood behind him. The old guy broke into a warm grin.

"Why Lieutenant Spracklin," he croaked with a noticeable Eastern European accent. "What a sight for sore eyes." He stood and extended his hand to Spracklin. When the Lieutenant extended his, he shook it firmly. "We've not seen you in months."

"Your boys here haven't killed anyone in months, Bogdan. No one we've found, at least." Spracklin sat on the edge of Polgar's desk.

The man behind Polgar glared at the policemen. Spracklin hadn't seen him before. He was built like a welterweight, narrow waist and strong shoulders. The Lieutenant made a mental note to make inquiries about the new henchman.

Polgar chuckled. "Is that any way to greet an old friend? Let's have a drink and a chat."

"Business hours, Bogdan," said Spracklin. "I need some information."

Polgar sat down. "You know me, Lieutenant. I'll always – always – do what I can to help the police."

Spracklin did know Polgar and he knew better than to be taken in by his charm. If you got sucked in by it, it was difficult to believe Bogdan Polgar could harm anyone. He was loved in Fillmore. Spracklin's file on Polgar was full of grey areas and questionable intel, but there was no doubt that the citizens of Fillmore adored him.

The files showed that Polgar had showed up in San Francisco in the late Forties. The most believable story Spracklin had heard was that Polgar was a Pole who had been caught behind advancing Soviet lines in 1945, and had decided the best route to the West was through Siberia. Legend said he had crossed the ice on the Bering Strait, but Spracklin believed he had worked on a fishing boat and defected in British Columbia. He'd shown up in San Francisco first by running numbers in Chinatown, and was soon investing in slums in Fillmore. It became his base. Polgar still lived there, and was active in the opposition to the redevelopment projects. Spracklin had heard that thirty-two people born after 1948 in the neighborhood had been named Bogdan. His tenements housed his chief lieutenants and their families. He had loans out to dozens of local businesses – not just bookies and pimps but shop-owners, barbers, and tradesmen.

Witnesses had told homicide inspectors of the casual ease with which Bogdan Polgar could pause during a cribbage game to put out a contract on someone who had crossed him. He had issued a death warrant on one of his key men, Jonathan Fraser, during a carol service on Christmas Eve, 1964. Spracklin had seven separate files spanning four years on homicides that he was sure were carried out by Polgar's men.

"The only help I've noticed from you, Bogdan, is that you keep us employed."

Polgar took a cigarette from a soft pack. He chuckled. "Why, Lieutenant Spracklin, you say such hurtful things. I'm a businessman." He held a cigarette to his lips and the athletic guy behind him reached forward and lit it. "You Kennedy guys," he said as he took a drag. "You'll need guys like me – businessman, active in civic affairs, respected by Blacks and Whites. Bobby knows it."

"Bobby would nail you so quick you wouldn't know what hit you."

"Bobby's doing a good job reaching out to black people. I heard about that rally in Oakland last night – even Black Jesus from the Panthers was impressed."

Spracklin hadn't read the papers that morning so he didn't know about the rally in Oakland. "I want to know about Andy Fox."

"I've heard the name."

"I hear he was moving in on Fillmore a few months ago."

"I think we're in different enterprises."

"Cut the crap, Bogdan. Tell me about Fox."

"I told you, I'm a businessman and – "

"I said, cut the crap."

Polgar held up a hand with the cigarette wedged between two plump fingers. He paused for a moment to make sure Spracklin wouldn't interrupt him. "And as a businessman, I know we need a stable environment in which we can conduct business. That's why I always go out of my way to co-operate with the authorities." He rolled the "r" in "author-r-r-rities." He took a drag and placed the cigarette in an ashtray. "I'm not entirely sure, Lieutenant, that Andy Fox understands the importance of a stable environment."

"What leads you to believe that?"

"Believed it for a long time."

"Why?"

Polgar smiled. "Because of Jamaal Roosevelt's toe." He laughed and shook his head.

"Tell me about Mr. Roosevelt's toe."

"If you don't know about Jamaal's toe, you haven't done your homework."

"Word on the street is you're bankrolling Fox, stability or no stability."

"I have a lot of economic interests in this neighborhood, other neighborhoods too." Polgar drew on his cigarette and wagged a finger at Spracklin as he exhaled. "I'll tell you, Lieutenant, I'd invest everything I own up around Haight Street. Folks from all over the world coming up there and spending money, and the business establishment downtown is turning up their noses at it. The place is a goldmine."

"You bankrolling hoodlums up in Haight?"

"I've invested in businesses there – legitimate, profitable businesses. I just like the economics of the area, Lieutenant."

"Is that a yes or a no?"

"Oh Lieutenant, I'd rather not get into the dirty details of business. Let's have a drink and talk about happier things."

"The only thing I could discuss with you that would make me happy would be confessions on Landry and Jason."

Polgar took a long drag on his cigarette. It was an excessively long drag. "Lieutenant, if I was as guilty as you say, you'd have found someone to testify against me. A clever dick like you – I wouldn't have a chance."

He'd put his finger directly on the kernel of the problem. Evidence. Everyone knew Polgar had ordered the killings of Jacques Landry and Emmett Jason, two of the three cases that Spracklin had failed to solve in 1967. Bogdan wanted everyone to know it. But Spracklin had come up against the universal problem in law and order: the citizens most victimized by crime were the least willing to fight it. It didn't matter if you were a black in Fillmore or a hippie threatened by heroin in Haight-Ashbury, the worse things got, the less you wanted to talk to the heat.

92

CHAPTER 19

Wearing his new belt, Fox watched The Seamstress fiddling with his old leather belt. After digging a buckle out of her knapsack, she struggled to stitch it on to the old leather. She talked as she worked, and Fox listened, nodding and taking mental notes about what made this girl tick.

"I just couldn't handle King's death," she said. She'd told him she had come to the Haight the summer before, making a living by sewing and doing embroidery for musicians like Chet Helm and the Family Dog. She'd been drawn to the visual artists at 1340 Masonic. Then she met Jake, an existentialist philosophy professor from the City College, during the Death of the Hippie Funeral. Fox remembered seeing them at the house, struck that the attractive young woman was with a nerd well into his thirties.

She and Jake decided to hitchhike to the East Coast, ending up in Greenwich Village. She mended clothes for a dry cleaner at Madison and 35th and became active in social reform in Harlem. Jake insisted he could survive without money or social revolution and the only way to ensure peace was for everyone to exist at subsistence levels.

"I mean, I'd come back to our pad on Bleecker Street after working and volunteering and had to listen to this existentialist crap about peaceful subsistence."

"Must have driven you nuts."

"I know, right? But like, I was in love." Her eyes returned to her belt and she forced a hole into the leather so she could bind it. "The King assassination was the end."

"I can imagine the pain Dr. King's death would have caused someone with your convictions. And Jake had none."

She tied a few more knots. Fox had learned to pay attention to two things when listening to people – the things they said and the things they didn't say. The things they didn't say told you what they were hiding, their weaknesses, their secret yearnings. And the way she averted her gaze now told him that they were getting to an important point. He had to say something that showed he understood her better than she understood herself.

93

"It reaffirmed your belief that you were placed here to make the world—"

"No," she said. Her eyes held his now. "I felt so inadequate. It's, like, man . . ." She had trouble finding the right words. "It's, like, I could never have King's devotion to the world." She put the belt down in her lap. "I couldn't even have my old man's conviction. You dig?"

They were reaching the point where people pause to make sure no one is listening, where they wonder if they can trust you.

"Your old man – Jake?"

"Not Jake. My old man, my dad." She blushed at saying the word.

"You said your dad was dead."

"Well, my step-dad. I called him Dad growing up." Her eyes shone. Fox had thought her art and social conscience obsessed and motivated her, but her step-father loomed large. "I hate what he stands for," she said. "But he put his life on the line for it. He was in Normandy at D-Day, attacked Germany. He was in Nuremburg during the trials. He devoted himself to defeating Nazism. I never risked my life for anything."

Her voice cracked. Fox saw the yearning she felt toward her stepfather. "He's a man of action, not someone who sits around rapping about the hierarchy of fucking needs." She wiped her eyes. "I left New York two days after Dr. King's death."

"You really love him, don't you?"

"My Dad? No." She shook her head. "I took off because of him."

"Then you did love him."

She looked down at her belt and began to weep. "I adored him – he was brave, kind, valiant. He'd take me to Veterans' Day parades. And fishing off Monterey. And to the shooting range every Saturday morning."

"The shooting range?" Fox said with a chuckle.

"Yes. I was twelve years old and he was teaching me how to shoot a handgun. He just couldn't get past the whole military thing. I grew up listening to his war stories, and I loved them."

"But you're not, I don't know, militaristic."

"I hate everything about the military. But . . ." Her voice dropped off and she took a deep breath. "When Dr. King died, I collapsed. I cried all day. I wondered how I'd go on. And I remembered Dad's stories from the war. He told me about having to keep driving forward after his best friend was shot. His devotion was so strong that he kept going. You've got to admire that."

Now it made sense. She was looking for a father figure, which was an opportunity for Fox. He could fill that need.

"And you feel both betrayed by him and admiring of him," he said. She closed her eyes and nodded.

"And the betrayal is all the more painful because you loved him so dearly," he said in a hushed voice. "You know, one thing I've learned over the decades – and now that I'm well past thirty it's even more evident – is that the deeper we love someone the deeper we're angered by their shortcomings."

He was about to continue when there was a knock on the door. Fox turned to see a husky guy. He had long hair but the crocodile golf shirt screamed college kid. "Good news, Paul," The Seamstress said.

"My belt's ready?" he asked.

Marie stood and held up the leather belt, now complete with a buckle. "Better than that," she said. "I found a leather belt for you – just like you asked for."

"I don't have to settle for rope?"

"Nope. Leather."

Paul stepped in, and studied the refurbished belt. "Cool," he said. "Already worn. How much? You want more 'cause it's leather?"

"Nope. Still seven dollars."

His smile broadened as he reached for his wallet before she changed her mind. The guy had wanted a leather belt, but Marie could only make one from twine. She probably had no money for leather, so the guy settled on rope.

"So you'd agreed to sell him this rope belt for seven dollars," Fox said with a smile as Paul left.

"You have a nicer buckle than what I offered to sell him, but yes." She was smiling now.

"So you made seventeen dollars off all that – not the seven dollars you'd expected."

"Yeah. Off an eighty-seven-cent ball of twine and a two-dollar belt buckle," she was leaning forward, savoring the moment. "I'd say I've learned the value of commerce, baby."

CHAPTER 20

Jimmy Spracklin flicked open his silver lighter, lit his cigarette and opened the folder on Andrew Fox.

In the hour since he'd returned to the Hall of Justice, he and Flanagan had tried to interview Reg MacIntosh. The guy was in the early stages of withdrawal, uncooperative and Flanagan had him placed in solitary. They booked four young people arrested at 1340 Masonic, including Gloria Vanhusen, who Spracklin wanted to interview. Burwell wanted to assist, but Spracklin needed to get her to talk. It was a job best done alone. And in the midst of it all, Flanagan had handed him a fat file on Andrew Fox. Spracklin bought a chicken salad sandwich at the canteen and took it and the Fox report to the interview room. He started reading while waiting for Gloria.

Fox was born in March 1933 in Manila, California, up near Oregon. His father was a fisherman, his parents happily married, and his older brother now owned a Ford dealership in Eureka. Fox worked as a hand on fishing boats as a teen, and took after his uncle, Burt Stepell, a petty racketeer. Fox had priors dating back to 1952, when he threatened a policeman in San Diego with a knife. He pleaded guilty to a reduced sentence of assault and was given a year's probation. He did six months in Corcoran Prison near Fresno in 1961-62 for assault causing bodily harm during a bar fight. During that time, his cellmate, Jamaal J. Roosevelt, entered the prison infirmary bearing knife wounds and missing a toe. Jamaal refused to say what happened. After his release, Fox became known to the narcotics task force as a supplier of drugs to Hell's Angels and an LSD pusher on Haight Street. Fox was known to employ a Cornell chemistry grad called Jeffrey Oakley to manufacture LSD. Oakley didn't fit in with the other kids on the street but Fox needed and protected him. Lately, Fox had graduated to selling heroin. The source of his heroin was not known, though his underlings said he imported opiates from Thailand and Burma through his contacts among the fishermen in Oregon.

Lucille Jenkins (aka Nebulous Neurocrank), a Nebraska native convicted of trafficking in Oakland in October, 1967, told police that Fox never took heroin himself. She said he prohibited junkies from working for him (though several underlings were known to be addicts). Fox had been arrested and arraigned on trafficking charges at the same time as Jenkins, but she declined to testify against him. She was sentenced to forty-eight months in prison. He was released.

The creased mugshot of Fox dating back to April 1963 showed a young man with short hair parted on the right. There were abrasions on his left cheek and a defiant expression. He had a scar on his chin. A 1967 photograph showed an older, hardened man with longer hair and a goatee – the man Spracklin recognized from the night before.

Spracklin flicked through the pages and found a psychologist's report. Dr. Ian Cheng had interviewed both Jenkins and Fox several times. Spracklin skipped to the conclusion.

> *Whereas traffickers commonly encourage their street-dealers to become addicted to narcotics so they can control them, Andrew Fox chooses other methods. He worries, says Jenkins, that addiction leads to carelessness and can harm the organization. He therefore controls his soldiers through paternalism and fear. Fear is the final weapon he wields, but it is by no means the only instrument in his arsenal. The first process he uses to establish his power over others is a sort of psychological seduction. Jenkins expounded on his methods for developing the devotion of his followers. In conversation, he probes his quarry until he identifies something needed or missing in their life or character. He then persuades them that he can provide what is missing in their life, that he and he alone can bring them fulfillment. He develops an almost religious position within these people's universe, and they eventually follow him. In the case of women, the seduction is usually sexual, and he becomes their source of sexual fulfillment as well as enlightenment.*

> *Jenkins revealed that Fox introduced violence into their relationship after he established himself as her master. When she refused to sell heroin, he became abusive, then threatened her with his knife. Given the example of Jamaal Roosevelt, it appears that he will resort to dismemberment with his knife, first removing digits and then threatening greater harm. There is no evidence that he has yet committed murder, but his violent tendencies certainly make it a possibility.*

Spracklin took a final drag, dropped the butt on the cement floor and ground it out with his shoe. He exhaled as a female sheriff led in Gloria Vanhusen. Spracklin gestured to the seat across from himself. The sheriff took her position by the door. Gloria sat and declined the cigarette he offered. He lit another.

"Isn't that other fella joining us?" she asked.

"Sergeant Burwell? No."

"No good-cop-bad-cop routine."

"I'm not a fan of that routine, Gloria." He wanted the tone conversational. "I find bad cop usually gets bad information, and that means a bad prosecution. If I arrest someone, the case has to be solid. In your case, for example, we have a baggie of marijuana in your bedroom with your fingerprints on it. It's one-hundred percent solid. You'll be deported back to Canada or go to prison."

They sat that way for a few seconds until he pushed the sandwich toward her. "I hope you like chicken salad. Best to eat here. You're going to the holding cells and the stench will kill your appetite." She hesitated and then unwrapped it.

"So which will it be?" she asked, with a wad of sandwich pushed into a cheek. "Deportation or jail?" She was pretending nothing worried her, but Spracklin thought the façade would crumble soon.

"It's up to you."

"Meaning ... "

"I want to know who murdered John Blakely and why."

She put the sandwich on the table. "I don't know."

"Who had reason to murder him?"

"I don't know that either."

"You're lying to me. That means prison. And with a mouth like yours, prison will be a grim experience."

She placed her face in her hands to try to hide her tears. He was surprised that her pretense of toughness was fading so quickly.

"Stop that now and answer me. Who had a motive for killing John Blakely?"

She glanced up. "I don't know, goddammit."

"Bullshit."

"I don't."

"Just last night you told Jasmine that John had crossed the line and some of you were right to be cruel to him."

She looked up, shocked, then seemed to remember something. "Oh no," she said. "I didn't mean we had anything to do with John OD-ing. It has nothing to do with it."

"Tell me what it is and I'll decide." She bit her lip and sullenly crossed her arms. Spracklin began to get up and collect his papers.

"John was ... " She searched for the right term. "Not a gentleman."

"I need facts – dates, names, places, evidence."

"John was a womanizer."

"It's the sexual revolution. Who isn't?"

"You don't understand. Women adored him." He sat back down. "John was handsome, never said much. He hung back from the crowd, always letting people come to him. Genius was part of his allure. It was an aphrodisiac just to be near him when he was painting. And he used it to his advantage. He'd ask chicks he dug to pose, then he'd get them to pose nude. That was the beginning."

"Consenting adults," said Spracklin.

"It wasn't always consenting. Jasmine didn't like it." She picked up his cigarette pack, shook one out and waited for him to light it. "Jasmine doesn't like boys."

"He raped her?"

"There are nuances. She didn't want to. He persuaded her."

"Did she resist? Tell him no? She seems ditzy enough to let any guy do what he wants."

Gloria looked at him with a stern expression. "She was educated at Princeton and writes beautiful poetry. But . . ."

"But?"

"She does a lot of acid. It gets to her. I don't know if she even realized what was going on."

"How often did it happen?"

"Once. I told him not to do it again."

"Did he do it again?"

"No. I think Jasmine actually dug him."

"Even though he raped her."

She decided she didn't like the cigarette and butted it out on the table. "She woke up beside him, and was upset. He didn't care – he just acted like sweet old John. Men liked him, women loved him. He broke so many hearts." She began to count on her fingers. "Joanie, Linda, Jasmine, The Seamstress, Sunrise, Evelyn . . ."

"The Seamstress?"

"This girl who lived at the house last summer."

"You didn't respond when I asked about her yesterday."

"She went to New York. There's a rumor she's back but I haven't seen her. She was just one of many. But you couldn't stay mad at John. He had this sweet nature, a sweet brilliant nature."

"What about you?"

"Me? John and I were friends."

"Cut the shit, Gloria."

"I liked him."

"Then why did you say last night that he crossed the line and you and Jasmine gave him what he deserved?"

"He went too far with Jasmine."

"It was more than that Gloria. Come clean or you're on your own."

"He never so much as looked my way," she said. She was beginning to cry. "He wanted all women, especially Jasmine, but he never so much as glanced at me."

"You were in love with him?"

"I adored him. But he'd just keep painting while The Mantis insulted me about my weight. So I got my revenge. Jasmine became my lover, and I loved to tell John about how great it was. And yes, I do feel guilty about that now."

Spracklin let her cry then adopted a lighter tone as he tried to find out other information, such as The Mantis' real name and whereabouts. She cooperated and he finally let her go. She was a woman overlooked by a womanizer. Was it a motive for murder? He didn't know. But he was glad she would be in a holding cell for the next few days.

CHAPTER 21

Spracklin leafed through some notes Tommy Jackson had given him as the elevator descended. In the basement, the door opened and he saw Ed Burwell was slouched in a chair in the reception area. "You're still here," Spracklin muttered.

"Where else would I be?"

Spracklin was too caught up in Jackson's notes to respond instantly. The cadet had talked to Julian Miller, the *Chronicle's* art critic, who spoke of Blakely's growing mystique since his death. Bryant Murray, his art prof at Stanford, had liked John but thought the boy should have had more sympathy for his father when his sister ran away. A.J. Vinnot, who owned Tableaux and Trinkets, said he sold twelve of Blakely's paintings at the exhibition, netting the artist $4,978. Jackson had talked to a guy called Simpson LaPierre, who worked at *The Oracle*, an underground paper on the Haight. LaPierre had little recollection of Blakely. Blakely had no record, no motor vehicle infractions, and his number had never come up for the draft.

"Okay Jimmy, I get that the kid in the freezer was hacked to death," said Burwell. "We've got at least one murder. But Blakely? Do we have anyone with a motive?"

They stepped into the coroner's office, which the staff had tried and failed to imbue with an antique charm. Someone had lined the shelves with old jars of specimens – a few eyeballs and dead salamanders – and dusty shelves filled with old volumes. But it fell short. It was simply a vast office that housed part of the civil service. The modern metal desks were neat and lit by long florescent lights that buzzed incessantly. Spracklin motioned Burwell to the desk and laid out the file. The top sheet was his own note.

Reg MacIntosh	*Artist – Rivalry? Stupid.*
Derek ???	*Teased about being soldier*
Jasmine (Real name?)	*Pressured into sex?*
Rupert Hill	*Vendetta against family.*
Gloria ???	*Loud mouth (harmless?)*
Raven (Real name?)	*Don't know enough yet. Withheld info.*
Andy Fox	*Drug dealer. Did Blakely owe him money?*
The Mantis ????????	

Spracklin filled in that Eleanor Jones was Jasmine's real name, Vanhusen was Gloria's last name and almost scratched out Rupert Hill. He wasn't sure the radical was still a suspect. He wrote in that Gloria Vanhusen was a jilted admirer. He explained what he'd learned to Burwell.

"And that's it," he said. "John Blakely had a few enemies, people jealous of his talent, women he'd bedded or rebuffed?"

"Did Gloria have the names of any former lovers?"

"Weird hippie names but nothing solid."

Ernie Swanson, a tall, orderly man in a well-pressed lab-coat, came in from the morgue. His glasses dangled on a string around his neck. He smiled and nodded. He would not show that he resented being there on a Saturday. Spracklin sometimes wished Ernie had some balls. There would have been something lovable about Swanson in any environment other than a police department.

Swanson led them into the examination room and they took up their positions on either side of the cadaver, which lay under a white sheet. They could make out the strange outline of a body missing its head, two arms and a foot.

As Spracklin leafed through the written autopsy, he felt that blend of nausea and intrigue policemen always feel when viewing a dead body. Someone would make a joke to lighten the atmosphere. It was only a matter of time. "The body was frozen about five to ten hours after the man died," Swanson said. "There was minimal decomposition."

"You can't tell how long it was in the freezer?"

"You said there wasn't much frost in it so I doubt it was long. Weeks probably. Obviously no one had looked in the freezer in a while. If one of the hippies had found a dead body in the freezer they would have. . ." Swanson started to snicker. "Put it out with the trash. Do hippies put the trash out?" There, thought Spracklin. The joke was out of the way.

Lifting the sheet, Spracklin examined the damage to the tissue around the shoulder and neck. The body couldn't possibly decompose, he thought, because there was too little flesh on it. The victim looked almost emaciated. His clavicle and ribs protruded. He checked the autopsy. Male, about five foot ten and one-hundred and fifty pounds. Probably in his mid-twenties. His body hair was brown.

"What can you tell me about the decapitation?" Spracklin asked.

"It took one hack, I reckon, with a heavy, blunt object, likely an axe," Swanson said. "The blade was more than six inches wide, more than that we can't tell. The blow entered from the left shoulder and moved down toward the shoulder blades. So the body was lying on its back, and the assailant was standing to the right." Spracklin crouched down and carefully studied the stump of a neck.

He moved to one side and lifted the sheet so the stump of an arm was exposed. He laid the sheet down across the chest. "And the arms?"

"Again the victim seems to have been on his back. The left arm was severed in one swipe, as was the right."

Spracklin walked around the table and studied the severed right arm. He moved to the end of the table and studied the severed foot. "Two strokes for the foot?"

"Two strokes," said the coroner.

"No sign of the missing extremities?"

"None that I know of. A head alone might be hard to get rid of but a head, two hands and a foot, they could be anywhere . . ." He stopped. "That's what I can't understand – why only one foot?"

Spracklin motioned to Burwell, asking him if he wanted to examine the corpse. He declined. "There's nothing that could identify this body," said Spracklin. "No teeth for dental records. No facial description. No fingerprints."

"But why one foot?"

"The hippies mentioned The Mantis was missing a toe. The assailant obviously wanted to make sure there was no medical proof that this was The Mantis, possibly to stop us from identifying him."

Spracklin moved around the table and studied the neck again. "Any indication of whether the head was injured before the decapitation?"

"None."

"So the severing of the neck caused the death?" He asked it as if it was a routine question.

"Did you read the report, Lieutenant?" asked the doctor.

Spracklin flipped to the second page and looked at the notes again. He'd assumed that the decapitation had killed the boy, so he'd just glanced at the cause of death. The man had died because of acute intoxication brought on by the effects of an opiate, namely heroin.

"Oh my God. He OD-ed?"

"We still need to get the toxicology report but the physical evidence – needle scars on the inner thigh and lower torso – indicate prolonged drug use. He bled very little, so he was already dead when his extremities were removed. The best guess is he died of a heroin overdose. All the axe-wounds were post-mortem. No blood was pumped through them. The wounds would have been darker otherwise."

Burwell stopped the doctor with a wave of his hand. "Hold on there. So The Mantis was already dead. Someone took him out and cut off all distinguishing marks, except his tattoo. Then they carted off his head, hands and one foot and left the rest in a deep-freeze?"

Swanson nodded. "Apparently, that's correct."

"Not quite correct," Spracklin said. He was studying the tattoo for the first time. "Answer one thing for me. Why did the assailant go to this trouble to remove the vic's extremities but leave the tattoo of the mantis on the right arm?" The spherical eyes of the bug gazed out of the dead man's shoulder at the investigator. "The perp could easily have cut the tattoo off with his axe." Spracklin frowned and bent closer to the tattoo as he noticed that the coloration was uneven. "Ernie, have you examined specimens with tattoos before?"

"Sure."

"And does the pigmentation fade or blotch after death?"

"Not as a rule. The point of a tattoo is it changes the color of the cells in the skin, in the epidermis and the layers beneath it."

"Yet this tattoo has gone all blotchy. Why is that?"

The doctor put on his glasses and studied the tattoo. He darted to a nearby table and came back with a magnifying glass and scalpel. He scrutinized the body for another half minute then gave Spracklin the magnifying glass. "Take a look at the surface," he said. "Look at the blotches of color."

"What am I looking for?"

"At the center of a lot of those blotches, you can still see tiny pin-pricks."

Spracklin squinted as he studied the blotches. There were indeed tiny holes. The doctor picked up a scalpel from a side table and bent over the cadaver again. He cut off a thin slice of the tattoo and took it to the desk at the side of the room.

"What are you thinking, Ernie?" Spracklin said.

The doctor placed the sample on a slide and put it under a microscope. "I'm thinking . . ." he said as he turned the knobs on his microscope. "I'm thinking . . ." He stood up. "Exactly. Go on. Take a look."

Spracklin gazed into the eyepiece and saw skin cells surrounded by green. "Now tell me what I'm seeing."

"A tattoo changes the pigmentation of skin cells, or macrophages. The artist takes a syringe and needle and injects ink into the cells, which retards their ability to cleanse the skin internally, even as the cells are replaced. But this ink never spread through the cells. It's just swimming around among them, and you can still find pinpricks where the needle went in."

"So . . ." Spracklin thought he understood but he wanted the coroner to say it.

"So this guy was tattooed after he died."

Burwell looked confused. Spracklin took the autopsy. "Ernie, we're going to need photos of your John Doe here – especially the tattoo."

The Lieutenant thanked the doctor for sacrificing his weekend, and said goodbye. Out in the hall, he gestured for Burwell to stop a moment.

Burwell took the lead. "Jimmy, Blakely did the original Mantis tattoo on the guy – I mean that guy the hippies call The Mantis, right?"

"Yeah, I think Derek told me that."

Spracklin was thinking things through as he spoke. "So if the intention here was to make the vic look like The Mantis, it's a safe bet that Blakely himself did this tattoo."

"Sounds reasonable," Burwell said. Spracklin could see where he was going but he wanted the Sergeant to work through it.

"So The Mantis owed Fox money. Fox has already cut off his toe. Someone ODs. The Mantis gets Blakely to do a tattoo on the body, then they dismember the stiff so he can't be identified. And The Mantis takes off hoping Fox will hear about this stiff and figure The Mantis is dead."

Spracklin wondered whether Burwell would finish the thought. He didn't, but at least he was starting to think.

"That also sounds reasonable," he said. "But there's more." Burwell looked at the Lieutenant. "Who's the only person who would have known The Mantis is still alive?"

"John Blakely."

Spracklin nodded slowly. "We've found a motive for someone to kill Blakely. I'd say we have to find The Mantis."

CHAPTER 22

As he stepped from his car on Saturday evening, Spracklin could piece together a theory on Blakely, but a few things kept nagging him. Why silver cyanide? Where did they get the body in the freezer? There was probably a gap of a few weeks between The Mantis leaving and Blakely's death. Why did it take Blakely so long to take the drug?

In the living room, Spracklin read the list of suspects again. It was mainly former lovers, jilted women and jealous artists. None had as strong a motive as The Mantis. *We have to find him*, thought Spracklin. *But we don't even know his name.*

"Any luck?" He wheeled around and saw Valerie in a yellow summer dress. She was wearing the smile he saw too often these days, a forced smile with which she tried to convince people nothing was wrong.

"We're narrowing it down. I have a suspect but only know him by an alias."

She paused, and continued to smile as she stepped to him and kissed his cheek. "I meant," she said, "when you looked for Marie today."

"Oh, no." He folded the sheet of paper and placed it in his pocket. "Naw, I didn't see her at all." He took his wife in his arms before she could move away. "But I did hear again that she's back in town." He settled in for a long hug, but she pulled back and held him at arm's length.

"Who? Who saw her?"

"I was interviewing a girl today, someone involved in this Blakely case. She said Marie was on the East Coast over the winter. Word on the street is she's back in town."

"What did the girl say when you asked where she is, Jimmy?"

"I didn't push it. I push it and everyone finds out she's a cop's daughter. Or she takes off again."

"But you've got to push it. Can't you dig just a little deeper?"

He placed his hand on her shoulders and looked into her eyes. "I love her, Val. I always have. But the last time I pushed it we lost her. We've got to be smarter this time."

He held her gaze for a moment, then she shook loose. Spracklin followed her into the living room. She sat on the sofa facing away from him.

"I don't want to fight about this, Jimmy," she said.

"I don't either."

She picked up a cushion and clutched it to her tummy. "You know, I just asked if you had any luck and you thought I was talking about the case. That's the problem. You can lose yourself in your work and your investigations. Even though you're responsible for her going." He was about to respond but she snapped, "Don't argue. Every minute of every day, there's a gnawing in my gut that's screaming at me that my girl is out there with those drug addicts and criminals. And now there's a murder. And you tell me you're not pushing it. I want to know my daughter is safe."

She left the room and he went upstairs and showered. He tried to relax in the hot water, but his fury was burning him. He'd done all he could to find Marie, to do what was best for his family. Yes, he tried to solve cases, but he had a sacred duty to find justice for murder victims and their families. He didn't know what else he could do to make Val understand that he loved Marie completely, every bit as much as his own sons. He'd adopted her, held her when she cried, took her to the park, and sailing in the summer. He did things with her even when Val was busy with the boys, like taking her and her little friend Raymond to the movies or the shooting range. *Raymond*, he thought. *Would everything be different if there had never been a Raymond?*

He glanced at the bedside clock as he toweled himself off. It was 3:25. He should go looking for Marie to placate Val. He'd planned to watch the debate that night between Bobby Kennedy and Eugene McCarthy. He could get to Haight Street and back in time for the debate, assuming he found Marie, and she was straight. If she was stoned, it would be a different story. He shuddered when he thought of the night the previous fall when he'd found his daughter, barefoot and braless in a basement on Page Street. She was in the middle of a crowd, swaying with the rhythm of some unfathomable music. As he tried to lead her out to the street, someone intervened. He'd punched the guy and taken her outside. All the way back across the bridge, she'd sat in the back seat mumbling about the plums on a dead tree that turned into prunes. She wept in her mother's arms once they were home, wailing about the prunes.

Three days later, Marie was gone again and Valerie suffered a complete emotional collapse. Spracklin called in sick for a few days so he could tend to his wife. Their friends from church rallied around, cooking and caring for the boys. The young ones couldn't witness their mother weeping for hours on end on her bed. The doctor sedated her and Val's sister flew in from Corpus Christi. In tiny increments, their life returned to a sort of normal. But Val seemed listless –

something vital was missing.

He had to stop by the kitchen before he left. His wife was staring out the window into the neighbor's back yard as he passed and tossed his dirty clothes in the washing machine.

"I'm going to look for her," he said. "I'll be a few hours. You're okay with the boys?"

She nodded, and he left the house.

CHAPTER 23

Fox liked the Drugstore Café, even though it had had to change its name. A year or two early, the California Pharmacy Board made the owner, Magnolia Thunderpussy, change it to the Drogstore Café. They said it wasn't legally a drugstore. That was the world every cat on the Haight was trying to escape, thought Fox. But you never fully escape human stupidity. He still liked to sit in the crowded diner, looking up at the high shelves behind glass and the railing around the mezzanine level. He liked the salads and fresh bread, though the servings were never enough to satisfy Jethro.

The big guy was waiting for his second sandwich when Fox pushed a paper napkin with some names on it across the table. Their new organization. It wasn't perfect, but Fox knew they had to put something together quickly. After glancing around for the waitress, Jethro read it and pushed it back.

"Soldier?" he asked.

Fox nodded. Jethro was right. There was a risk in putting Derek on the list. He was mainlining, and they'd just disciplined him. Derek would resent them and couldn't be fully trusted. "It's temporary."

Jethro nodded. But only once. He wanted it to be very temporary. "There's women," he said.

"Salesmen. Distributors."

"Two have aliases." A waitress brought him his ham and cheese sandwich. He took a big bite and mumbled, "I never like aliases."

Raven and The Seamstress were listed near the bottom. "We've checked out the first one," Fox said in a low voice. They'd gone over this. Raven's name was Elisha Twain and her Maryland driver's license showed she was from Baltimore.

"And the other one. . . ." Fox's voice trailed off. "I spent a long time chatting with her today. She's straight. She likes money. You can . . ." He thought back to the time he spent with The Seamstress in the office at Vague Dimensions. "You can connect with her. I think we could control her."

Jethro stiffened. There was a girl standing by their table, about twenty years old. She wore a floppy felt hat and granny glasses. Her rainbow skirt and halter-top

113

suggested she was trying to fit into the previous summer. She was trying too hard, Fox thought as he looked up.

"Hey, Andy." The girl was trying too hard to sound casual. "We were rapping at the Red Victoria the other night, and . . ." She giggled. "I'm just wondering if we can chat."

He looked at her again. A cop? No way. A mole? He doubted it. She was pretty but she was careless. He turned back to Jethro and began to talk about meaningless crap. She tried talking again, but Fox ignored her. He talked more nonsense, imagining he was slicing her cheek off. He just kept talking until she finally slipped away.

Jethro swallowed and whispered, "The Seamstress. What's her name?" He wasn't going to let it rest.

"I'll get it."

"We need it." There was an edge to Jethro's voice. He was getting restless. Fox thought the incident with the Soldier the day before should have calmed him down.

"I have a good feeling about her," Fox said. He recalled how her green eyes gazed at him, saw him. "She's impressive. We need good people fast."

They were in a public spot so he didn't mention the other thing that intrigued him about The Seamstress—the fact the homicide detective Spracklin had been asking about her.

Through another mouthful, Jethro said something else. The only word Fox understood was the last one: "Numbers."

Fox raised his eyebrows.

"Yer too worried about numbers," Jethro said more clearly. He took another bite.

"We need people."

"We need good people."

Fox pushed his empty plate to the middle of the table and leaned on his elbows. "So you think we should only bring on one-hundred-percent proven people?"

"Yeah," said Jethro. "And get rid of cats who aren't."

CHAPTER 24

The hippie in the Victorian cloak and top hat didn't remember how Spracklin had scowled at him an hour earlier. The Lieutenant had spent the late afternoon shouldering past the flakes and weirdoes who came out on a Saturday evening. He was once again searching for the daughter he allegedly didn't love enough. Jesus Christ, what did he have to do to prove his love for that girl again? He'd been wandering up and down the streets in the Haight, searching for Marie and cursing her mother, getting more and more furious. He stopped outside the free clinic on Stanyan. He needed a drink to calm down. He was about to head to the car where he had a fifth of scotch in the trunk, when the kid in the top hat twirled himself around a lamp post like Gene Kelly.

"Hey dude," the kid said with a smile. His hair waved as he swung. "Wanna score some peyote?" He swung around the lamp post again and added: "Three bucks a button."

Spracklin believed there was a law against stupidity. It wasn't written in any penal code, but the biggest reason people got arrested is they were just plain stupid. Most prison inmates were idiots, so it stood to reason there were criminal levels of stupidity. This kid, who should have at least suspected Spracklin was a cop, was a classic case. Spracklin paused and studied the kid and wondered if he should run him in. He lit a cigarette and thought of the paper work it would create. He couldn't be bothered. He'd let the asshole get over his high and crawl back into the Haight Ashbury Community Clinic. His eyes left the hippie and moved up to the clinic's oval wooden sign that hung nearby. Haight Ashbury Community Clinic. It triggered some sort of memory. HACC. Something twigged as he studied the blue Victorian structure with semicircular bay window hanging out over the sidewalk. John Blakely had scrawled HACC at the bottom of his drawings that looked like corpses.

Spracklin walked in and up a flight of stairs to a big waiting room, lined in a cream wainscoting with grey paint above. On one wall, a great psychedelic mural seemed to spring from the wainscoting. It showed a tangle of vines that bore cheerful human heads as fruit. All the figures were lined in rainbow contours.

"Can I help you?" A man with greying hair walked from the office with a clipboard. He wore a button-down Oxford cloth shirt, rumpled trousers and a badge that said Dr. Leger.

"I'm Lieutenant James Spracklin, SFPD." Spracklin showed his badge. "I'm looking for some information." The doctor looked at the ID and badge, studied Spracklin, and nodded. He led Spracklin back into his office and sat on the edge of a neat desk, clutching the clipboard to his chest. "An artist died on Haight-Ashbury last week," Spracklin began. "John Blakely. Did he ever come here?"

The look of caution turned to one of surprise. "Yes," the doctor said. "An intense lad. He used to help out during the night shift."

Outside, someone began singing an Irish folk song about the road to Dublin. "What sort of work?"

"He'd volunteer. He helped kids who were distressed, talked them down, checked to make sure no one needed attention, in case of an OD. It's becoming an epidemic, you know…" The doctor sighed. "We were all shocked about John's passing. His heart was in the right place. And he was so devoted to his art." He shifted and went silent.

"What happened to the kids who OD-ed?"

"What you'd expect — we'd call the coroner's office, record the details of their deaths, arrange for them to be taken away."

"And John Blakely would sketch them?"

The doctor jumped. "Absolutely not."

"Dr. Leger, he left behind a stack of sketches of dead guys – and he wrote HACC at the bottom of each one."

"I don't know anything about it." The doctor looked away.

Spracklin didn't know how good a doctor this Leger guy was but he was one lousy liar. He paused to let the guy squirm, then said, "I have this stack of sketches and they're one of the few clues I have in a murder investigation. I can discreetly look into them, or I can be pretty public about it."

"We work hard here, Lieutenant."

"I don't doubt that."

"We're understaffed, underfunded and John was a wonderful person who volunteered his time. He'd check the patients all night long, once every week." He paused and picked at the edge of his clipboard. "And if someone's breathing stopped – heroin is a respiratory suppressant – John immediately began AR and called for help. That boy saved lives – lives, plural. We were devastated when he died, and the irony that he died by an overdose haunts us all. We –"

"Dr. Leger, I want to know about the sketches."

The doctor took a deep breath. "People die, young people, and it's a heart-rending experience. Sometimes – a few times it happened – I came back to the patient after filling out paperwork or calling the coroner, and I found John drawing the deceased. I told him not to – told him repeatedly. He always promised not to, and he always did it again."

"You let him continue working here?"

"Dr. Don never knew it," said Leger, as if Spracklin should know who Dr. Don was. "John argued every artist needs to work from the human body. Rembrandt and Leonardo did so. It was harming no one. I figured it helped out one of our volunteers."

Spracklin figured the guy was a flake, letting hippies run around a health clinic sketching the deceased. "I understand John was nervous the last few weeks of his life. Did you notice that?"

"He left us a few weeks ago. Pulled a prank and we never saw him again. Odd really."

"Tell me about it," said Spracklin, leaning forward. "Every detail is important."

"It was about four in the morning. I believe it was two weeks ago last Thursday. John and I were down here, reviewing what needed to be done. Suddenly I heard all these obscenities being shouted upstairs. I thought someone was having a bad trip. I went up and found the noise was coming from a locked room, a store room – the door was jammed. When I finally got the door open, I found someone had taken my cassette player and recorded a bunch of swearing at the end of a tape. John had started the tape, cranked up the volume and jammed the door. So there was fifteen minutes of silence and then this hideous swearing. I turned off the tape and came downstairs and John was gone. I never saw him again. Two weeks later I heard he was dead from an overdose."

"You're sure John put the tape recorder in the store room?"

"I don't know who else could have."

The doctor seemed hurt that Blakely had parted with playing a prank on him. "So John was alone downstairs for how long? Please think carefully," Spracklin said. "This is important."

"Four, maybe five minutes," the doctor said. "You know how hard it is to judge time." He went over it in his mind again. "I'd say five minutes."

"Was anything else missing when you came downstairs—any thing or person?"

The doctor stroked his chin. "Well, yes, now you mention it." He turned and pulled out a hardback notebook and flipped through the pages. "Here we go. May 17." He studied the page. "We keep a record of everyone who comes and goes. One young man that night – we never got a name – came in, obviously with an adverse reaction to narcotics. He was in a room John had been monitoring. But when I made my next check, he was gone as well. I'd assumed he recovered and left – it happens you know."

"Do you have the boy's name – the one who disappeared?"

"I thought John had signed him in, but I could find no paperwork for him." He looked into Spracklin's face. "Lieutenant, we handle upward of thirty cases a night, many of them critical. We deal with the flow as best we can. It was a fraught night that John decided to pull his prank. And if I'd taken the time to follow up on that missing boy, other young people who needed my attention would have died."

Spracklin knew all about the constraints of proper funding. How many times had he faced the parents of a murder victim to explain his department would have to leave their case unsolved in order to move on to other homicides?

"You never saw either of them again?" The doctor shook his head. "The deaths you've seen around here – mainly from heroin?"

"All from heroin. I've seen no evidence that hallucinogens like LSD are lethal."

Spracklin nodded, thanked Leger and turned to leave. The doctor might have said good-bye, but Spracklin didn't hear him. The wheels were turning and he was getting a better picture of what John Blakely was up to in the last month of his life.

CHAPTER 25

Spracklin was lost in thought as he joined the line-up for Vague Dimensions behind a group of flower children. He was piecing together the scheme that The Mantis and John Blakely had come up with. It was just a theory with little evidence, but it made sense. He snapped out of his thoughts as he realized he was standing in the entry hall nodding to himself. The narrow room was lined with glossy pictures of the Vague Dimension's performers. Some, like Janis Joplin or the Chet Helms and the Family Dog, were allotted two frames. The two women in front of him – one in a flapper's dress and purple Converse All-Stars, and the other in coveralls made from an American flag – had gone through the swinging doors. A woman sat at a desk reading A. A. Milne and eating a carrot. Orange epaulets hung from the shoulders of her blue velvet tunic.

"Is there a cover charge?" Spracklin asked her.

"Tony says a cover creates the rigidity of a master-servant affiliation," she snapped, "and denies a performance the spirit of a shared experience."

"Tony."

"Tony's our impresario. He once staged *Aida* in the belly of a whale."

Spracklin concluded there was no cover charge. He stepped into the great hall, where a crowd of about fifty hippies was watching a trio play electric blues. Spracklin searched for Marie and some of the hippies from 1340 Masonic. Even in the darkened space, his eyes were drawn to the high walls, to the cartoons of different animals playing musical instruments. His mind kept wandering back to the case. He now understood where Blakely and The Mantis got the body from – they found a poor kid who'd died at the clinic, stole the body, dismembered it and tattooed it. But he was no closer in learning who or where The Mantis was.

One final thing nagged at him: would Blakely have held on to the heroin for twelve days before taking it? Spracklin doubted it. He was gaining a picture of Blakely as an obsessive man – a heroin addict, a fanatic artist, a sexual predator. He'd taken Marie as a lover. The prick. He may have broken her heart. Spracklin had come to terms months ago with the fact that his little girl had grown up quickly. He knew he had to love and protect Marie, just as he had to find justice for John Blakely. Sometimes Spracklin wondered what had become of his daughter. What drugs had she taken? Had she had graduated to heroin? Could she have turned to prostitution to support her drug habit. He couldn't imagine his wonderful daughter debased like that, but he knew this was Haight-Ashbury. If he could see her, he'd know whether she'd hit rock bottom.

On the stage, an overweight black man in striped bell-bottoms was playing a sloppy electric guitar. He was backed by a thin blond bass player with puffed sleeves and a drummer with buck teeth. The band's name was painted on the bass drum: Tomorrow's Leaders. The fat guy stepped to a microphone and sang scat.

> *I am Mankind's whipping post*
> *I am the cosmic spittoon*
> *Me, I'm broken-hearted*
> *'Bout how troubles started*
> *But I'll be 'ccused of 'em soon*
> *I'm up to me eyeballs in blame*
> *Biggest scapegoat there could be*
> *When the world got disjointed*
> *Then fingers got pointed*
> *Cause all the world's shit on me*

Spracklin noticed a dark dome of black hair against the crowd of people, and recognized the gold hoop earrings dangling below the afro. It was Raven, watching the stage and nodding her head to the beat. Spracklin stepped up beside her and said hello. She glanced over with a smile, her look hardened once she recognized him. She looked him up and down and said, "Dressed to blend in, didn't you?"

Spracklin grinned as he glanced at his windbreaker and khaki trousers, and then at her lavender Nehru jacket and Levi jeans.

"About as close as I can get," he responded. "C'mon, I'm not the only old guy here." He nodded to a fit-looking guy in his fifties talking to three young women. Spracklin wanted to be conversational. Her eyes always betrayed keen intelligence and he wanted to get through to her.

"Tony," she said. "He runs the place – big man in the arts around Haight-Ashbury."

Spracklin nodded and said, "We've got to have a chat soon."

"About John?"

"About John," he said nodding and looking around the room. "And the Mantis, and a few other people. The Seamstress, for example."

"The who?"

"The Seamstress. Know her?"

"Nope. And I haven't seen The Mantis in two weeks." Her voice carried above the music and people were looking at them. "And I really don't need you to bust me for smack while you're pretending to do homicide. My landlord will be here soon. He wouldn't like me talking to you." She walked across the hall to join a group of people standing to the right of the stage.

He wanted to bust her now, but he knew he had to be calm. He could apprehend her the next day and take her downtown for questioning. He began to meander through the hall again looking for Marie. He wondered if the place was licensed – he could use a drink. He sidled up to one young man, a fairly clean-cut guy whose blond hair was neat but fell over his eyes. "Know where I can get a drink?"

"Juice?"

"Hmm, a beer would be great."

The guy shook his head. "Only juice here." He nodded his head to a table at the side with a pitcher of juice and a stack of paper cups. A few kids were helping themselves. Spracklin thanked him and joined the kids, getting a cup. Orange juice, he thought. At least it was wet. He continued his scan of the room and shook his head. These punks thought they'd invented every vice imaginable and they were drinking OJ on a Saturday night.

The hall was darker now. He checked his watch. It was 8:15. If Marie was going to come, when would she be here? He didn't know. Fox was coming. That was fine. He'd like to talk to the guy. He had forty-five minutes until the Kennedy-McCarthy debate started. He could miss the beginning. He had hoped to question Jasmine. He'd have to take her outside, as he could hear little above the sound of the band.

> *. . . So now I stand before you*
> *My crown of dung upon me*
> *'Cause I made my abode*
> *'Neath mankind's commode*
> *And all the world's shit on me*

Tomorrow's Leaders finished their set and left the stage. Spracklin put his empty cup down on the table and clapped. He'd always liked the blues because of the links to jazz, and he thought these kids were pretty good. They were fun and talented and the crowd loved them. The hall was beginning to fill up. Looking around, he saw groups of freaks standing around the overhead projectors, flashing their messages up on the wall:

> *Shouldn't LBJ be succeeded by MCK?*

And

> *Why do they call chili chili when it's hot?*

Spracklin thought he heard kids laughing. He got the sense eyes were staring at him, although they did not meet his when he looked. Was he being paranoid? He moved to the back of the hall and leaned against the wall. He wanted to bust The Mantis. He'd murdered his best friend, who'd tried to help him. Talentless, abrasive, murderous – it would be a pleasure to arrest and convict this guy.

The room was now dark and only a black light was shining above him. High on the wall, a horn-playing goose shone, its pink eyes fiery. Spracklin realized he felt strange – fatigue? Stress? He leaned against the wall to steady himself, and saw a message beamed up on the wall for someone called Jimmy:

> *Jimmy! Jimmy!*
> *We know you feel*
> *Things don't seem real.*
> *Just why, we can't reveal.*

The young dreamy faces were staring at him. Someone was laughing.

Jasmine was on stage. He was feeling light-headed. Should he eat? He saw a chair nearby, groped toward it, and sat down. Jasmine was singing about an all-American dandy who fights crime. Spracklin smiled. He closed his eyes and the song enveloped him.

> *He was born in a log cabin and he'll never tell a lie*
> *He hates the Warsaw Pact and loves his mom and apple pie*
> *He loves the flag, the eagle, and all noble hearts and minds,*
> *He loves his country like himself, but he don't like my kind.*

He opened his eyes. The cat with a clarinet painted on the wall seemed to be pulsating. Spracklin thought he saw it move. There were more messages flashing up from the overhead projectors.

> *What can you say bout a gumshooooo*
> *Who's on the case but don't have a cloooo*

Jasmine's voice surrounded him. He shut his eyes and let that enchanting voice flow through his mind. She seemed to be singing about a policeman.

> *And he's got in his secret files*
> *Foolscap notes that run for miles*
> *And seven denim body bags*
> *Dental charts and ten toe tags*
> *And evidence and alibis*
> *'Bout the way an artist dies*

And who was there and then who wasn't
And four John Does and one Jane Doesn't
And one murderer who won't admit it
And the hall where Colonel Mustard did it . . .

The throbbing lights – purple, crimson, yellow – beat out the rhythm. They came in wave after wave and distorted the writing on the wall. He pondered her words: "The way an artist dies." He wondered if there was some meaning in the song that she hadn't told him. He had to interrogate her. He felt light beaming through his eyelids. Opening his eyes, he saw someone on a ladder on the far wall was pointing a spotlight at him, and in the glare he could see the silhouettes of the hippies staring at him. The wall of hippies changed into a single entity with frizzy edges that swayed to the beat of the music. He tried to suppress his fear of this beast, to control the reasonable portion of his consciousness that told him he had a gun in his shoulder holster. Still, he felt fear rising, and his chest tightened as he gazed around the room.

He focused on a message on the far wall.
He may fill me full of lead
But I think Jim's an acid head

Someone was crouching beside him. It was Raven. She leaned in, spoke quietly. But he couldn't hear her. Tomorrow's Leaders were on stage playing with Jasmine and the sound was deafening. He leaned closer to Raven.

"There was LSD in the juice," she whispered. "Get out of here before Fox arrives." He wondered if she was an illusion.

She leaned away, and when there was a silence before the next song, she looked back at him and said, "Lieutenant Spracklin, go home. Fox's people are here and he's on his way."

CHAPTER 26

Fox was coming. The news jarred Spracklin, and he felt an unaccustomed fear welling up from the pit of his stomach. Why? He'd learned in Normandy to control panic. Maybe it had something to do with the LSD. He could tell the hippies were staring at him. He would reveal his fear to none of them.

"It's okay," he said, feeling his tongue heavy and slow in his dry mouth. "I'm armed."

Raven smiled. "Lieutenant, leave your sidearm in its holster."

She laughed inexplicably and looked back at one of the green-rimmed silhouettes—the silhouette seemed to be melting. She turned back to Spracklin. "I told the others I came over here to play games with your mind. Now leave." The big smile persisted. "I'm in trouble if anyone finds out I've helped you."

Several lights shone on the crowd around him, and if he stood up he'd be in the light. Their colors kept changing. A strobe flashed behind a group of kids dancing, each flash produced a new distortion. On stage, Jasmine and Tomorrow's Leaders were playing a song about a child being born to give the world hope. High on one wall, Spracklin noticed his name glowing in the darkness.

What will the judge give Lootennant Spracklin
when they learn he's an acid head.

As he focused on the words, he saw the cartoon animals at the periphery dance with their instruments. He understood. They'd drugged him and now they were going to call his bosses and colleagues and have him jailed. He'd lose his job, his standing with Bobby Kennedy. He wouldn't be chief. He'd lose the respect of his boys and wife. He'd never reconcile with Marie. Panic welled, dark and wild, inside him. He tried to control it. He sat rigidly in his seat, breathed deep. He had to leave, but it was even more important to control his emotions.

Then there was another girl at his side. She held her head low so her blonde hair fell over her face. She took his right hand in both of hers and stroked the back of his hand. Each of her fingernails was painted a different color. "You have to go, Lieutenant," she said. "Fox is coming and he has Jethro with him." He tried to look at her face, but the thick hair hid it. She stood and pulled gently at his hand. He realized the spotlights were now pointing at the stage, where Jasmine

125

was singing.

> *A child is born 'mid blackened brick*
> *To lift the low and soothe the sick*
> *A tired man, his broken mate*
> *Speak no word but celebrate*

The verse ended with a heavy drum beat and the band fell silent. The hall seemed to freeze. Then the band took up the melody again and played right into the next verse.

> *A beam of light breaks through the mist*
> *And highlights all ambition's grist*
> *Dead eyes open, fabric's torn*
> *One simple act: a child is born*

"Lieutenant Spracklin." A voice in his ear. Raven again. She was so close her afro brushed his forehead. "There's a door to your right. Go through it and run. Your life is in danger."

The blonde girl with the painted fingernails was gone. Turning his head, he saw the glowing exit sign above the glowing mass of young people. He took a deep breath, stood up, tried to ensure he had his bearings.

On the stage, Jasmine was playing with the three misfits. And by the lit entrance, Andy Fox and his big blond friend were entering. Spracklin gazed at them, remembering the note with human flesh Fox had left on his car that morning. Fox and his muscle were in the hall. He wanted to bust them. They couldn't intimidate him. The big blond guy caught his eye in the dim light. They glared at each other across the crowded hall. Spracklin's muddled senses told him to get out, but he wanted those two thugs to know he didn't fear them.

The blond giant started to wade through the crowd. Spracklin wanted Fox to come over as well, but the drug dealer was drawn to someone else. It was a woman, with wavy hair. Was it Marie? The girl was smiling and talking to Andy Fox. Spracklin closed his eyes, squinted and looked again. Marie was laughing and talking with Fox, and the blond giant was coming toward him, seeming to grow larger with each step.

"Lieutenant, you have to go." It was Raven. She was still there, hunched beside him, trying to hide her body behind his.

"Not yet."

"Yes, now."

The giant was pushing people out of the way. Another few seconds and he would reach the detective. Spracklin clung to his reason, fought the effects of the drug. He had to decide whether to flee or try to get his daughter away from

126

Fox. Fox was smiling, reaching out to touch Marie's hair. Spracklin felt his jaws tighten. The latent fear was now turning to rage as he studied his daughter and the torturer. And the giant was looming larger as he was getting closer.

> *A child is born, too weak to cope*
> *Yet bears the weight of our great hope*
> *The strength to suckle one small boy*
> *And fill the craters of Hanoi*
> *And East Berlin and Central Prague*
> *Till roses fill each burnt-out crag*
> *A child is born, so carry on*
> *So carry on, so carry on.*

Spracklin moved. He shouldered his way past clusters of hippies and pushed open the door. He flew through a dim corridor to another door. He burst through and felt the cool night air hit his face. He was in an alley. At the end of it, Raven was standing under a streetlight. She must have gone out another exit and circled around to meet him. He flicked his hand, messaging her to leave, then he stepped behind the door he'd just exited. The door looked molten and kept changing color. Fear sparked again – he couldn't trust his senses. He breathed—be logical, think. Get behind the door. It will work. He took out his revolver and made sure the safety was on.

The door flew open, and the blond giant came out. He stopped, gazed down the alleyway, his back to Spracklin. Music poured from the hall. Spracklin could feel the sheer bulk of the man. Spracklin drew back his hand and smashed the butt of his gun against the giant's skull. The big man sank to his knees and fell over on his hands. He was stunned, but the blow hadn't knocked him out. Spracklin considered hitting him again, but he had to be careful not to kill him. This was simple payback for one of Fox's people braining him the night before in the basement of the house on Masonic.

He skirted around the fallen giant and dashed to the end of the alley, turning right as he'd seen Raven do. He'd run a block, when she called to him from an alley.

"Where's Jethro?" she asked. All he could see was the gold hoop earrings glistening in the streetlamp's faint light.

"I slowed him down."

The walls of the alley seemed to be closing in at the top. He felt a prickle of panic—the two of them would soon be swallowed up, he felt sure. She came into his line of sight, and he saw a furrow between her brows. She took his hand and led him down the block and uphill toward Haight Street.

He ignored the rust-colored flames in the trees and the organ music emerging from the sewer drains. He was hustling uphill, past the undulating lines of Victorian houses, which swayed to the music still ringing in his ears. He looked up at the orange eaves of the houses. The sound of each footfall reverberated in his ears. All perspective was exaggerated and the architectural details of each house stood out in perfect clarity. It was incredible. He must ignore it.

He couldn't tell how long they walked. The hallucinations took over and he had no choice but to trust Raven as she held his hand and led him. He was beginning to feel safe when he saw something move between two houses. It was a warrior astride a giraffe. Then he realized Raven was at his side pulling at him.

"Come in here." She was standing by an open door.

He stepped inside, and she shut the door. Her hair was now amber and moving as if it were alive. Outside, he heard men's voices.

"It's Jethro, maybe Fox. Come on."

She tried to lead him further inside. He held back. "Who are you?"

She glared at him, pulled him by the hand toward a narrow stairway, but the walls surrounding it were melting. "Who are you?" he said.

The voices outside stopped. Raven's hand shot out and hit the bolt-lock as the doorknob turned and the door rattled. Spracklin took out his gun. Raven grabbed his arm and pulled him up the stairs. They came to a hallway wallpapered with labels from beer bottles. Raven looked out a window then skipped past it. She stopped on the far side, looked out again and motioned him forward. He dashed past the window then followed her down the hall.

"Where are you leading me?"

"We're getting out of here," she whispered.

She stopped by a door and looked through a crack. She turned back to him. "Put your gun away."

"No."

"Put it away. We're going through this room. There's a window here that overlooks another yard. We'll go through and be a block away from Fox. Put the gun away."

He put the gun in the holster and followed Raven into the smoky room. Seven naked people were sitting in a circle and chanting. Three columns of smoke rose from joss sticks that encircled them. Indian music played on a portable record player. Spracklin heard the door crash open down at street level. He and Raven moved swiftly through the room. No one seemed to notice. Raven opened the window and stepped out on to the ledge. He followed her, thinking he heard footsteps in the hallway.

"Jump," whispered Raven.

He looked into the blackness. Was this the hippies' latest prank on him? "You're trying to get me to break a leg?"

"I'm trying to save your life."

"Why should I believe that?"

"Because I'm a federal agent."

She gave him a nudge, just enough that he was forced to leap into the darkness of the next yard.

Sunday, June 2, 1968

CHAPTER 27

In the depth of the night, he perceived the darkness. Rainbows no longer ringed the full moon outside the window. The outlines of the trees had stopped glowing. He hadn't had to run to the toilet in about half an hour. Jimmy Spracklin was beginning to see straight, but was he thinking straight? He'd seen Marie, his lovely Marie, with Andy Fox. Could he have been hallucinating? He yearned for his daughter so much he wondered if the drugs created images of her. He hoped so. The thought of her with Fox was too maddening to ponder. But he was rational now and he knew he'd seen them.

"You coming down?" Raven whispered.

"I'm sobering up." They were in a disheveled bedroom off some street in Haight-Ashbury. He had vague memories of Raven leading him there. Then she'd tried to calm him down, which was difficult as she'd kept looking out the window, or checking the door. She wouldn't allow any lights, not even a cigarette. They'd sat in the darkness on the single bed and waited.

"You're not hallucinating anymore?"

He shook his head. It made him dizzy. He took a breath and looked around the room. There was a selection of wigs and hats on the dresser and Andy Warhol posters on the wall. Warhol. The poor bastard had been shot the week before. He noticed a bottle of Drambuie on the dresser. "Where are we?"

"A friend's place. She's out of town. Modeling in Chicago. She lent me the key. I come here sometimes to escape 1340 Masonic. You okay?"

"Yeah, just a bit light-headed." She was sitting close to him, and the sag of the bed forced them toward each other. "But I had the weirdest dream. I imagined you said you were an FBI agent."

She looked tired. The enchanting grin was gone. "I said federal agent. Bureau of Narcotics. My name is Elizabeth Watkins."

"And the reason I should believe this is . . . "

She was already convincing him. It was the way she exhaled and slouched, relieved to shed her disguise. Spracklin had seen it before – the decompression that undercover operatives experience when they're among cops again.

"For verification you can call Superintendent Joshua Rosenfeld at the Bureau of Narcotics in Washington." Spracklin knew the name. When he was in Washington, Rosenfeld had been at a Midwest bureau of the FBI, Missouri or Kansas. Had he moved over to Narcotics? Raven handed him a matchbook. She'd written a phone number with a Washington area code inside the cover. She checked the window again. "If you call, tell him my mother's first name is Clarissa and my childhood hero was Heidi. I've been undercover for six months. We're watching Fox."

"I remember Josh," Spracklin said with a smile. "My wife and I had dinner one night with him and . . ." He snapped his fingers as he tried to remember Mrs. Rosenfeld's name. "You know, his wife."

"Shh," she said, looking at the door. Then she whispered: "Janet."

He felt the smile fade from his face. "No. Diane. Rosenfeld's wife is Diane." He began to wonder who she was and what her game was.

Now Raven smiled. He was still high enough that her teeth seemed to glow. "Inspector Rosenfeld left Diane for Agent Janet Lubinski two years ago." She shook her head. "Some detective you are."

He smiled with her. She was as clever as Marie, and then he thought of Marie, smiling with Fox. Marie. Jesus, seeing her again ripped at the chords of his heart. He wanted to head back to Vague Dimensions and look for her, but he had to stay in this apartment until he was stronger. He also knew Raven – Elizabeth Watkins – needed human contact.

"Tell me about your assignment, Elizabeth."

"I'm getting close." She leaned back on her hands. "About a year ago, we noticed a huge increase in the flow of opiates from Southeast Asia, and Andy Fox was identified as one of about a dozen kingpins. I went undercover in November and I'm getting closer."

She drew a deep breath and looked at him. "It's been getting tense, really tense." She was trembling. "One guy at the house called The Mantis disappeared, then John OD-ed. Then you said John was murdered. Reg, Gloria and the others were busted. And, and . . ." Her voice began to crack.

"You were close to John?"

She sighed. "I was close – am close – to all of them. They've become my friends. They're dead, busted or vanished, Lieutenant. I wasn't supposed to get involved."

She fought off tears, and Spracklin resisted the urge to reach out and hold her. "Elizabeth," he said. "This happens undercover. You grow close to people.

You've done brilliantly just hanging in there this long." He placed his hand on her knee. "Now tell me why you say you're getting close."

She leaned toward him and spoke in a hushed voice. "Because Fox's organization is collapsing. The Mantis and Reg were key lieutenants, and now they're both gone. It used to be that one of them would get shipments from Jethro and they'd distribute it among us to sell. Now they need a new lieutenant fast."

"Why fast?"

"Fox has to cover his losses from when you busted Reg – at least that's the word on the street. He's got a shipment coming in and he needs people to sell it."

Spracklin's mind drifted as she spoke. Fox was recruiting and he was hanging out with Marie. Was he seducing Marie to get her to join his gang? "Is he recruiting street dealers?" Spracklin interrupted.

She looked at him impatiently. "Did you hear what I said?"

"Sorry. Go on."

"Fox has let us know we should be calm – that more stuff is coming in. Then today, he shows up at the Mime Troupe at Golden Gate Park. I have a job there, as their barker. He shows up and asks me if I have a driving license. I say yeah, but I don't have a car. He says don't worry about that. There's an errand Tuesday night. He told me to get lots of sleep 'cause I may be driving most of the night."

"Yeah?"

"So I ask him where we're going and he says Arcata. Tuesday night."

Spracklin tried to piece it all together, but he was still light-headed. Arcata, he knew, was a little coastal town near the Oregon border. "So his stuff is coming into Arcata on Tuesday night."

"If not Arcata, then near it. He's from up around there and we believe he's using fishermen to smuggle stuff into the country. He wants me to be his donkey. I'll be there when it lands. With luck, he'll give it to me himself, or I will bring it to him."

"Do you need backup from us?"

"Out of your jurisdiction. I hate going near a phone and I won't see my local contact Max till late tomorrow. The Bureau's field office has a young agent that checks on me each week at the Mime Troupe. I want you to get word about the drop to Superintendent Rosenfeld. You have to be fast. The drop-off's in three days."

Spracklin nodded, then laughed.

"What's so funny?"

"Yesterday, I wanted to arrest you and now you're ordering me to stay clear of your jurisdiction." She smiled. She'd seemed to relax during the debriefing. Official business seemed to calm her. She was an impressive young woman, courageous and intelligent.

"I'll do anything I can for you," he said. "Let's take down Fox and get you back to D.C. Anything else I can do?"

Her eyes took on a mischievous glow. "Well, Lieutenant, there is one thing you could do to help a lady in peril."

"And what's that?"

"You could forgive me for knocking you out last night."

The smile faded from his face. "You were the one who whacked me."

"Sorry," she said. "I had no alternative."

He sighed and looked away. "I'd say not knocking me out would have been a good alternative." He took the bottle of Drambuie from the dresser. Without asking if it was all right, he uncorked it and took a sip.

"Well," she said. "Last night, after Reg got busted, Fox and Jethro called a meeting at the house. While they were inside, I snuck out and searched their van. I found nothing but weapons, then I snuck back to the house. I wanted to listen to what was being said so I went down to the basement, to the room below the raccoon room, where they always meet."

"Why not just go to the meeting? You live in the house."

"Because Fox has these little side meetings with people. He's big on getting inside people's heads and manipulating them." She took the Drambuie from him and sipped. "So Fox had just taken Gloria into The Mantis' old bedroom, and suddenly I hear someone else in the basement. I thought it might be Jethro, but you flicked on your lighter in the pottery room. Then you came into the room where I was hiding. I hid behind the door when you flicked the lighter on again. Then you fell off the freezer. Fox and Jethro were coming. If they found me there with you, it would – my mission would never recover. I knew how to get out – there's an old coal chute across the hall. I whacked you with a piece of two-by-four, tipped you over the freezer and bolted. They caught a glimpse of me, and followed me. I don't think they even knew you were there."

Spracklin closed his eyes and let the little lights swim around for a moment. He took the bottle back from her and drank. He shook his head and drank again. "I need The Mantis," he said.

She sounded surprised by the change in the conversation. "He's gone. I don't know if Fox killed him but I haven't seen him in weeks."

"I think he's alive and that he killed John Blakely."

"The Mantis? He worshipped John."

"Tell me about him. I need a name and home town."

She thought for a moment. "I just don't know. He was – he never used a real name, didn't have parents." Spracklin gave her a sidelong glance. "It's the economics of the Haight. Most kids get money from their parents. The only time you learn their real name is when they get checks in the mail from Mom and Dad – the real name's on the envelope." She laughed. "As for The Mantis, I got the sense he was from the Midwest, but I don't know for sure."

"You've been here six months. You must know something about him."

"He was a big, athletic guy with a big mouth. He'd studied biology. He could be funny. He liked to brag he'd had sex with Janis Joplin, like it was something to be proud of. A tattoo of a praying mantis on one shoulder and an eagle and a dog on the other arm. He owed Fox money, Fox cut off his little toe and then he disappeared. He and John were both scared shitless toward the end." Her expression and gestures grew more intense. "At least, they seemed scared. Maybe it's just that everyone's scared. Maybe it's just that I am."

"Elizabeth, you're cool as a cucumber."

"I can't imagine he would hurt John."

"All we've got is a theory now." They shared the liqueur as he told her about the body in the freezer, the post-mortem tattoo and what he'd learned at the medical clinic. "So Blakely was working there each night – he liked drawing kids who'd overdosed. What I think happened was he kept an eye open for some poor sucker who died, so he could steal the body. He'd prepared for it by making a tape full of yelling. And when he found one, he created a diversion with the tape and called in The Mantis to help him carry the body out –"

"Football," blurted Watkins. She put her hand on his forearm and laughed. He felt the warmth of her fingers on his skin. "The Mantis played college football – I heard that about him."

He tried not to notice how the warmth of her touch spread up his arm. "Sorry," she said. She took her hand of his arm and reached for the bottle. "Go on."

"So," he said. "When the doctor was upstairs, he and The Mantis took off with the dead kid. My bet is they took him into Golden Gate Park, into the bushes, where they used an axe to remove the extremities, anything that could identify him. Then Blakely, the guy who'd done the original Mantis tattoo, did a tattoo on the stiff."

"Sounds desperate."

"The Mantis was desperate – Fox was ready to kill him."

"And you think they put the body in the freezer. And as The Mantis fled, he gave John a vial of poisoned heroin."

"Yes. To cover his tracks."

She placed the Drambuie back on the dresser. "I can't see The Mantis doing that."

"Murderers never seem to be the type to kill someone, not in my experience."

She thought about it and tried to smile. "Like I said, I've made friends here, and most of them are either dead or busted. I feel some days I'm going nuts."

He put his arm around her and pulled her close – to comfort her, he assured himself. Her head dropped to his shoulder and stayed there. "You're doing brilliantly, Elizabeth," he said into her hair. "In a few days you'll nail Fox, and it will all be over."

CHAPTER 28

Light from two candles flickered across the corrugated metal above their naked bodies. It illuminated the plaster cast sculptures that surrounded them – a horse's head, a car with a smiling face, a baby-blue unicorn. The props from recent plays and pantomimes at Vague Dimensions had been painted in bright colors, but the hues were dull in the weak light. With her chin resting on Fox's chest, The Seamstress studied each one and looked around the storage area.

"So this is where you live?" she asked, shifting on the bare mattress.

"A guy I work with showed me this place – I crash here sometimes," Fox murmured. He was fighting off sleep. He wanted to be with awake with her, to talk with her as long as he could. The Seamstress had been impressed that someone his age liked rock, and even knew some of the bands that performed at Vague Dimensions. Just before the last set finished, he'd taken her by the hand and led her behind the stage's rear curtain to a rickety ladder that led up to the metal catwalk. Off to the side was a storage area, with a mattress on the floor. He lit a candle and they lay down. She was nervous, even a bit reluctant at first. But he used gentle persuasion, told her she was special, beautiful. She was comfortable in her nakedness, let him kiss her, eventually responded passionately. She was nervous, Fox knew, and the next time their passion would overcome the tension.

"I live in my van," he told her. "Where do you live?"

"Tony found me a place."

"Didn't want to move home with your gun-toting dad?"

"Not my gun-toting dad. Not my over-protective mom."

"I thought it was dads who were over-protective." She didn't respond. "He wasn't protective?"

"What? Oh, uhhh. Yeah, yeah. In his own way he was protective."

He couldn't see her face but there was something in her voice that said she was smiling. "How?"

"He taught me to protect myself. That was his form of caring. He told me, never drink too much, never get in a car with a drunk boy." Her voice drifted off.

"And he taught you how to shoot a gun."

She was about to agree and caught herself. "To use a gun. To clean it, aim it, how the safety worked."

"Life lessons from an aging Republican."

"No." She lifted her head, turned to him and smiled. "No, a Kennedy Democrat. But very, *very* big on military service."

"The World War Two generation. Even their liberals are fascists."

"Right on."

"So is that why you left home? Because he wanted you drafted."

It was a lame joke and it fell flat. "No," she said. "My friend Raymond."

"Boyfriend?"

"No, no. Raymond was this goofy kid who lived next door. We always played together." She smiled. "I think I liked him 'cause I always won when we wrestled. Even though he was two years older than me." She rolled over so she was lying on her belly and dropped her face into her hands. "Didn't have an athletic bone in his body. My Dad would get us out playing baseball – Raymond always wanted to be outfield 'cause he figured everyone would leave him alone if he was out there. He was probably gay. He didn't live long enough to find out. He died in Vietnam."

She tried to say it nonchalantly, as if she had long ago come to terms with Raymond's sad story, but it was unconvincing. She looked at her clothes, draped over a steamer trunk a few feet away. She stood and walked over to the trunk.

"Are you leaving?"

"Gotta piss."

"But first you have to answer a question?" She was about to step into her panties but stopped. "Why do you blame your father for Raymond's death?"

She pulled her panties up, put on her jeans. Had he pried too much?

"Tell me," he coaxed. "It's good to be open about these things."

She sat down beside him, took his hand in hers. He squeezed her fingers. "Raymond got drafted," she said. "No one was ever worse suited to the Army than Raymond. I told him to go to Canada. We were in my parents' kitchen. Dad heard us, he came in and gave Raymond that line that the Army would be good for him, that it would toughen him up. We fought. Raymond listened to Dad, not me. He wanted to serve his country."

"And he bought it in 'Nam?"

"First month. Stepped on a Claymore – one of our mines. I'll never forgive my father. Raymond would be alive and in Canada if it weren't for him."

She wasn't close to crying, but she had the solemn tone that said she had shed tears often for Raymond over the last year.

He nodded. "It's so tragic when young people die. Did you hear about a cat on Masonic, an artist called John Blakely?

She'd picked up her bra, and her arms tensed when he mentioned the name. "Yeah," she said. "It was sad."

Clothed, she stepped around the mattress and left the storeroom. He listened to her footfalls against the metal grating then reached over and grabbed the handbag she'd left beside the mattress. He took out her wallet and flicked through her identification cards. She had a California driver's license that gave her name and address. Her name was Marie. He slipped the license into the pocket of his Levis. He returned the wallet to her handbag long before he heard her climbing back up the ladder.

CHAPTER 29

Spracklin opened one eye and saw the mesh curtains billowing in the morning light. Raven, the athletic black woman from the house on Masonic, was standing at a broad mirror, fussing over the puffy sleeves of her shirt. It took a second to remember. Vague Dimensions. Her mission. Hallucinations. Marie. Marie and Fox.

"Good morning," Elizabeth said, smiling at him in the mirror. She'd changed into a white silk shirt and purple bell-bottoms. Dressing in mod fashion seemed to have brightened her spirits. Spracklin felt dizzy and his mouth was desperately dry. He noticed he still had his shoes on.

"Where did you say we are?"

"My friend Natalie's flat, on Cole Street. She's a model, and when she's out of town she lets me stay at her place. That means I can borrow her clothes."

"Fantastic." He stood and stretched. In the mirror, he could see himself: five o'clock shadow, bloodshot eyes, waxy complexion, grass stains on his pants where he'd landed after jumping from a second story. He walked into the bathroom and cupped some cold water to his mouth. He walked out and shook a cigarette from the pack. "I have to know about Fox's organization."

"You can't smoke in here," Elizabeth said. He gave her a look, asking why not. "Natalie doesn't like it."

"I need details on Fox."

"He didn't kill John."

"There are people of interest we think are in his organization." How much should he say? He didn't want Raven to know about his daughter, not yet. "I just need details."

She looked perturbed. "I told you: Fox, then Jethro, then a bunch of dealers. Jethro will give the stuff to one dealer – it was Reg before Friday. We never see Fox with the stuff."

Spracklin nodded. "Yes, yes, you can't nail Fox yet."

"Not for narcotics," she said.

Spracklin paused. "What could you nail him for?"

"Assault with a deadly weapon. As long as I can find The Mantis." He wasn't following her. "Fox was the one who cut off The Mantis' toe because of a debt. Jethro and Reg held him, but Fox cut him. The Mantis told me. If we can find him, he'd testify in exchange for immunity." She returned to the mirror and made sure her earrings were secure. "I have enough on The Mantis to put him away for a long time."

"You can get a conviction for The Mantis?"

"For four months, I received heroin from him. I swapped it for cash with my contact Max and The Mantis took that money. We have records, dates, places, photos – I have enough to nail The Mantis." She picked up her suede handbag.

"You know of a girl known as The Seamstress?"

"The who?"

"The Seamstress. She does embroidery, makes clothes."

"Never heard of her. Why?"

"I'd like to ask her a few things."

"You'll have to tell me more later. I have to get to work – handing out flyers for the Mime Troupe at Free Street."

She leaned over, kissed his cheek, hugged him quickly and was gone. Free Street, he thought. He remembered Derek had told him it was the name for the market that took place on Haight Street every Sunday. He lit his cigarette. It wasn't a street at all – it was a market, a place where local craftsmen bartered their stuff. If Marie was anywhere on Haight-Ashbury, he thought, she'd be on Free Street selling shirts and wall hangings. He needed to get down there, but a lot of hippies would recognize him. He looked like hell, and he needed to be less conspicuous.

He walked over to the clothes rack and studied the hats on top of it. He tried on a panama with an aquamarine band, checked himself in the mirror then pulled the band off. The hatband was too conspicuous. Without it, he looked like a rummy and would fit in with all the drifters on the Haight. He could pull the hat just low enough that people wouldn't see his face.

Outside, Haight Street was bustling. Spracklin stood on the corner and gazed at the freaks milling about the blankets that were spread all over the sidewalk. He saw no sign of Marie – just the usual weirdoes picking over the crafts, clothes and foods. Most vendors were offering food. He meandered through the crowd. Outside the Red Victorian Hotel, he drew up beside a woman who was offering scarves. She drew a blank when he asked her about The Seamstress, and he moved on.

Spracklin estimated the merchants took up about four blocks on both sides of the street, from Shrader to Masonic. He stood tall, gazed east, and spotted an afro bobbing among the distant crowd. He could imagine Raven handing flyers to the hippies and passersby, none of them knowing she was on the verge of a bust that could make her career. To keep up appearances, he stopped to check out some cheese, wrapped in wax paper and spread out on a blanket.

"How's it shakin'?" asked the young cheese-maker, a slight hippie with a Ho Chi Minh goatee. He peered at Spracklin through granny glasses. Spracklin shrugged. "Like some cheese?" the kid asked. Spracklin shook his head. He had nothing to trade. "I don't need anything for it," said the vendor. He smiled faintly. "Go ahead."

Spracklin realized he was hungry. He took the chunk of the brie and nodded his thanks. He stood in an alleyway as he ate it. It was delicious—salty and creamy. He noticed a newspaper box. The *Chronicle* headline screamed that Kennedy had gained a slight edge in the previous night's debate. Spracklin rolled the wax paper into a ball, tossed it in a trash can, and walked north, where's he'd seen Raven. He stopped at a phone booth on the corner of Clayton Street. He checked the people nearby, stepped in, closed the door, plugged in a dime and dialed Ed Burwell's home number.

"Burwell."

"Spracklin."

"Where the fuck you been? Your wife's looking for you."

Oh shit, he thought. Spracklin knew Val and the boys would be getting ready for church, but he'd have to miss the service that Sunday. "Some kid slipped me a mickey. I'll explain later. Gotta pen?"

"Yup."

Spracklin read out the number for Rosenfeld in Washington, and made Burwell read it back. "Tell Superintendent Joshua Rosenfeld – Got that?"

"Joshua Rosenfeld."

Spracklin looked around. "Tell him Elizabeth Watkins' mother's first name is Clarissa and that her childhood hero was Heidi."

"What's this — "

"No time. Top secret. Then tell him Fox wants Watkins to go with him up to Arcata on Tuesday night. Up near the Oregon state line. She thinks it's for a drop. Top secret. Highest priority. "

Spracklin waited while Burwell read it back. Down the crowded sidewalk, Raven came into view. She stopped to chat with people bartering clay jars. It reminded

Spracklin that he would probably run into Derek selling his pots. Spracklin noticed a quick motion at the edge of his vision. A man ducking into an alley. He looked over, and saw Andy Fox peering out of the alley at Raven.

"Now I got to tell you –" said Burwell before Spracklin cut him off.

"Gotta go." It would be fatal for Raven if Fox saw Elizabeth even glance at Spracklin.

"Your wife called."

"Is there a problem?"

"They're all okay. Al Morton is with them and we have a squad car in your driveway."

"What happened?" Spracklin could see Fox sinking back into his alley so he wouldn't be seen by Raven.

"When she opened the living room curtain this morning, 'I want my horse back' was spray-painted all over the living room window. She called me and went nuts. I calmed her down, but she's upset. You better get home."

Raven crouched to look at something on one of the blankets and Spracklin lost sight of her. Fox was lingering. *Why was he spying on Raven? Had he made her or was he just suspicious?* Spracklin's own suspicion persisted. *Why was Fox so interested in Raven? What had he seen last night?*

"Jimmy?" Burwell was still on the line.

Spracklin knew he had to make a decision. "You say there's a patrol car in the driveway?"

"Yeah."

Val and the boys were safe. He was more worried about Raven and Marie now. Marie was obviously part of Fox's gang – who else could have given him the address of the Spracklin home? Fox could lead him to Marie. "If she calls again, tell her I'll be home as soon as I can."

Spracklin hung up, dipped the hat to shield his face and walked back toward Cole Street, near where Raven was. He stopped in front of a blanket, where a pimply kid was selling hand-carved pipes and letter-openers. He could see Raven, but not Fox. He had to get a lead on Fox. What had he done to Marie? Spracklin thought back to the psychiatric report that he'd read. Fox had a knack for making his followers think he'd formed a deep psychological bond with them. Had Marie been persuaded to betray her own family?

Feeling the muscles in his jaws tighten, Spracklin wondered if he could lure Fox into an alleyway and take care of him. Fox probably had a knife. All Fox had to do was pull the knife and Spracklin could finish the job. Fox obviously knew that Marie was Spracklin's daughter. How else could he have got his address from her? The cocksucker. Rage pulsed in Spracklin's temple. *I could kill him, then Raven's assignment would be over.* Spracklin walked about half a block, keeping his eyes peeled in the alleys for any sign of Fox. The fuck might have moved without him noticing. Spracklin was pulling up near the Psych Shop window when he saw Fox's mauve shirt. He was crouching behind a parked truck. All Spracklin needed to do was walk by him into an alley and Fox would follow. He'd decided that's what he would do when a scream pealed across Haight Street. The sound came from the direction of Golden Gate Park. Pandemonium was breaking out. A girl was running away from an alleyway screaming, and several people were shouting.

"He's dead," a woman yelled. "He's dead!"

Spracklin took one last glance at Fox, and turned toward the screaming woman. He shouldered through the crowd, and forced his way into the alleyway, coming to a parking lot in the rear. Three hippies were gathered around a figure slumped on the ground.

"Police," Spracklin said. "Stand back, please."

They looked at him doubtfully. Removing the Panama hat, Spracklin pulled out his badge and they stepped back.

"It's the pig who was tripping at Dimensions last night," said someone in the crowd.

"Don't touch anything," Spracklin said. "This is a crime scene."

Spracklin held out his arms, ushered the kids back and turned to face the poor barefooted bastard slouched against the brick wall. The color was drained from his face, he'd vomited and his lips were blue. Spracklin made the customary check of his pulse. There was none.

The rubber hose was still tied around his upper arm, and Spracklin could see the scar tissue around his major veins. There was a vial, spoon with a burned bowl and a little flask of white powder near him. Vomit caked the stubble of his chin and his shoulder.

"Lieutenant Spracklin?" said a man's voice. Spracklin looked up to see a patrolman, about thirty, with a bit of a belly. Looked like a career patrolman. "Lance Schmidt, sir. Patrol, Park Station."

Spracklin stood and they looked down at the corpse.

"We're seeing more of this, sir. Lot of ODs."

"This was murder," Spracklin said. Schmidt looked puzzled. "This boy's name was Derek. He was a Vietnam vet. I interviewed him two days ago about a housemate of his who was also murdered."

They stood above the kid who'd survived Vietnam only to be murdered in a community that celebrated peace and understanding. "I haven't heard of any murders around here," Schmidt said.

"An artist called John Blakely. Same MO as this one." The constable still looked doubtful. "Constable, ever see an OD where the victim barfs while he dies?" Schmidt shook his head slowly. "That's because it wasn't an OD. It was cyanide poisoning."

The patrolman clearly wasn't convinced yet, so Spracklin took a handkerchief from his pocket and delicately picked up the syringe. "Smell," he said and he held it to the patrolman's nose. Schmidt sniffed it tentatively.

"Almond," he said. "It smells like almond."

"I figured as much. Someone cut silver cyanide with his heroin, same as with Blakely." Spracklin took one more look at Derek and then told the patrolman he was going to get his kit to begin to work the crime scene.

CHAPTER 30

Back in his driveway, Spracklin was relieved when patrolman Herb Frank, the constable who'd parked all day outside the Spracklin home in Marin, accepted a cigarette. As Spracklin held out the lighter for Frank, he studied his house and vandalized window. Valerie had found some turpentine and cleaned off the graffiti, though some pink smudges remained on the plate glass. From inside the house, Spracklin could hear his boys' music booming from the HiFi. The Beatles. Sergeant Pepper's. Marie had played that album non-stop in the weeks before she left. There was one tune she'd chosen again and again. After she ran away, Spracklin realized it was called "She's Leaving Home".

Marie. He visualized her smiling as she looked into Fox's eyes.

"Another homicide?" Frank asked. Spracklin knew he had to go in and face his wife and another fight, but he could chat with the patrolman for a few minutes.

Spracklin nodded. "Soldier – just back from Vietnam. Now he's dead on Haight Street."

The fact that Derek Hodgson had been a soldier made his murder all the more tragic, Spracklin felt. He'd called the Boston Police Department to request they inform the parents. He imagined the despair of the couple who would have feared that call while their son was in the combat zone. They must have thought the danger had passed.

"Same MO as the murder we've been investigating the past three days," he said. "Poison. At least, we think it is. Autopsy pending."

Spracklin had called Ernie Swanson but couldn't get him out to perform his second unscheduled autopsy of the weekend. The Lieutenant was proceeding under the assumption it was the same murderer and he or she had again used silver cyanide. Spracklin had worked the crime scene and found nothing. He'd had the uniforms canvas the people on Haight Street. He knew it was futile – the murderer was nowhere near the Haight. Spracklin himself had gone through Haight Street looking for anyone that matched the description of The Mantis, still his main suspect. Another pointless exercise, but he used it as an opportunity to look for Marie. He couldn't escape the image of her smiling at Fox. He'd put out an APB for Fox and the paisley van.

147

"So we have a serial killer on Haight Street?" Frank asked.

"Looks that way. The press will be all over it in the morning."

They finished their cigarettes in silence. Spracklin didn't want the media crawling all over this case. It was too personal now. He dropped his butt on the asphalt and stamped it out.

Valerie didn't turn from the stove when he came in. The kitchen smelled of the chicken she was frying, and the spattering sound drowned out the Beatles. He stepped over, placed a hand on her shoulder and kissed her cheek. She didn't recoil, but she didn't respond either. She'd been cool when he'd called earlier – she didn't believe his story that someone had slipped him a mickey. The news of another murder concerned her only because it might affect Marie. Spracklin squeezed his wife's shoulder. Now he would have to lie to her – this courageous woman who'd already lost a husband and a son – and tell her he hadn't seen Marie.

"Any leads?" she asked flatly as she stirred the chicken breasts with a fork.

Spracklin thought before answering. She'd used the word "leads" so she must be talking about the case, not Marie. "Nothing. We think it's the same perpetrator as the Blakely murder."

"That Fox character?"

"We're not sure." Spracklin took two glasses from the shelf. "I think the same person committed both murders." He took an ice tray from the freezer, pulled the metal lever and a few cubes flew out. He plunked them in the glasses and floated them in scotch. "But we have a warrant out for his arrest – for what he did here."

"Oh yeah, that. I forgot about that."

He fought the impulse to react to her sarcasm. In the next room, the Beatles record finished, and they heard another disc dropping down the spindle. The boys had been delighted at Christmas when they got the cabinet stereo with the record changer that could hold five LPs. They'd been torturing their parents with it ever since.

"Val, I had to take that case. I found the body. It's likely the same perpetrator as the last one. The guy was a soldier, for Godsakes."

"Don't you use that language with me," she hissed. Neither of them wanted the boys to hear them fighting again. "I have to bear all this on my own. You tell me my daughter's back on the Haight just as all these murders are happening. And now this maniac is targeting our house. How the heck he knows where we live is beyond me."

"We're looking into it."

She turned down the heat under the chicken and lit the flame under the carrots. She turned and studied him. "And there's no more news on Marie?"

He shook his head and took a sip of scotch.

She held her gaze on him a second longer than he liked before returning to the stove. The music coming from the next room sounded familiar to Spracklin. He thought he'd heard the driving rhythm and blues beat and scat singing before, but he couldn't place it.

He placed his glass on the counter and wrapped his arms around Val's waist. He just held her, hoping the touch of his body would be more soothing than words. She held her frame rigid and continued to stir the carrots. He held on, sure she'd soon relax and their bodies would meld together. She turned off the left element. The sizzling of the chicken began to die down, and the boys' music filled the house. She turned to the carrots. Spracklin felt his spirits lift as he listened more closely to the lyrics of his boys' record.

> *I am Mankind's whipping post*
> *I am the Cosmic Spittoon*
> *Me, I'm broken-hearted*
> *'Bout how wars got started*
> *But I'll be blamed for 'em soon*

Tomorrow's Leaders. His sons were listening to a record of a band he'd stumbled on last night. It brought back the image of Marie and Fox. He couldn't escape it.

Valerie broke away from him and moved to the refrigerator, checking for something in the vegetable crisper.

He'd tried. She was in pain but she was only seeing things from her side. She didn't understand the responsibilities he had to other people, living and dead. With his head held high, he walked past her and went upstairs to have a shower. He tried to calm down. Maybe things would settle as the evening went on. He'd have another drink, watch Walt Disney with the boys and have an early night.

He walked into the living room, where the boys were playing a game of Mousetrap – rather they were trying to play the game, improvising with popsicle sticks and bottle caps to make up for missing pieces. "Need a hand, fellas?" he asked. They were too consumed with the game to look up.

"I bet I can help you with that," he said. But again they ignored him. They were focused on trying to fix one of the plastic gizmos.

Spracklin was about to crouch beside his boys, when he noticed the record was now featuring a female vocalist. It was Jasmine, singing the song he'd heard her sing in the sunshine the first day he took the case.

> *Just a whiff of mischief*

Under crackling summer stars
A fiendish laugh and darting eyes
A lung of smoke and flash guitars
The rugged, roguish boys
Run with Satan's Earthly flock
It's just a whiff of mischief
And it's only two o'clock

Spracklin looked at the pile of records and discarded sleeves the boys had tossed beside the big wooden console. He saw a multi-colored sleeve with psychedelic lettering reading "Tomorrow's Leaders." He flipped it over and saw several photos of the band and its three members, and one of Jasmine. It noted she provided backup vocals and wrote the song "Whiff of Mischief". Beneath it was a description of her. "One of the leading songwriters in Haight-Ashbury, Jasmine combines haunting lyrics and doleful melodies to create a unique sound. She is a pioneer in 'living music', believing a song is never finished, that it must be rewritten as the artist evolves. This rendition of 'Whiff of Mischief' preserves the song as it was when she and Tomorrow's Leaders recorded it."

Spracklin paused and listened.

Fathers weep with acid tears
To see such wanton waste
Tears flow of citrus juices
Leaving furrows cross each face
This mischief is the stuff of life
The reason to draw breath
Without it life is pointless
He found it and found death

Spracklin stepped into the office and picked up his briefcase. Something was bothering him. He remembered the song mentioning Jesus and Old Glory, but he hadn't heard it on the record. He reached into the briefcase, and plucked out the ring binder he'd taken from Jasmine's room. The label read Jasmine's Secret Songbook. He flipped through until he found "Whiff of Mischief." He noticed the date at the top of the page – May 29, 1968. He read through the lyrics, and found the verse.

And Jesus wore Old Glory
When He came to claim his soul
In faded stripes and fraying stars
He pondered boyhood's toll
This mischief is the stuff of life
The reason to draw breath
Without it life is pointless

He found it and found death

She'd changed the song on May 29 – the day after Blakely died. He was reading the words again when he noticed he wasn't alone. Val was leaning against the doorjamb.

"You haven't a clue, have you?"

His weary mind seized on the word "clue". He believed he'd actually found one that could mean something.

"Not a blessed clue," she repeated.

"Honey, I don't know—"

"Those boys are furious, and they have every right to be."

He slowly lowered Jasmine's notebook and glanced toward the living room. He looked back at his wife, puzzled.

"All week, all I heard from those two was 'Planet of the Apes' on Sunday' and . . ." She kept talking. He didn't hear. He was remembering his promise to take the kids to the movies. It was Sunday. He hadn't thought of it in twenty-four hours as the tensions of the case mounted. Oh damn, oh damn, damn, damn.

"I'm so sorry, Honey. I was looking for Marie last night and—"

"Don't you pin this on Marie. You chose to take this case today."

"It's the same perpetrator as the case I'm working."

"Your sergeant coulda handled it."

"No he couldn't. He has no skills as an investigator. Do you want me to tell people I can't do my job because I have to see a movie?"

Her bloodshot eyes burned as she stared deep into his. "Yes, Jimmy, that's exactly what I want." He was about to respond but she put up a hand to silence him. "I want to feel, to really believe, that you're focusing on our family."

"I am giving all the time I can to our family."

"It's not enough."

"I've been searching for Marie, Val," he yelled. "That's family time."

"Those boys need you more than the SFPD does. If this case shows anything, it shows that young boys need guidance, Jimmy. They'll be teenagers soon and they'll be wanting to head down to Haight Street. They need a father to set them right. And you need them more than you need to be Police Chief."

"I give everything I can," he shouted, his grief and tension exploding. "It's who I am. It's who I was when you married me. You knew I was ambitious. I'm the same man you married."

She nodded for a moment or two. "Yessir, you surely are." She always exaggerated her Texan drawl when they fought. "But the situation changed. And family is more important than ever."

"I am who I am. If a soldier is murdered, I investigate it. And yes, I hope to move higher in my job."

Tears began coursing down her face. "Dammit Jimmy, you drove my daughter from our house and now I just want you to be a good father to our boys."

"I did not drive Marie away!"

"If you'd shown compassion for poor little—"

"I did what was best for that boy." He stepped forward, grabbed his wife by her shoulders and pulled her closer. He felt he should hug her, but his arms remained tense. "And I love that girl. I'd do anything to bring her home. Surely you know that."

He released his wife, picked up his briefcase and threw the notebook in it. He left her leaning against the wall. He paused at the living room door and looked at his sons. They were pretending to still be working on the Mousetrap game. They didn't look up. He wanted to say something, to hold them, to tell them he loved them. They didn't want to talk to him. He left by the front door. Constable Frank looked over as he strolled to the Monaco. He nodded, got in the car, engaged the clutch, turned the key and revved the engine. He had work to do in Haight-Ashbury.

CHAPTER 31

Jethro had left the door to the can open while he went in and tried to scrub the blue spray paint off his hands. Fox moved to the window and pulled back the drapes. By stretching his neck, he could just make out the Econoline parked near the corner of Leavenworth and Geary. Even from the fourth floor of the Ambassador, he could tell how bad the paintjob was. It was parked outside a bar. Every time its pink neon martini glass flashed on, Fox could see the rough patches on the roof. He'd wanted to paint it fast, so they'd gone to a garage owned by a friend of Bogdan Polgar and painted it themselves.

They should have let it dry before moving it, but Fox wanted to get away from Haight-Ashbury. Fast.

Earlier that day, Fox had been on the Haight, trailing Raven, after deciding that Jethro was right and they needed to check on her. There'd been some sort of a frenzy in an alley near Cole Street – a crowd gathering, people screaming. Fox asked someone what was going on and she said a kid had OD-ed. Fine, he thought, but a few minutes later three cop cars pulled up – three black and whites because some loser OD-ed. And then he saw the cops talking to Spracklin. Fox didn't know how he could have shown up within minutes of the body being found. It didn't make sense, and he didn't like it.

He glanced over to the bathroom door and saw Jethro standing there. Jethro had barely spoken all day.

"Afraid someone's going to steal it?" he asked.

"Just checking."

"Worried about the pigs?"

Was he worried about the pigs? He was wondering why the cops were showing so much interest in two ODs in a week. It didn't make sense. He knew Spracklin was a homicide cop and not vice, but why was he spending so much time on Haight Street? He and Jethro had waved a red flag in Spracklin's face by spray-painting his house. The guy was obviously searching for them now. He was sure the cops were looking for a multi-colored van on the Haight, but he was also sure that a blue van in the Tenderloin was safe.

"Naw," he said. "Just checking. Force of habit."

Jethro threw the towel back over the sink and wandered to his bed. "I hope Spracklin comes looking for us," he said.

Fox pretended to agree with him. He knew the big guy wanted to settle scores with the homicide detective.

"You did a number on his house last night," he said. "Just knowing that we know his address must be driving him nuts."

Fox had made Jethro promise to do nothing more than spray paint the house. They just wanted to put the cop on edge, show him they had stuff on him. But there was something in Jethro's manner, something unsettling.

"I don't want to just toy with him," Jethro said, sitting on the edge of his bed.

"I know," Fox said. He'd seen it before. It was blood lust. Some people spoke about it just to mean sadism, but he was certain it was a psychological condition. He'd seen it in the joint. There were guys who yearned to see blood like it was pussy. And soon it became hard to satisfy. Once they got blood lust, it only got worse. Jethro had been edgy lately. He needed to satisfy a yearning.

CHAPTER 32

His search for Marie and the paisley van led nowhere, so Spracklin decided it was time to check the house on Masonic. He had to talk to Jasmine and he hoped Raven would be there. He wanted to see Raven. He wanted to chat with a woman who respected him.

He found Jasmine alone in the room with the raccoons, wearing a cream-colored night gown and playing her guitar by the light of a few candles. Her friends were dead or in jail. Her house was almost empty, but she was here, strumming her songs as if nothing had happened and singing in perfect pitch.

> *Shuffled south on Broadway*
> *Had tea on Lafayette*
> *Drifted through the Village*
> *'Mid the hip and languid set*
> *Benched in Central Park*
> *I thought of you at home*
> *I'm swamped in New York City*
> *And I'm feeling all alone*

He stepped into the room. "Jasmine?" The music stopped, though she continued to tune her guitar.

"How are you tonight?" He walked round to face her.

"Probably the same as I was all day," she said. "Though you'd expect people to be happier in sunlight."

"Your singing sounds beautiful. Actually I heard you playing last night."

"Here?"

"At the Vague Dimensions."

"Oh." She nodded. "The strobe lights kept screwing up my rhythm. Did you notice? I think it was last night."

"I also heard you on an album today." She made no response. "With Tomorrow's Leaders." She nodded. "Do you play with them a lot?"

"They do some of my songs," she said. "We started jamming at one of those

155

fifty-cent jam sessions up at 1090 Page Street. Remember them?" She looked at him, expecting an answer. He nodded. "They've been using my stuff ever since."

She began to tune the guitar again. "You told me once you were playing on your ledge the night John died." She thought for a moment then nodded slowly. "And you were singing `Whiff of Mischief'?"

"I think so." She gazed from the window. "I've sung a lot of tunes since then."

"But the version on the album is different than the version I've heard you play before."

"The song's alive. It has to grow."

"Yes, I know. But the new version talks about Jesus coming to take someone's soul. Was it John Blakely's soul?"

"I already told you, didn't I? I saw Jesus come to take John's soul. He was wearing one of those…things."

"What things?"

"You know."

"I don't."

"Sure. Those things the Pranksters wore."

"Kesey's Merry Pranksters?"

"Yeah. They wore those clothes made out of the flag." Spracklin wasn't sure he knew what she meant, but he seemed to recall photos in *Life* of Ken Kesey and his followers sitting around in coveralls made of the Stars and Stripes. A girl had been wearing one at Vague Dimensions the previous night.

"That's why you said Jesus wore Old Glory."

"I guess. I don't remember."

He sat down on the sofa in front of her. "Jasmine, this is important. I want you to tell me exactly what happened the night John died. You were playing on the window ledge, right?"

"Yeah. Most of the time. Sometimes I got cold out there so I came in to warm up. I'd rap with John, then go out to play more tunes."

"Did John say if he was expecting someone? Or if he was planning to shoot heroin?"

She looked out the window at the moonlight shining through the rustling leaves.

"I don't remember."

"Did he talk of suicide?"

She thought for a moment. "I don't remember him talking about suicide. Such a downer for a guy like John."

"Now one time when you came in, you saw something different. Someone was with him."

"Jesus was with him."

"Tell me about it."

"I was on the ledge and I saw Jesus standing by John. He was wearing the flag. It was pretty freaky, man. Um, and John was, like, on his back. Belt around his arm, needle in his forearm. Jesus looked at him, touched his neck, and left. I realized later he took John's soul. It was beautiful."

"Did Jesus see you?"

"I don't think so. I was at the window. No, I don't think so."

Spracklin took a folded paper from his pocket. "Would you recognize Jesus if you saw him again?"

"Sure."

He gave her the paper and she unfolded it. It was Rupert Hill's campaign flyer that he'd taken from his apartment. She read the caption under the picture. "Yeah. That's the dude." She laughed out loud. "I thought he was Jesus. Too fuckin' much!"

Spracklin shook his head. "This is a man called Rupert Hill. He was a friend of John's. "

"You want to bust him, huh?"

"I'd like to talk to him. Is this the man you saw?"

"I think so. Yeah, I'm pretty sure."

Spracklin took the pamphlet from her and asked it was all right if he looked around the house. She nodded. He was about to leave the room when he realized he still hadn't asked her the most important question. "Jasmine, who do you think killed John?"

She frowned. "Haven't thought about it really. Does it matter? He died peacefully."

He said nothing, and she dropped her head and was soon tuning her guitar again. Spracklin went up the back stairs. The second floor was dark and silent. He wandered into John Blakely's room and flipped on the light. There were a few new sleeping bags rumpled in the corner. The easel was broken, and Blakely's painting was facing the wall beside the broken wood. Spracklin flipped it over and looked at the dead flowers. If Blakely did indeed leave a suicide note, it wasn't that foolish piece of orange paper. It was this magnificent painting with its perfect detail and stark message. After replacing it, Spracklin turned off the light and looked out at Jasmine's perch.

He moved up to the third floor. It was dark but light and the sound of music were coming through the crack under one door. He knew the music – Simon and Garfunkel. He'd heard the duo in the car when he'd turned the dial to KFRC to please the boys. He felt a pang of guilt at the thought of the boys – he'd let his sons down. He knocked twice, and pushed the door open.

Raven was lying on her bed in jeans and a T-shirt, reading a paperback called The Confessions of Nat Turner. They held each other's gaze for a moment, until Spracklin mouthed the word, "Alone?" She nodded. He noticed the perspiration on her forehead.

He closed the door and turned up the volume on her cassette player. He bent down so his mouth was beside her ear and said, "You okay?"

She nodded. "You can't be here."

"The house is empty. I'm sorry about Derek. I know it's hard."

She nodded again.

He lowered himself on to the bed beside her. "I need your help," he said. "Who would have wanted to kill both John and Derek?"

She shrugged her shoulders. "Everyone respected John. And poor Derek, he – he just never fit in."

"Fox?"

"Fox attacked Derek two days ago – sliced his shoulder with his knife. But giving people tainted heroin doesn't make sense." There was a break between songs, and Mrs. Robinson began to play.

"I saw Fox today," she said. "Just after I heard about Derek. He was in a blue van – I think they painted their van."

"Was a girl with him? Brunette?"

"Just him and Jethro that I could see. He looked tense, frustrated. One thing about Andy is he's cool, always in control. But he looked tense today."

As if he hadn't heard her, Spracklin reached into his windbreaker pocket and pulled out a photo. "This girl. I think she was at Vague Dimensions last night. Was she with him today?"

Raven studied the photo and handed it back. "Never seen her. Is that The Seamstress?"

"Yes."

"And she's a suspect in John's case?"

"I need to talk to her. And I need to talk to Fox. They may be together."

"You've got to stay away from Fox."

"I have to —"

"You've got to understand something," she said. He saw a desperate look in her eyes. "We are at a critical juncture in this investigation and we don't need anyone fucking things up. This is not the time to go after Fox."

"I have a murder investigation —"

"And we both know he's not a suspect. Stay off his back."

"He's threatened my family. He spray painted a threat on my house last night. If I don't go after him, he'll get suspicious."

She was quiet. They were sitting so close that he thought he could feel her trembling. He told her about the note on his car and the spray paint on his house.

"Things are going to hell," she mumbled.

"It's tense around here."

"You have no idea, no idea. Fox was low on stash before you busted Reg. People were…anxious for it. Now the Haight's been dry, no heroin at all, for three more days. People are on edge."

He understood. It was a community of addicts. He noticed the beads of perspiration gathering on her forehead. He knew of the dangers of undercover agents working among drug dealers, and he felt certain Elizabeth Watkins was taking heroin.

"And now Derek, simple, awkward, earnest Derek, is dead." She dropped her head to her hands, began to sob. "And all I know is, I've got to get out of here. I'm cracking, Lieutenant. I've got to nail Fox."

He wrapped an arm around her and held her close. She took her hands from her face and wound both her arms around him. She pulled him tight to her body. He rocked her as she buried her face in his shoulder and cried. He could feel her breast pressing against his chest. He held her and rubbed her back.

They stayed bound together for several minutes.

"You okay now?" he asked.

She nodded, and wiped her left eye with her wrist. "Not very professional, was it?"

"It was human. You have to be strong now. And I have to get home to my family."

"Yes," she said. "Yes, it's late on a Sunday."

He stood, and she rose with him. They faced each other, then they hugged again. He held her for a long time. They parted a few inches and looked into each

159

other's eyes. Slowly, their faces came together and they kissed. Their mouths were wet and strong and they kissed passionately until she pulled away.

She held him at arm's length. Her expression told him she was longing for him but scared of what they were doing. "As you said," she whispered, "you should go home to your family."

He knew she was right. "You're going to be fine, Elizabeth. You'll be home soon."

He kissed her cheek, rubbed her shoulder and left the room.

Monday, June 3, 1968

CHAPTER 33

Spracklin figured he had enough time to have a word with Tom Jackson before Burwell returned. He'd reviewed the department's cases with other inspectors, gone over two with the prosecutor's office. He'd cleared his administrative tasks, but there was one last thing he wanted to do. He knew Burwell could get back at any moment, so he came right to the point when Jackson entered his office.

"Tommy, you gotta take more care with your work," he said, spreading out the boy's latest report – three typed pages, summarizing the documents they'd found in Blakely's closet. Jackson had researched and categorized everything – Blakely's twelve returned letters to his sister, the carbon copies of fifteen letters to art dealers, three letters to his father that he hadn't sent, receipts from the sale of his paintings.

Jackson looked up through his thick glasses. He was one of those earnest baby-boomers that Spracklin felt a special fondness for – kids with energy and purpose, kids who strove for something more than drugs and sex. Like Marie. Like Raven. Like Raven.

"Sir?"

"Your research, organization, they're great. You need to be more careful in writing your reports."

"I hoped to get everything in to you by the end of the day on Friday."

"That's good. But always remember you're preparing evidence for a court of law. And anything you write can be torn apart by a defense attorney." Spracklin took a pencil and pointed at one passage on the second sheet outlining Blakely's letters to his sister. "Look here," he said. "You've written, 'Blakely tells Julie in four letters their father has become "unhinged" since her disappearance and had to move in with Geoff.'" He looked to see if Jackson understood that he'd made errors. "The girl's name is Julia, not Julie. Jeff Blakely spells his name with a 'J' not a 'G', and I've gone through the letters. Blakely never uses the term 'unhinged'." Spracklin let the cadet study the notes he'd made on his work, then Spracklin shifted the pencil to the third sheet, where Jackson referred to a letter to a studio owner. "And here, where he's sneering at Reg MacIntosh, you've spelled "MacIntosh" three different ways."

"But that stuff might not be used in a trial."

"It doesn't matter. A good attorney can use it to show there was sloppy police work."

Jackson nodded. "Now, when we catch Blakely's killer, I hope we'll get a confession and avoid a trial," Spracklin said. "But we have to have everything iron-clad." He paused so Jackson would understand the gravity of the next sentence. "At the Bureau of Inspectors, once we catch murderers, they don't get off. Our clear rate was 68 percent last year – that's really good, but we have to improve it."

Jackson gazed at the sheets through his thick glasses and nodded. "Yes sir, in our criminology course –"

"Criminology."

"Yes sir. My minor's in chemistry. I want to work in forensics, crime scene investigations."

Spracklin couldn't help himself. He'd heard universities were teaching something called "criminology," and now he was working with a kid who used the term in conversation. "The investigating officer has to investigate the crime scene," he said, "not a scientist."

"Well sir, the way police work is heading, at least this is what the profs said, forensic science units are the way to go. Bring criminalists in to investigate all crime scenes."

Spracklin was about to respond when they were interrupted by a ruckus from the elevator lobby. Burwell was arriving.

"Let go of me, you Fascist!" a man's voice yelled. Spracklin had expected as much – it was largely why he'd let Burwell bring in Rupert Hill.

Burwell had Hill by the upper arm as he pushed him into the office. Hill massaged his arm in pain as he was released and scowled at the Sergeant. "You're just demeaning me because I have long hair."

"I'm demeaning you because you're an asshole," Burwell said. "Sit down."

Spracklin nodded to a straight-backed chair. He told Jackson to be more careful and sent the cadet off to rewrite the report.

"My rights have been violated," Hill told Spracklin.

"Yeah, we'll give you a form to fill out about that," Spracklin said. "Now take a seat."

Hill sat as Jackson left the room.

"I need to know when you last saw John Blakely."

"I told you, I last saw John alive on –"

"I didn't ask you when you last saw him alive, Rupert." Spracklin got up, sat on the edge of his desk and leaned toward the hippie. This was not an interview that called for good manners to coax out information. "I asked when you last saw him."

The hippie shifted in his chair. "And I gave you my answer."

Spracklin looked over at Burwell, who shook his heavy head and offered Spracklin a cigarette. They both lit their cigarettes then faced Rupert Hill.

"Don't lie to me."

After about four seconds, an eternity in an interrogation, Hill said, "I last saw John a few weeks ago, maybe more."

"Would you swear in a court of law that was the last time you saw John?"

"Your courts are farcical."

"But if you lie in one, you end up in jail, and jail's a damn hard place to start a revolution."

"That's not funny."

"Rupert, when's the last time you saw John Blakely?" Hill looked down, licked his lips. "When did you last see him – alive or dead?"

"The night he died."

"Where?"

"At that house. On Masonic."

"Why'd you lie about it?"

"I didn't lie. The last time I saw him alive was about a month ago."

"Aw Rupert," said Spracklin. He took a long drag on his cigarette. "I could get you on perverting the course of justice. Save me the trouble – tell me what happened."

The boy collected his thoughts and said, "When I saw John a month ago, we had a big argument. He started telling me I wrecked his family. I told him he got his sister into drugs just as much as me. It degenerated into this real tit-for-tat bummer. He swore at me and I stormed out."

"When did you talk to John Blakely again?"

"The day he died."

163

"Go on."

"I'd just announced I was heading a delegation from Berkeley to attend the Democratic Convention in Chicago in August. My picture was in the Chronicle so I heard from a few old friends. I'm easy to find at the Student Council office."

"He called you?"

"Yes, it was early afternoon. The phone rings and it's John. Said he saw the picture. I said I'd read the reviews of his show."

"No sign of resentment?"

"It was awkward but we were old friends. We arranged to get together for a beer that night. I had a meeting of the social justice committee and then I'd go to his house."

"Just a beer."

"I don't do drugs. Saw friends messed up by it. We agreed to meet at his place. I think I mentioned to you that I was one of Kesey's Pranksters for a brief spell. So for a ruse I put on my American Flag overalls – all the Pranksters used to wear them. I arrived after midnight." He took a breath. "As I walked up to the house I heard this haunting music – a woman on an acoustic guitar. No one answered the door so I walked in, and the weird thing was the music got fainter when I stepped inside. I was walking through all these weird scenes, you know, fish in one room and raccoons in another. But no people."

The office was growing smoky and Hill gave an exaggerated cough. Spracklin opened the window.

"On the second floor, and . . ." His voice faded. "It was surreal. And dreadful. The room was painted like a clearing in a forest. And a painting of dead flowers in a vase was on an easel. And a girl playing guitar outside the window, and John just lying there."

He gulped.

"There was – John lying on the mattress. There was a tourniquet around his upper arm and a needle stuck in his arm. I spoke to him. No answer. I nudged him with my foot. He didn't move. I felt his throat for a pulse. Nothing. He was dead. Stone dead."

"So you called an ambulance?"

"He was dead. I got out of there. And the girl was there. She'd stopped singing."

"Shouldn't you even have reported the death?"

"You don't understand. I'd already been kicked out of one university because of drugs. I'm clean. I didn't want my name dragged through the dirt at Berkeley as well."

"So what you're telling me, Rupert, is that you valued your political career more than your friend's life."

"He was dead."

Spracklin held Hill's gaze long enough to let the boy know he wasn't buying it. "So were you there when he injected the heroin?"

"No."

"Where'd he get the heroin from?"

"I didn't know he was a junkie. Last time I saw the guy he'd do nothing harder than acid."

"Now tell me about Derek."

Hill stopped – he was surprised and his patience was waning. "Who the fuck is Derek?"

Spracklin knew that was the right answer but pressed on. "And I should believe you because . . ."

"Because it's the truth. I don't know a Derek. Why would I lie to you?"

"You lied to me on Saturday."

"I've told you enough today to get me in a lot of shit. And what motive would I have for killing him?"

"Revenge, for getting you kicked out of Stanford."

"You're framing me. In some democracies, a man is innocent until proven guilty."

"Cut the shit, sonny." Spracklin stood. He wondered why Hill had to make a speech each time he opened his mouth. Why couldn't he have strong convictions but be subtle about it, like Raven? "I want you to take a polygraph test, Rupert."

The boy paused, then said, "Of course."

Spracklin called for a constable to take Hill to the interview room. A technician would conduct the interview. Spracklin watched him shuffle off, a man more humble than when he entered.

"Think he'll pass?" asked Burwell.

"Polygraph test? He'll pass the important parts."

"Think he did it?"

Spracklin put out his cigarette and shook his head. "It doesn't make sense, doesn't fit." He sat back in his seat. "He and Blakely had both moved on. I don't have any evidence. Nothing links him to Derek Hodgson." He took out his cigarettes. He was about to offer one to Burwell but the Sergeant was still working on his.

"No, I don't think he killed John Blakely. If I were to make a guess right now, I'd say The Mantis is still our guy."

"But The Mantis disappeared too long ago to have anything to do with the Hodgson murder."

Spracklin thought and nodded. "That's why I think The Mantis had something to do with it. But maybe there was more than one person involved."

CHAPTER 34

As they broke apart from a kiss, The Seamstress slipped her arms around Fox's neck and pressed her body to his. He ran his fingertips up and down the dry warmth of her bare back and breathed in the scent of her neck. He pulled away, and his eyes slipped down her naked body. She returned his gaze, then reached out to touch the scar on his shoulder. "What happened here, Andy?"

"It's not important," he whispered. He smiled. "I want to call you by your name."

"Marie. Call me Marie. But only when it's just you and me."

"Marie," he gushed. "It's such a beautiful name." And it was. It was beautiful to hear her say it, the name she hid from everyone else. It was another part of their intimacy.

"We're two weird hippies," she said with a chuckle. "Your secret pet name for me is my real name."

He burst out laughing. It wasn't that funny, but he was delighted at the little secret he shared with this beautiful, intelligent woman. He held her face in his hands and kissed her again, pressing his lips against hers for several seconds. "Marie," he whispered again. "It's a beautiful name that matches your own beauty."

"You're so lovely, Andy," she said. She sighed. "I wish we didn't have to go."

He lay back on the bed and nodded. "Me too. I wish we had forever in this . . ." He waved his arms around the room. "In this little paradise."

She laughed again and eased herself from the bed. "But I have to head to Chinatown."

He also had to go – to patch things up with Jethro. There'd been a knock on the door that morning and Jethro leapt from bed and grabbed the revolver from his coat. Fox got to the door first, made sure it was Marie then delayed her while Jethro put the gun away. The big man had glared at his friend as he walked to the bathroom in his shorts, his clothes slung over one arm. Jethro was furious Fox had revealed where they were holed up. The two men agreed to meet for breakfast at 10, and Fox now had only a few minutes to get to the greasy spoon.

"So what's going on in Chinatown?" he asked Marie.

"Bobby Kennedy's making an appearance. A parade or something."

"Kennedy?"

She smiled. "He's the closest thing we have now to Dr. King. I want to go to his rally."

"McCarthy? Dylan?"

"If Kennedy becomes President, he'll get us out of Vietnam."

"In what century?"

"You don't know Bobby Kennedy," she said, stepping into her embroidered jeans.

"And you do," he said. "You'll have to tell me about your weekends at Hyannis Port."

"If you're lucky," she said. She leaned across the bed and kissed him. "But I might be too busy having tea with Jackie and Ethel." She kissed him again, turned and left the room.

He fell back on the bed. He reached under the mattress, grabbed his knife and stuck it in his sock. What a woman she was. He'd have to call her later and find out about the meeting at Chinatown. He wanted her again. Soon. But now, he had to meet with Jethro. They had work to do.

CHAPTER 35

Spracklin knew he wouldn't get anywhere near Bobby Kennedy at the parade. But when they met later that afternoon, he'd at least be able to tell the candidate he'd been at his event in Chinatown. With the King assassination, Spracklin had been too busy to help out with the campaign. The only consolation was that Bobby of all people would understand the importance of police work. Spracklin had hoped to make eye contact with RFK in Chinatown, but he could see the crowd was too huge, and too hysterical.

People lined the sidewalks seven or eight deep. He could hear the drums from a dragon dance at the far end of Grant Avenue. He assumed the Senator was on the other side of the street. All he could see was a swarm of people pushing out from beneath the lanterns and Chinese store signs to get close to Bobby Kennedy – housewives, black families, professionals and their secretaries on their lunch hours, whole classes of inner city school kids. Two hippies with antiwar posters were on Spracklin's right and three Korean War vets in their legion uniforms stood behind them. A Kennedy could draw all of them, Spracklin knew that but still felt awed.

"Hell of a sight, isn't it?" a voice yelled in his ear.

Spracklin turned, saw a face he recognized but couldn't place. Then he remembered – Nick Muto, a member of President Kennedy's staff who was now working Bobby's campaign. They hadn't seen each other since the assassination in Dallas. They shook hands and hugged. "Hell of a sight," agreed Spracklin.

The sound of the drums was too loud to chat, but Muto reached over and hollered, "The candidate's looking forward to seeing you."

So Muto knew he was supposed to meet with Bobby. That was a good sign. He was on the radar of the organization. "Not as much as I am," he shot back.

"You're with SFPD now?" Muto asked.

Spracklin nodded. "Head of Homicide."

"Bobby knows it –" Muto paused as he was drowned out by a chorus of cheers from the crowd. "He's starting to think about good people for his administration."

Spracklin nodded then pointed to the ground and mouthed the word, "Here?"

Muto looked in his eyes and mouthed, "Wash-ing-ton."

Spracklin understood. The meeting that afternoon at the Pacific Club wasn't just a meet and greet. Spracklin would be sounded out for a position in the second Kennedy administration. In Washington. In the city Raven would work in once they nailed Fox. He thought of her again, of holding her, the taste of her kiss. He longed to hold her again.

The sound of gunfire shattered his daydream. A string of six rapid-fire shots rang out through the canyon of buildings. Gunfire at a Kennedy event sent a wave of panic through the crowd. The drums stopped. Screams pierced the air. Across the street, a mother grabbed her baby from his pram and pulled him to her. Policemen placed their hands on their pistol grips and looked around wildly. Spracklin stepped forward and surveyed the street. Then they all started to smile.

"Firecrackers," Spracklin said to Muto. His voice sounded light and buoyant in the brief silence. Muto laughed, and Spracklin felt the people around them relax. Four and a half years had elapsed since the President's assassination but the sound of gunshot near a Kennedy was particularly unnerving. "Chinese firecrackers," Spracklin said again as the drums resumed.

He shook Muto's hand and they agreed they would get caught up at the Pacific Club that afternoon. Back in the car, he checked his watch. He had work to do on the Blakely and Hodgson cases and realized he would have to be fast. He had to focus on The Mantis. Ideally, he had to figure who the guy was. If The Mantis had been part of a conspiracy to commit two murders, there must be collaborators still in San Francisco. Had The Mantis left clothes, papers, letters behind when he fled? Even though the house on Masonic had been cleared, there must still be hippies hanging around who knew The Mantis. He had to find them. He would check with Raven. Yes, he would have to ask Raven. There must be clues about The Mantis at 1340 Masonic.

The old house was silent and felt deserted. As he walked through the main floor, he couldn't even hear Jasmine's guitar. He wondered if Raven was upstairs. If so, they might have the house to themselves. He ran up the stairs, telling himself not to be a fool. He reminded himself of Val and told himself only to talk to Raven. But he could still taste her kiss. He wanted to make sure the house was empty. He checked in Blakely's room. No one there. Up the stairs, Raven's door was closed. Gloria's door was slightly ajar. He pushed it, then jumped back in shock.

"Oh Jesus no," he yelled. "No, no, no, Sweet Jesus, no." He paused, fighting the urge to weep, to vomit. He turned away. He couldn't touch her, not yet. He had to hold his emotions in check. He stood, trembling. He breathed deep, and slowly felt his self-control returning. He must remain an officer. The killer could still be in the house. He withdrew his Smith and Wesson and stood listening. He would check the house and call for back up. He turned, looked at the horror in front of him.

Raven was hanging by a satin scarf from a ceiling pipe in the corner. Her throat had been slit and blood covered her clothes and the floor beneath her. Spracklin had to fight the temptation to cut the rope. He couldn't risk destroying evidence, but he felt the human urge to ease the suffering and indignity of a dead body. He longed to lower her lovingly to the floor. He knew she was dead but he followed proper procedure. He tiptoed up to her to check her pulse and make sure Federal Agent Elizabeth Watkins was dead.

CHAPTER 36

Spracklin heard the patrolmen from Park Station moving through the house, searching each nook of the dreadful place. Soon they'd canvas neighbors, then the merchants on Haight Street. They had to find Fox. But all he could do was stand at the door of Gloria's room and gaze at Elizabeth Watkins hanging by her neck.

There were shoe prints on the floor. The dust emitted when he pulled the section of plaster from the wall had settled into a delicate layer. He could make out two faint sets of footprints encircling the body – a large pair of shoes, possibly boots with flat soles, and a smaller pair of running shoes. The problem was they were in thin plaster dust on light wood. Photographing them would be difficult, and lifting a print could disturb the dust and ruin them.

There was a single blood splatter on the wall, and a pool of blood where she'd fallen when killed. He would have expected more blood, given that it was a knifing.

Someone was coming up the stairs. Jackson had fetched the evidence kit from the Monaco. Spracklin nodded to the floor as Jackson set the case down.

"Tom," he said. "Remember the room with the coral reefs?"

"Jasmine's room?"

Spracklin nodded. "Go get the black light in that room."

Watkins' body, hanging from the scarf, didn't swing at all. She'd always moved with such athletic grace. Now her body seemed leaden at every point. The corners of her mouth hung in a gruesome frown. Her head, clenched at that unnatural angle, strained the tendons in her neck that hadn't been severed. Her limbs stretched toward the floor. Her sleeves were heavy with blood. Jackson returned and placed the black light – a fluorescent tube in a white plastic holder – beside the evidence case.

"I want you to take dictation," Spracklin said. He was surprised that his voice sounded calm and even.

Jackson took a notebook and pen from a pocket. "The victim," Spracklin said. He studied her a moment longer, glanced away. "The victim was found hanging

173

from a satin scarf attached to a pipe in the third floor room with an eastern exposure." He described the positioning of the body, the head and the blood below.

"The floor is coated with thin plaster dust," he said. "The result of damage to the east wall during a police action Saturday morning." He wanted a cigarette but couldn't risk dropping ashes on the crime scene. "There is a plume of blood on the undamaged sections of the east wall." Another pause. "There is what appears to be an imprint of a body and moderate blood collection stretching two feet to seven feet from the wall, indicating that is where the body fell." Spracklin rubbed his eyes and continued. "It appears that the assailants lured the victim into the room. When she was facing the wall, they took her from behind, attacked her with a knife and lowered her to the floor."

Spracklin opened his evidence kit and withdrew a camera. He counted eighteen flash bulbs. He placed one in the camera, looked down into the viewfinder, and flashed a shot of the room. "All shots were taken with a Kodak Brownie Auto 27 camera, 1964. Frame one, blood splatter on the east wall." He then took a photo of the body imprint, and Jackson recorded the shot.

Spracklin took out a tripod and set it up. "Tom, I want you to notice the floor around the body." The cadet crouched, studied the scuff marks and shoe prints in the filmy dust. "We were in here two days ago, and I returned yesterday to pick up a piece of Blakely's work. So my shoe prints are in this room. But I see two main shoeprints around the victim."

Jackson nodded. "Looks like a running shoe and a cowboy boot."

"Cowboy boot? I thought it was just a hard-soled shoe."

Jackson gestured with the pen. "You can make out a pointy toe right there. Looks like a cowboy boot to me."

Spracklin studied the print and nodded. "Write it down." He plugged in the black light and found its glow lost in the daylight. He walked along the west wall to the window, and drew the long curtains, being careful not to disturb the plaster dust. The room was dark, but in the black light the plaster dust glowed against the wooden floor. "It worked," Spracklin muttered.

Attaching the camera to the tripod, he adjusted the lens to get the best shot he could of the running shoe. "Write this down: frame four, aperture setting f2.8, shutter speed of one sixtieth of a second." He clicked the shot, and repeated the process several more times with the other prints. He walked around the perimeter and looked up at Elizabeth Watkins.

"The victim has three stab wounds in the chest area, judging by the tears to her blouse. The largest is just below the sternum. The relative lack of blood indicates the first stab hit the aorta, killing the victim instantly. No cuts or slashes on the arms, no defensive wounds, indicating the victim was unconscious or dead before she realized she was being attacked. The assailant was experienced in attacking with a knife, knowing to aim below the sternum and ribcage and thrust up to the heart."

"He snuck up behind her?"

"I think he lured her into the room, and his first motion was to come up behind her and grab her mouth or throat with his left hand. The next was to stab her in the lower chest. She…she fell to the floor there and he stabbed her twice more, to be sure, possibly in anger." Spracklin placed another flash bulb in the camera so he could photograph the body hanging from the pipe.

He focused on the throat. The knife had been sharp and cut cleanly into the flesh. But again there was little bleeding. "Dictation: the cut to the throat begins under the left ear and extends to within two inches of the right ear. It appears the trachea has been severed. The lack of blood again indicates it was a postmortem wound, inflicted purely for effect."

He could visualize Andy Fox standing over her and slashing the throat just to desecrate the body of his former collaborator. The hatred, the sheer evil of that move made perfect sense to Spracklin. The only thing he didn't understand was the location of the murder. *Why Gloria's room?* He stepped out into the corridor and walked to Raven's room. He stared at the bed where they'd sat together the night before, then looked up at the ceiling. There were no pipes in Raven's room. Fox had lured Raven into Gloria's room simply so he could hang her from a pipe. Spracklin's stomach spun with disgust and grief. Fox had been determined to make Agent Elizabeth Watkins look as grotesque as possible.

CHAPTER 37

Fox was always intrigued by Jethro's glow after a bloodletting, especially a killing. Fox himself never felt any emotion after he'd killed or mutilated someone. He was interested in the effect it had on people. But it didn't satisfy a craving. He recognized the emotional release Jethro underwent after a murder. The big guy seemed calmer now, breathed more deeply. As long as he could feed that, Fox knew Jethro would be a loyal soldier.

He'd let Jethro kill Raven because Jethro had needed to. As they'd mounted the stairs of the old house, Fox had given Jethro the knife. They'd paused at the top, and Fox had burst through Raven's door, demanding to know who left their stash in the wall of Gloria's room. Raven denied anyone had, and he told her to come with him. She followed Fox into Gloria's room, and Jethro grabbed her from behind. The job was done by the time Fox turned around to look. Jethro was an accomplished killer and Fox believed he mutilated her heart with his first thrust.

Afterward, they'd crossed the Golden Gate Bridge to Marin County. It was a cool, sunny morning, and Jethro tapped his thumbs on the towel-covered steering wheel to the beat of The Byrds playing on the radio. They drove up to Bolinas Point, checked there was no one around, and began a familiar ritual. They brought firewood, hotdogs and beer from the back of the van and soon had a little fire going. They checked all their clothes for blood stains. They found red patches only on Jethro's shirt and jeans, so these were tossed into the fire. They added the towels they'd draped over the dashboard and seats of the van. They stripped down and jumped into the ocean, which gave Fox a chance to wash the blood from his knife.

Soon they were sitting on the warm rocks in fresh clothes, eating hotdogs and washing them down with warm beer. Almost all the fabric had burned and the evidence was destroyed. They were pros.

"Things are goin' good," Jethro said. He twisted open another beer and downed half of it.

Fox nodded and wondered where he was leading with this. Jethro often got talkative after an operation. "Yessir, they are," Fox said.

"We're getting the bad apples out," said the blond giant.

Fox nodded.

"It's good," Jethro repeated, "Good." He looked down the shore to where some sandpipers were wading in and out of the water. "Now we gotta keep them out."

Fox tossed an empty beer bottle into the flames and pulled another from the six pack.

"Meaning . . ."

"I think it's obvious."

"Enlighten me."

Jethro finished his beer and opened the final one. "We've had traitors, thieves, junkies . . ." He thought for a moment. "Idiots. We need good people."

"I agree," said Fox

"I want to know who I'm working with." Jethro leaned back against a boulder, closed his eyes and turned his face to the sun.

"Anyone in particular?" asked Fox as he fished his wallet from his back pocket.

"I don't know that girl's name." Jethro said it kind of casual, eyes still closed.

"Sure you do. She's The Seamstress."

"I can't check up on her."

"We need a few people, good people, just for a few days."

"Everyone we take on is a liability."

"We're marked men. We need a messenger or two. Just for a few days."

"We haven't even tried the Arcata test."

"Don't think we can use that one again," Fox said. They both knew the Feds would know now that they only used Arcata to test snitches.

Fox flicked The Seamstress's driver's license so it landed in Jethro's lap. "Here's her driver's license." Jethro opened one eye and looked down at the card. "I've been checking her out," Fox said, "asking around and she's clean. We've got her name and address. Marie Mercer, a sixteen-year-old runaway from here, in Marin County. She's – she's just too young to be a narc or a snitch. She's smart and she's in with us."

Jethro smiled slightly, as if to tell Fox he admired his moxie for pinching her license. "Marie Mercer," he said. He slowly finished his beer and pocketed the card.

CHAPTER 38

How did Fox find out about Raven? The question began to eat away at Spracklin as sat in his office. *How the Hell did he find out that she was a narc?* The drop in Arcata must have been a set-up. Must have been. On Sunday morning, Spracklin had called Burwell and asked him to call Washington. He made the call probably around 10 am. And twenty-four hours later she was dead. Had Fox been testing her? He couldn't have found out that quickly, could he? Maybe one of the other hippies had heard Elizabeth and Spracklin in the house the night before. Fox knew his own address, and he had found out about Elizabeth. How? As he stubbed out his cigarette, Spracklin saw Burwell walking toward him with a young man with long hair.

There was no sense of tension between the hippie and Burwell. Long brown hair, long beard, white T-shirt, red pants and sandals. It wasn't Rupert Hill. He'd passed the polygraph test and they'd released him. So who was this kid, coming in voluntarily?

Burwell nodded toward an interview room, and the boy walked in. Spracklin stood as Burwell reached his office door.

"Kid here you should talk to," Burwell said as Spracklin joined him outside the interview room. "The hippies call him Retrorocket. Real name Anthony Luccello."

Spracklin stepped up beside Burwell and looked at the boy in the glass room. His eyes were red from crying. "Raven mentioned to us she worked with the Mime Troupe," said Burwell. "I went over to the park to talk to the Troupe. Anthony here took it really hard, asked how he could help."

Spracklin knocked before entering, and the guy looked up. "Anthony, I'm Lieutenant James Spracklin."

After they shook hands, Spracklin sat beside the kid so they wouldn't be facing each other over the table. He didn't want anything that felt adversarial. He offered his condolences and asked when the boy last saw Raven.

"Yesterday, at work. She was laughing and hustling for coin."

"You didn't see her at the house on Masonic?"

"I don't live there. I have a room in Castro."

"Do you know of anyone who would want to hurt her?"

Luccello paused, then answered. "There's a guy, Andy Fox. I've heard he's a dealer. He owns the house she lived in. He'd come around the Mime Troupe looking for her."

"When's the last time?"

"A few days ago. Saturday maybe, the day his house got raided." The boy stared at the floor again. "He used to come around with a big blond guy, and another guy, a muscular jock who called himself The Mantis. They'd take her aside and discuss things. Raven would always say it was stuff to do with the house where she crashed."

Spracklin offered him a cigarette. The boy declined, so Spracklin put them away without lighting one. "You knew The Mantis?"

"I met him."

"And John Blakely?"

"Yeah. I was down in Carmel the night he died but I knew him."

"Any idea who could have killed him?" Luccello shook his head. "Do you know if The Mantis had anything against John?"

Luccello looked shocked out of his gloom. "Naw," he said. "He seemed to worship the guy. I spent a bit of time at that house but you could see he respected John. Always telling everyone he was a genius."

Spracklin wondered how he could ask whether the guy knew anything about Arcata. As far as he knew, the feds still had an operation there and Spracklin couldn't say anything to jeopardize it. He'd keep asking about Blakely until he could figure a way to test the boy's knowledge.

"Anything else you can tell me about Blakely and The Mantis?" he asked.

As the boy answered, Spracklin thought more about the trip to Arcata. It was likely the key to Fox learning about Raven's cover. Spracklin had read in Fox's rap sheet that he'd worked on a fishing boat. Maybe he had people in Arcata who worked at hotels and the Feds' first move was to book rooms.

". . . And I figured he went back to Fresno."

Spracklin looked over at Luccello. "What was that?" The boy gave an exaggerated sigh. He realized Spracklin hadn't even been paying attention. "Just tell me what you said," the Lieutenant said.

"I said The Mantis probably returned to Fresno."

"Why do you think he was from Fresno?"

"I don't know if he's from Fresno, but he went to school there. At Fresno State."

"He told you that?"

"Not exactly. He used to talk about playing football – talked about it all the time. And he had a Bulldog tattoo on one forearm."

"Bulldog. I heard it was an eagle and a dog."

The boy nodded his head. "And the dog was a Bulldog, like the Fresno State logo. He played linebacker, some defensive back. Never gave his name or his school, but I figured it was Fresno State."

"He never mentioned Fresno himself?"

"No, sir."

They had a lead – a weak lead but a lead – on The Mantis. After days going in circles, he could pursue something. Spracklin stood and motioned to Burwell to join him in the hall. He wanted the Sergeant to keep the boy talking but not to mention the operation in Arcata. Spracklin felt something kindling within him. He could act rather than mourn. They had fourteen cars patrolling the Haight-Ashbury and the surrounding neighborhoods looking for Fox or find his van. Now there was something he could do.

He waved off an inspector who wanted to discuss a case and strode out to the reception. Melanie was at the switchboard, sitting erect reading a magazine called *Crawdaddy*. "Melanie." She put the magazine down. "I need the Fresno Police Department – chief if possible. Or a senior detective."

He noticed the stack of pink phone slips in his tray. He flipped through them on the way back to his office. Most were from reporters – word had got out that a federal agent had been killed. He'd expected calls about the two poisonings, but an undercover agent being knifed was bigger news. Community Relations could handle it. He tossed most of them into the wastepaper basket when he reached his office. There were five messages he set aside on his desk – one from Val and four from the Chief. Shit. He knew what the chief wanted. Elizabeth Watkins was a federal agent, which meant the case belonged to the FBI. Spracklin should have notified Field Agent J.P. MacLean immediately. MacLean had probably gone to Bud Hawkings rather than call Spracklin directly. As soon as they caught up with him, Spracklin would be taken off the Elizabeth Watkins case. He had to avoid the Chief as long as he could. It wasn't simply a matter of turf war. It was a matter of Spracklin not believing MacLean had the ability to come up with an airtight case against Fox.

The phone rang. "Lieutenant, I have Chief Gary Barrow from Fresno on the line," Melanie said. Spracklin was relieved. He knew Barrow from forensics conferences.

181

"Gary, Jimmy Spracklin." He heard his voice sounding firm, professional.

"Sounds like you guys are having yourselves a bad day out there, Jimmy." News of Elizabeth's murder was spreading. "What can I do to help?"

"I've got a want on a related case. We believe a suspect has gone to Fresno, where he was a student."

"I'll do what I can. Details?"

"Male with the alias The Mantis. Caucasian. Twenty to Twenty-Five. Brown hair. Muscular build. Tattoo of a praying mantis on one shoulder and a Bulldog tattoo on the other arm. Known to –"

"Did you say a praying mantis?"

"That's right. A tattoo of a praying mantis on his right shoulder."

"Heroin addict."

"Severe, from what I understand. And missing a little toe on the right foot."

"We have your man. But I'm afraid you're too late for him."

The Mantis was dead. Spracklin wondered if he had killed himself, possibly due to guilt about poisoning John Blakely.

"The details please, Chief." The disappointment in his voice was evident. Five minutes earlier, he'd been ready to push for the gas chamber for the guy. Now he was shocked by his death.

"Lemme grab the file." Spracklin could hear papers shuffling. "Cyclist found a john doe in some shrubs in Roeding Park at 0645 May 28. We declared it a homicide immediately. Vic was stabbed in the lower chest, the knife entering the heart. There was slashing of the victim's throat, but it was a postmortem wound."

Spracklin slumped in his seat. "Estimated time of death?"

"About midnight on May 27."

The Lieutenant nodded slowly. "No identity yet?"

"No sir."

Spracklin sighed and told Barrow what he knew of The Mantis. "My advice, Gary, is to contact the football coach at the university and show him a photo of the vic. I believe he played football there and they might be able to identify him. We would certainly be interested in learning his identification."

Spracklin thanked Barrow, asked him to Telex over the details of the case and hung up. He sat staring at the wall. He felt inexplicably shocked that The Mantis was dead. Maybe it was simply that here was a death he didn't have to investigate. Maybe it was just that another American had died too young.

Burwell was leaning against his door. Merrill Flanagan stood beside him, clutching a large manila envelope.

"The Mantis is dead," Spracklin said, and told them what he'd learned from Fresno. "Same MO as Elizabeth Watkins."

Burwell shrugged. "Another dead junkie."

Spracklin shook a cigarette from his pack and stuck it in his mouth. "So it's Blakely, Derek, Raven, and The Mantis. Four talented kids who died too young." He lit the cigarette and slid the pack across the desk toward the other two. "And that kid in the freezer. We'll probably never find out who he was."

"Kids these days," said Flanagan. "If Nam doesn't kill them, their own drugs will." He took a cigarette. "If it keeps up, you'll have to open an office on the Haight."

Spracklin gave a thin laugh. "Haight-Ashbury Homicidal," he said. "Now open for business."

The words hung in the air. "I'm going to interrogate Reg MacIntosh in a few minutes," said Flanagan. "The time is right."

Spracklin knew "the time is right" meant the boy was going through withdrawal from the heroin. He may crack. "They're going to take the Watkins murder from us."

"Feds?"

Spracklin nodded. He had to finish interviewing Luccello and he had to make a call. "I'll join you downstairs in a few minutes." He watched them walk down the hall then picked up the phone, asking Melanie to put him through to Ernie Swanson.

He paused after thanking the deputy medical examiner for working on Saturday. He had to choose his words carefully. "Are you doing the autopsy on Elizabeth Watkins?"

"The federal agent? Yes, but I'm not sure I'll get to her till, probably, tomorrow."

"That's fine, Ernie. That's fine." He took a long draw on his cigarette. "She was a courageous officer who died in the line of duty."

"Yes. I understand that's the case."

"I believe you'll find she died from a knife wound to her chest. I also think you'll find traces of opiates in her blood. Possibly some scar tissue on her arm. If those assumptions are correct, could you omit references to the opiates in your report?"

There was silence on the other end. Spracklin had never made such a request before. He knew the drug use had no bearing on the cause of death. He could hear Swanson's breathing, and then he said, "I understand. If it's not germane to my conclusions, I should be able to do that."

Spracklin thanked him and hung up. He hadn't been able to save Elizabeth Watkins' life, but he would help to preserve her reputation.

CHAPTER 39

The smell of vomit in the interview room was overpowering, and the sound of Reg MacIntosh retching grated on Spracklin's ears. Manacled in a metal chair, MacIntosh's yellow skin shone with sweat beneath the fluorescent lights, and a string of vomit stretched from his mouth to his lap. His shivers rattled the handcuffs. Spracklin took up a position next to a table with a stack of glossy photos, a tape recorder taping the session, and the bag of heroin they had taken from MacIntosh on Friday.

"We got you on Safety section 11350, possession of opium or a derivative thereof," Flanagan said. It was about fifteen minutes into the interrogation, Flanagan was standing over the kid, sleeves rolled up, reading the rap sheet. "Section, 11379, trafficking in a controlled substance. Section 241, battery against a police officer. Section 834, use of force when resisting arrest." He dropped the papers on an empty table in front of MacIntosh. "Make it easy on yourself – tell me about The Mantis and Fox."

"They knew each other," the boy whimpered.

"Did they do any business together?"

"Gimme some water."

As Flanagan worked on the hippie, Spracklin glanced at the glossies. They were his shots of the stiff they'd found in the freezer, including details of the tattoo of the praying mantis. Spracklin started to understand where Flanagan was taking this. He also realized the vice squad head had placed the heroin right in MacIntosh's line of sight.

"I need a drink."

"I need answers."

The boy continued to stare straight ahead, in the direction of the baggie of heroin. Occasionally, he strained weakly against his chains.

"I need information on Fox," said Flanagan, stepping in front of MacIntosh to block his view of the heroin. "Tell us when he gave you the stash."

MacIntosh looked up and mumbled, "He didn't."

185

"Who did?"

The kid lowered his head and said, "He never hands over stuff. He's too smart."

"So who did give it to you, Reg?"

"Gimme a drink."

"We need information." He got no response. "I can get you a drink, but I need to know about Fox and The Mantis."

MacIntosh raised his head. "He owed Andy money."

"Yeah."

"He wasn't paying so Andy had to frighten him."

"Yeah."

"Andy sent word that Mantis and me had to meet him in Oakland." His head drooped, the strain of talking was tiring him. "There were two guys with Andy when we got there. Jethro and a guy I didn't know. We held The Mantis in a chair while Andy cut his toe off with his knife."

"How much did he owe Fox?"

"About ten-thousand dollars gimme a drink for godssakes find me a drink."

Flanagan nodded to Burwell, who left. Flanagan paced the room. Burwell returned with a cup of water and held it to the hippie's lips while he drank. It revived the boy slightly and he tugged at his chains. "Lemme scratch my arms," he slurred.

"We have —"

"Lemme scratch my arms. There are things crawlin' in my bones. They itch."

"Did Fox know The Mantis was getting ready to split?"

"Andy was on to him. No surprise when he eighty-sixed."

"Were you in on the plot to track him down and kill him?"

"Who? Mantis?"

"Yeah. Mantis."

"There wasn't a plan."

"Sure there was."

Flanagan picked up two of the photos of the kid in the freezer and threw them down on the table in front of MacIntosh. The boy screamed when he saw the shot of the tattoo. "We want to know when Fox began planning it," said Flanagan.

MacIntosh's teeth were chattering louder as he looked at the photos in front of him and began to cry. Flanagan was breaking him.

"I didn't know anything about it," said MacIntosh.

"Of course you don't."

"I swear to Jesus," he said, gulping for breath, "I didn't."

"But Reginald, we know you were Fox's point man at 1340 Masonic."

"I was a donkey. Oh Jesus, give me a drink."

"You were key to his distribution. You collected money for him. You went up to Arcata to get the stuff."

"Arcata?"

Flanagan wheeled on him. "Arcata. We know about Fox's operation and we know you helped him import drugs."

MacIntosh leaned to his left and shook his head. "Naw, naw naw. Arcata was a test. When Andy wants to see if he can trust someone, he tells them about a drop in Arcata."

"I need details."

"He has friends there who tell him if narcs move in. Hotel bookings and that."

"Who did he test this way?"

"Everyone. Before I was busted he gave this girl in the house, Raven, the Arcata test."

Flanagan looked at Spracklin and then back at MacIntosh. "But there was no drop?"

"No. It was a test. It was always a test."

Flanagan began pacing again. "Where's the real drop, Reg?"

The boy paused for a second then said, "Only Andy knows."

"We need to know where and when." That split second of hesitation told Spracklin that MacIntosh knew.

"I told –"

"Where and when?"

"I don't know."

"Where? And When?

"I told you. I don't know."

Flanagan walked to the table and rested on his hands. "You know we have enough on you now to put you away for ten years, at least." He shuffled through the papers and photos. "Right Reg, you know that?" The hippie said nothing.

"The thing is, Reg, I think we can get life for you."

MacIntosh looked up. He was confused. Flanagan turned with a few photos in his hand.

"We've got you on accessory to murder of a federal agent."

"Fuck off."

Flanagan slowly flicked the photos on to the table, one at a time, as if he were dealing cards. They were Spracklin's photos of Raven hanging from the pipe, her throat slit. MacIntosh screamed and struggled, but he couldn't divert his eyes. Flanagan threw down five photos and then walked away. He turned off the tape.

MacIntosh strained at his chains. He howled. He mumbled several syllables, but Spracklin couldn't understand him. The boy's eyes, wide in horror, were held by the photos. Flanagan grabbed a chair, pulled it over and sat next to MacIntosh.

"We have you on tape, Reg, admitting to holding The Mantis while Fox cut off his toe." He held MacIntosh's gaze as he spoke. "We have tape with you saying you knew Fox was testing Agent Elizabeth Watkins – a woman you knew as Raven."

Flanagan wanted it to sink in that Raven was a federal agent and that Fox murdered her. The guy needed to know the stakes were higher than he'd realized.

"Now you can imagine, Reg," said Flanagan. "You can imagine what it will mean when we play that tape . . ." He made sure the boy understood him. "For Andy Fox."

"For Andy?"

"We're going to catch him. We'll use that tape to get a confession out of him."

MacIntosh started crying again – not a gentle weeping that he tried to suppress but loud wails of grief and horror. He unleashed a babble of syllables, the only thing Spracklin could understand was the word "no" repeated several times. Then he gave way to more sobs, and tried to say something else. Flanagan let the boy cry out. Finally, he sat panting.

Flanagan started to say something and MacIntosh screamed, "He'll kill me. Torture – it'll be torture." When Flanagan tried again, he yelled, "He enjoys it, thinks it's interesting."

Flanagan held up a finger. "We don't want that, Reg. We really don't." Spracklin thought Flanagan was going to say more, but there was no point. They all knew what Flanagan wanted. They all knew MacIntosh had it.

He was exhausted now. He slurred his speech as he spoke. "It comes in by air."

Flanagan nodded his head. "We need details."

"It may already be here." The boy looked at Flanagan, pleading to be believed. "I, I don't know what day it is today."

"Just tell me the date of the flight.

"June 4," he said. "Andy told me we had to make the stuff he gave me last week last till June 4. Late June 4. And the stuff comes in from Hong Kong."

"Who's carrying the stuff?"

"Dunno."

"Don't fuck with us, Reg."

"I don't know. A month or two ago, Andy gave me some stuff. It was wrapped in a newspaper. It had Chinese writing – couldn't read it. But at the top it had the name of the paper, and at the bottom it said Hong Kong. And it had the date. The date was the day before he gave me the stuff. So I figured Andy's stuff came from Hong Kong and it had to come by air."

"How do you know he's not just testing you?"

"He already tested me." He seemed calmer now. Spracklin wondered if he was working his way through the cold turkey. "I already passed the Arcata test."

Flanagan kept talking to the boy, but Spracklin knew the interrogation was over. It would continue on June 5 if they came up with nothing the next night. He opened the door and slipped from the room.

"Cold turkey," said a voice behind him. It was Burwell. "No form of torture like it." Spracklin kept walking to the elevators "Self-inflicted. No scars."

They stood and waited for the elevator. Spracklin shook a cigarette half out of the case and offered it to Burwell. "Now let's hope he was telling the truth."

CHAPTER 40

Fox sat behind the passenger seat, out of view, his ass growing numb on the metal ruts of the van's cargo area. They'd passed through the wooded stretches of the Presidio and were in the urban section of the north panhandle. "Shakin' All Over" was on the radio, but Jethro wasn't tapping his fingers to the beat.

"You know we have to line up a driver," Fox said. Jethro's window was open and his big arm was half out. "Lookit, we may have something on her," Fox said.

"I'm listening."

"That cop, Spracklin. He was looking for her when he was asking questions about Blakely."

"So?"

"So she knew Blakely. He broke her heart."

The van came to a stop at an intersection. Jethro dipped the rim of his baseball hat, shielding his face from someone across the street. "She killed Blakely?"

"I don't know. She has a hardness, a resolve. I want to find out."

As they pulled through the big intersection at Van Ness, Fox crouched between the front seats and scouted the street. He'd called Marie and asked her to meet him in front of her place. His heart jumped when he saw her waiting on the sidewalk. She was wearing a beige sweater that looked too big and a grey mini skirt. Her large dark eyes gazed out from beneath a floppy felt hat. Jethro pulled over, Fox slid open the heavy door and she jumped into the back.

"Where we going?" she asked.

"Let's you and me go for a walk, okay?" said Fox.

"Wanna tag along, Jethro?" she said. He didn't turn around.

"Let's take a walk," said Fox. He scanned the street before he and Marie jumped out. After the van drove off, he grabbed Marie's hand and they sauntered along Union Street toward Coit Tower. They passed a few beatniks campaigning for McCarthy in the next day's primary and headed into the parkland around the tower.

"Man, does that cat hate me?" Marie said with a laugh.

191

"Jethro? He's just moody."

"C'mon Andy. He doesn't even try to hide it."

He scanned the park as he led her toward a bench. "He, well we – we've got a lot on our minds right now."

She took his hand in hers once they were seated in the shade of a tree where a few wild parrots were roosting. Their green plumage was barely visible against the spring leaves. "You okay, baby?" she asked.

"It's tense, Marie. It's heavy right now. You know I'm in business, and it's a tough business." She nodded. She squeezed his hand and he gazed into her eyes. "Marie, I'm in some trouble."

"What sort of trouble?"

"It's hard to talk about. It's –" He looked away then back at her. It had to be sincere. "I'm trying to get out of trouble. I don't want to end up like – well you know. Like John Blakely."

"You're not a junkie."

"It's not that. John, he had some enemies. You know what I mean. The cops are treating it as a murder. Someone killed him."

She didn't flinch. There was no change in her voice or in the pressure she applied to his hand. Without missing a beat she asked, "Do you know who did it?" If she did kill Blakely, she was good. Cold as ice. "Oh my God, you're not in shit with John's killer, are you?" she said.

"No, I don't know who did it. But I'm in debt, Marie. Big debt to a bad man. Have you ever heard of Bogdan Polgar?" She shook her head. "Bogdan's the boss of Fillmore. I owe him money. I'm in big trouble if I don't pay him soon."

They sat listening to the squawk of parrots. "And you'll end up like John if you don't repay him."

He nodded.

"I don't have any money to give you."

"I don't need that. I wouldn't take it. What I need is a favor tomorrow night."

"Anything."

"I need you to pick up a friend at the airport."

CHAPTER 41

"Christ Jimmy, you look like hell," said Bud Hawkings as Spracklin and Burwell stepped into the Lieutenant's office. Spracklin knew The Chief wasn't going to bawl him out for ignoring his messages. The Chief understood why Spracklin was avoiding him. He probably respected it. And Hawkings, standing there with the Field Officer from the local FBI office, obviously wanted his tone to be pleasant and respectful.

"It's been a busy few days," muttered Spracklin. He nodded a hello to the Chief and to Agent J.P. MacLean.

At 62, Bud Hawkings was still not fat, though his muscles had long since settled. His face was jowly rather than square, his neck most notable for the double chin in front rather than the bullish heft behind. He was still a dominant presence – and a terrifying individual when he was angry. He towered over MacLean, who stood silently behind him.

"No time to answer your phone messages," said the Chief. He nodded to the pink slips on the desk. He was smiling, but the message was clear.

"As I said, I've been busy."

"You must know Agent MacLean," said Hawkings. They nodded a hello to each other, and then reached out to shake hands. MacLean's gold cufflinks flashed as he stretched out his arm.

"We're old colleagues," said MacLean. "Lieutenant Spracklin used to be with us in Washington before he took his current position." There it was, thought Spracklin. The first sentence out of his mouth highlighted that Spracklin had left the Feds. MacLean saw himself as a cardinal and Spracklin a defrocked priest. MacLean always radiated a sense of superiority – he dressed well, understood wine and collected art. He was a tall man with a deliberately formal manner – like Inspector Erskine on the FBI television show. It was the one show Spracklin refused to watch with his boys. He didn't like thinking about the FBI. Whenever he met MacLean or his kind, he wondered if he was being too sensitive around them. But they always brought up that he had been with the Justice Department, and chose to leave for a local police force.

"Just felt police work was my calling," said Spracklin. "What can I do for you gentlemen?" He took the chair behind his desk.

"We're here about the Watkins investigation," said Hawkings. "How are things going?"

"We're making great progress, sir," Spracklin said. He always addressed the Chief formally when they were in the presence of other people. "Prime suspect is Andrew Fox. We just interviewed an associate, who said Fox is importing a shipment tomorrow night at the airport. Flight from Hong Kong, we think." He paused. Outside the open window the traffic rumbled on. A horn honked. "We look forward to intercepting the shipment and apprehending Fox."

"Lieutenant," began Hawkings. "Elizabeth Watkins was a federal agent." He didn't need to say the rest. "Field Officer MacLean has been good enough to discuss the case with me," Hawkings said. "I've told him we will co-operate fully."

Bud Hawkings was going to follow the politically convenient path even though it might reduce the chance of actually catching and prosecuting Fox. Spracklin knew he'd lose the battle but he had to give it a try. "With all due respect, I think it's best handled by homicide investigators," he said.

"We have a team of investigators flying up from L.A. right now," said MacLean. "Two investigators and a forensic scientist."

"And I've assured Field Officer MacLean that they will have complete co-operation from us," said Hawkings again.

The strain of the day was wearing on Spracklin. He wanted to tell them to fuck off, the two of them, even Bud Hawkings, who he liked and admired. But he had to be cannier than that. He told himself the forensic team would hopefully come up with evidence that would ensure a prosecution. "All right," he said. He reached in his drawer and pulled out a pack of cigarettes. "I have a cadet, Tommy Jackson, transcribing my crime scene notes. I'll hand them over as soon as I've proofread them." He lit a cigarette, not offering one to anyone else. "We'll have the autopsy tomorrow – you'll have that as well. The big thing to do now is coordinate an operation at the airport tomorrow night. I think Merrill Flanagan should head it."

"Hold on a second," said MacLean. "Do we know who's bringing the stuff in? What flight? Any details?"

Spracklin pulled the cigarette from his mouth and shot a stream of smoke to the ceiling. "The only thing our witness could tell us was that it's coming by air tomorrow night, likely from Hong Kong. We checked. The only flight from Hong Kong is Pan Am, refueling in Hawaii. Lands at 12:25 a.m."

"How good's your source?"

"A Fox Lieutenant. Heroin addict going through cold turkey."

Spracklin waited for him to respond that the witness was unreliable. He would counter-punch by asking him what sort of witness MacLean was expecting from inside a drug ring. They both knew it was the best information they were going to get.

"Where's the witness?"

"In lockup."

"Can we interview him?"

"It's your case," said Spracklin. He took the cigarette from his mouth and swiveled in his chair so he was looking at MacLean. "You can do whatever you like. We're just here to help. But we have to focus on the airport now because it will take coordination – FBI, SFPD, Customs."

"We're talking importation of a banned substance," said MacLean. "Clearly federal responsibility."

"Yes, let's make sure the operation's headed by the best narcotics officer in the region. No one's better than Flanagan. And it will free you up to work with your team on the murder investigation."

MacLean was silent. He was obviously wondering what the Lieutenant was up to. For the first time in hours, Spracklin felt happy. He was messing with MacLean's head.

"As I said," MacLean said, glancing at the Chief, "it's a federal operation and I'll take charge of it. I'd be delighted to have Lieutenant Flanagan's cooperation as we prepare."

Spracklin took another long drag on the cigarette and tapped a length of ash into the ashtray. "It's your call."

He was too worn out by murder and interrogation to care about a pompous shit like J.P. MacLean. He was glad that MacLean was fidgeting, obviously looking for a reason to leave before the locals got nasty about losing the case.

"This will let you guys focus on the Blakely case," said MacLean. Spracklin looked up at him.

"You know about the Blakely case?"

"The Chief was telling me about it, and I've read about his exhibitions. I was telling the Chief that I was reading in the *New York Times* today about Andy Warhol getting shot the other day. Must be open season on artists." He laughed at his own lame joke. Spracklin said nothing. MacLean had let them all know he read the New York Times and was up date on the latest trends in art. Typical. "So what else should I know about Fox?" asked the FBI agent.

"Psychopath. Lives in a van. Controls heroin trade on Haight Street. Travels with a goon known as Jethro." Spracklin flipped open the file and looked at his notes from his discussion with the coroner. "And he's dangerous. He killed Agent Watkins – instantly, from what I could tell. He used a knife with a blade at least four inches in length – up and into the heart. There were two other chest wounds."

"What else did you find at the crime scene."

"Shoeprints. We have a good imprint of" – he checked the notes again – "a running shoe, size nine-and-a-half PF Flyers. We have the model number."

"We'll have our forensic team go over the crime scene one more time," said MacLean, nodding his head at the Chief as if to say he had what he came for.

"Great," said Spracklin. "Hopefully they'll do the same bang-up job you boys are doing on catching Dr. King's killer."

"These guys have state of the art techniques—"

"State of the art? I have a 68 percent clear rate. You guys can't catch a hillbilly in Memphis who shot a national leader."

"Jimmy," said Hawkings.

"It's all right, Chief Hawkings," said MacLean. He summoned a smug grin. "Demotion is painful."

Spracklin stood, ready to respond. MacLean knew Spracklin left Justice because he was a Bobby Kennedy man and had no future in the Johnson administration. Bud Hawkings placed his massive body between them and raised his hands. "You've each had a shot at each other," he said. "Jimmy will get you the report, J.P. I'll see to it. We've probably reached the end of this meeting."

MacLean grinned as he stepped past the Chief and out of the office. Hawking, Spracklin and Burwell watched him go and the Chief turned to the Lieutenant. "Was that necessary, Jimmy?"

Spracklin tossed him the pack of cigarettes, and sat down. "Necessary? No. But it was worth it." Hawking took a cigarette and threw the pack to Burwell. "And it will be my job to make nice with him, I suppose," added Spracklin as he lit his cigarette.

"You're the perfect man for the job," said the Chief. Spracklin gave a weary smile. It was like the old days for a moment, Bud and Jimmy busting each other's chops.

The Chief leaned against the wall. "We have to work with them on this case. I'm getting heat."

"Lot of heat?"

"Christ, Jimmy," he growled, shaking his head. "The Washington Post called Community Relations this afternoon about the Watkins murder. It's big. Only news other than the Democratic primary. The mayor's feeling the heat, and as you know. . . "

"Heat descends in the civil service."

They always understood each other. "I had the mayor on the line today goin' apeshit about this whole fuckin' hippie thing." The Chief reached in his pocket and pulled out his notes. "Get this: some Georgia paper is reporting that a Mrs. J.G. Hillsdown of Atlanta was held up at knifepoint on Haight Street on Friday." He flicked some ash into Spracklin's ashtray. "It seems Mr. and Mrs. Hillsdown and their three kids took a holiday in California. A few days in Disneyland, then they came North 'cause they wanted to see the hippies on Haight-Ashbury. She arrives looking for peace, love and fucking harmony, and some junky threatens to cut her tits off if she doesn't hand over her purse."

Hawkings laughed and shook his head. "People are rating Haight-Ashbury with Disneyland on their holidays. And the mayor is upset because one of the hotels has cancelled its summer bus tours of the Haight. What is it with these hippies, Jimmy?"

Spracklin looked back with a blank expression. As he thought about it, he realized it was a good question. What was it with these hippies? Who fucking knew? He just frowned and shrugged.

Hawkings turned to leave then turned back. "How's it going with the other cases – the dead artist and that junkie?"

"We'll clear them."

"You know you have to."

"I get that," said Spracklin. "The mayor's tourism strategy depends on it."

Hawkings smiled and left the office. Spracklin and Burwell watched him wander around the corner to the elevator lobby, and Spracklin reached into his desk and took out a bottle of Black Label and two glasses. Burwell tossed the pack of Chesterfields down on the desk. "So what were you trying to keep MacLean away from?"

"Huh?" asked Spracklin, handing him a glass of scotch.

"You gave in too quickly, letting him take the case from you. Then you picked a fight to divert him. What were you up to?"

Spracklin sipped his drink, looked over at the Sergeant and appraised him.

"The writing was on the wall, Ed. We knew they were going to get it. And we also knew we already solved it – it was Fox. But I wanted to keep him away from

The Mantis investigation for now. We'll get the credit we deserve for that one."

He couldn't tell Burwell what was really going on – that his priority was to make sure the FBI didn't conduct its own autopsy on Elizabeth Watkins. He was also wondering if Burwell was a better detective than he'd previously given him credit for.

CHAPTER 42

Marie glanced up when the street light flicked on and, for a second, Fox caught a glimpse of her beautiful face. In the dusk, he could only make out her silhouette but in an instant he saw her green eyes and full lips. He could see the curiosity, the intelligence in her features.

"So you're not going to tell me anything else?" she asked.

He wanted to hold her in his arms and confess everything. He couldn't, and he had to go soon. He'd been in the open too long.

"Honey, you're going to have to trust me," he said as she took his hand in hers. "The next forty-eight hours are key to my business. If things go well, yeah it will be great for me. But it will be great for both of us. You and me together, baby."

"That's cool, Andy. And I'm there for you. But we both know that the more I know, the more I'm prepared."

"Marie, baby, the less you know, the better for all of us. Trust me."

She pulled him in and kissed him, a long slow kiss. "But you have to promise me something," she said, pulling away.

"I'll do my best."

"You have to promise that when I get in, we watch the returns from the primary."

"What?"

"Kennedy's going to win tomorrow night. I want to watch it."

He kissed her. "I think we can manage that."

"And I get to tell you how great Bobby –"

She was interrupted by a massive form sliding on to the park bench behind them. The cops, Fox thought. As he swung around, he dropped his hand to the knife in his sock. But it was Jethro. He'd come out of nowhere and was sitting beside them.

"Jesus, dude," Fox said with a laugh. "You scared me." Jethro had a crazed look in his eye. "What's going on, man?"

"You should ask your little friend there," Jethro said. Fox didn't turn around to look at Marie, but he could feel her squirming.

"Me?" she squeaked.

"What are you talking about?" Fox asked.

Jethro smiled and reached over and handed something to Marie. She snatched it and held it in the light of the street lamp. It was her driver's license. "What the fuck is this?" she said.

"The question is," Jethro said, "who lives at 17 Juillet Crescent? Marie Mercer, my ass. What's your real name?"

"Fuck you. It's my parents' place. What are you doing with my license?"

Fox held up a hand to silence her. He didn't know what Jethro was up to, but Jethro wouldn't ambush her without reason. "Let him speak."

"When I saw her license, there was something fishy. The address looked familiar, so I drove over to Marin County to check it out. It's that house where that cop, Spracklin, lives."

"Andy, what's going on?" asked Marie.

"We checked on you. We have to do that." Fox said it with a tone that suggested she should know as much. "And the address on your license is the home of the detective that's been busting my balls."

He was trying to control his reaction. It had been bad that Raven was a narc. But not Marie. He just couldn't handle Marie being a narc.

"I told you about my step-father," she said. "What I didn't tell you – what I don't tell anyone – is that he's a cop. Jimmy Spracklin married my mother when I was five. I used the name I was born with on my driver's license, but my legal name is Marie Spracklin. And that's it. I can't help who my mother married."

"And the reason you didn't tell us is . . ?" said Jethro. He was aggressive in his tone.

"I didn't tell anyone. He's responsible for my friend's death and I want to forget him."

Her voice quivered as she spoke – not with fear but with emotion. Fox felt she was telling the truth. Maybe he just wanted to believe her, but for now he trusted her. Cops don't use their sixteen-year-old daughters as under-cover agents. But he had to keep Jethro away from her – at least until she helped them out the next night. After that it might prove more difficult.

CHAPTER 43

It was early evening by the time Spracklin finished reading the report Jackson had written. It was clean and accurate. He tucked the report into the folder with a label that read:

ELIZABETH WATKINS
(AKA RAVEN)
060168-F-030

He handed it over to the cadet and asked him to take the file to Bud Hawkings. The Lieutenant realized, as Jackson left the room, that he needed another whiskey. The horror of what had happened to that beautiful young woman was setting in and a drink might numb the suffering. He poured one for himself and another for Burwell, who sat across from him. The phone rang.

"Lieutenant Barrow from Fresno," said Melanie.

"Put him on," said Spracklin. "Then head home." The girl was working late, doing her part to help on a busy day.

He heard the click of the cables connecting and Melanie telling Barrow to go ahead.

"What's the news, Gary?"

"Coach Jenkins identified him," Barrow said. "Name's Daniel Lake. Played back-up linebacker for two years before dropping out as a sophomore in '66. The coach described him as a good kid, a good student, though a bit reckless."

"Done a search on him?"

"Youbetcha. Arrested on vagrancy in San Mateo January 17, 1967, and December 21 for possession of cannabis on Haight-Ashbury."

Across the office, Spracklin saw Melanie wandering toward his office with the last batch of phone messages for the day.

"Forensics?"

"Murder weapon was a knife, five-and-a-half inches in length, single-edged, half an inch wide, with a nick on the blunt edge."

Spracklin nodded again. It might be a match for the weapon that killed Elizabeth

Watkins. It meant Fox kept his knife, probably had an affinity for it, and may still have it on him. Melanie came toward his desk. She smiled at him and handed him one last batch of pink phone messages for the day. *Yes*, he thought, *when we finally catch Fox tomorrow night, he'll have the single piece of evidence. . .*

Spracklin never finished the thought. As Melanie reached out to give him the phone messages, her hand caught his attention. He reached out and grabbed her wrist. She squealed and tried withdrawing her arm, but he held fast. The pink slips fluttered across the desk as her hand opened.

"Ow, Lieutenant," she squealed. Burwell looked over at them. "You're hurting me."

Still staring at Melanie's hand, Spracklin muttered into the phone. "I'll call you back, Gary." He was already lowering the receiver when Burwell asked what was happening.

"Lieutenant, let go."

"Melanie," he said slowly, "could you step into the interview room, please?"

"I just told you. I have to go."

"That room over there."

"Look, I'm running late and my mom is waiting for me."

Spracklin stood and pointed to the room. Running late, Jesus Christ, he thought. He would have to wait for his scotch and Melanie's mother would have to wait for her daughter.

"Look, what is this shit?" she asked. "I have to – "

"Interview Room B," he said.

"Look, I just have to visit the ladies' room and then I'll – "

"Get the fuck in there." She moved through the Homicide Department to the interview room. Burwell followed, trying to figure out what was going on.

Melanie stood there, twirling her hair around a green-ended index finger. Spracklin pointed to a chair. She sat and her act dissolved. She started to cry. "Keep your hands on the table," he said. The ten fingers, the nails highlighted in green paint, touched the vinyl surface, and her face crumpled into sobs.

Spracklin looked at the fingernails. At the edge of the green paint, he could see the remnants of her last nail job. At the edge of each nail, diluted with nail polish remover, were signs of what the previous colors had been. Each nail had been painted a different color until she had redone them all in green. Spracklin thought back to Vague Dimensions. One of the girls who had calmed him down had had different colored fingernails. He hadn't seen her face, but she spoke like they knew each other. Melanie had obviously been at Vague Dimensions, seen he was in trouble, tried to talk him down without letting him see her.

"You were at Vague Dimensions," he said to her. "Saturday night."

"There were lots of people—"

"But you knew what Fox and Jethro were planning." He looked at her with disbelief. One of his staff members was in with Fox. "Empty your pockets and your handbag," He turned to Burwell. "Ed, get a female sheriff up here."

Burwell was puzzled, but obeyed. Out in the bureau, the few inspectors who were working late were watching through the glass wall.

"What is this all about?" asked Melanie, between sniffs.

"Just empty your pockets and handbag."

Slowly, she emptied the contents of her handbag on to the table. Spracklin took a pen from his pocket and pushed aside makeup and chewing gum. He sifted through her wallet and found nothing. Inside her glasses case he found a pair of sunglasses with heart-shaped lenses. He told her to stand and he studied her. Her pockets were clearly empty. He'd have the female sheriff search her when she arrived.

Spracklin took one final look at the glasses. He tipped them out of the case and felt the case bottom. There was something under the lining. Melanie began to cry again as he used a fingernail to pry away the backing. There were six perforated squares of cardboard, each about a half-inch squared. Each square had a little picture of a skull with a lightning bolt through it.

"What's this?"

The girl simply sobbed.

"We're going to find out. What is it and where did you get it?"

She sat with her hands still on the table, crying too hard to speak.

"Deadhead acid," said a voice behind him. Spracklin glanced up to see Burwell looking over his shoulder. Behind him was a sheriff from the women's lockup. "It's LSD soaked into blotter paper and stamped with the logo of the Grateful Dead."

Spracklin looked down at the papers, and at the sobbing girl. He recited her rights then placed one hand on the back of her chair and the other on the table. "Melanie, you're going to tell us where Fox is."

Melanie glanced up and saw Spracklin's glare. She was used to the genial Lieutenant but now she saw a man looking for a killer.

"Where's Fox?"

"I don't know any Fox."

"He was the one who murdered that black woman you saw at the club two nights ago. She was a federal agent."

Melanie burst into tears again. She sobbed uncontrollably for a minute or more. "My father's going to kill me," she blurted out.

"Least of your worries. Where's Fox?"

"I want a lawyer," she said through her tears.

"Make it easy on yourself, Melanie. Just tell us where he is."

"I want a lawyer."

"You thought it was cool to hang out with Fox, didn't you? You led a boring life in the suburbs but all the rebels up on Haight Street were cool. You could be cool too."

"No."

"You knew everything Fox was planning two nights ago. Where is he?"

"I was trying to save you, asshole."

"So you do know him."

"I want a lawyer."

"Where's Fox?"

"A lawyer," she said, bursting into a fresh round of sobs.

Spracklin thought about the lawyer. He didn't care about prosecuting her on the LSD charge. But he knew he might need her to testify against Fox. He was worried his reluctance to get her a lawyer would have an impact on her testimony in the case that mattered. He asked the sheriff to watch her while he and Burwell conferred.

"What the fuck is this all about?" asked Burwell when they were out in the hall.

"Other night, when I was drugged, a girl who talked me down had multi-colored fingernails – a different color on each finger." He started to walk out of the room toward the reception area, and Burwell filed in behind him. "She spoke like she knew Fox." Spracklin looked at the old switchboard, a tangle of cords and plugs. He'd learned to use it over the years. A call came in, the receptionist answered, put the plug in the socket, then pushed a button to release the call. But if she didn't push that button, she could listen to everything being said.

"Ed, did you and I talk about Fox, or about Raven, on the phone this morning?"

"You thinking she eavesdropped?"

"It would have been easy. You called Rosenfeld in Washington from home, right?"

"Yup."

Spracklin tried to recall who he'd talked to in the last few days. Melanie had probably heard his conversations with Barrow down in Fresno. So Fox probably knew everything about that investigation. He now wondered what she'd heard wandering through the office. What notes she'd seen. What information she'd got from flirting with young officers. She must have been the one who told Fox where he lived.

"Oh shit," said Burwell.

"Oh shit is right. I'm wondering if I mentioned Arcata to anyone on the phone."

"If so, she would have had to get in touch with Fox real quick," said Burwell. "She must have a phone number for him."

Burwell ran back to the interview room to check her handbag again. Spracklin rummaged through the drawers at her desk. He found her phone lists on a clipboard in the second drawer.

"Ed," he yelled. "Bring the reverse directory."

Jackson stepped out of the elevator and watched as the Lieutenant and Sergeant studied the clipboard. The margins were covered with pink and green doodles of peace signs and hearts and Grateful Dead skulls and names with phone numbers. Inside one heart were the initials "J.S." – Jimmy Spracklin. Could she have helped him at Vague Dimensions because she had a girlish crush on him?

Most of the jottings seemed to be personal numbers with a San Jose exchange and names of her friends beside them. There were two local numbers, a boy called Freddie and a couple called Helium and Shelium. And there was one number with no name written beside it. It was in a little box at the lower right hand. Burwell looked up the number in the reverse directory and read out the address. "One-thirty-two Lyon Street."

"Vague Dimensions," said Jackson. "That's the address for Vague Dimensions. I've been there plenty of times and I'm sure that's it."

Vague Dimensions. Spracklin knew Fox had been hanging out there the other night. Could that be his headquarters? It was worth checking out. "Ed," he said. "I want you to take charge of Melanie. Have the sheriff search her. Get her a public defender and interrogate her. I want to know about her and Fox. We need to know what she told him and when. Try to find out if she gave Fox my address."

Burwell nodded, and the Lieutenant turned to Jackson. "Tommy, you and I are heading over to Vague Dimensions."

CHAPTER 44

Spracklin and Jackson drove in silence through a light rain along Market Street toward Haight. Spracklin knew the chances of Fox being at Vague Dimensions were slim. It was eight on a Monday night. But he had to check.

"What's going to happen to Melanie, sir?" asked Jackson as they turned on to Haight Street.

"First offence for drugs with a San Francisco judge – stern warning," said Spracklin. He accelerated up the hill through Lower Haight. "But if she abetted in a homicide of a federal agent, things change." Spracklin accelerated up the hill. "Probably ten years but it'll be hard to get a conviction."

"I don't think she's a bad person."

Spracklin heaved a sigh from deep in his chest as he pulled up at a red light. "Tom, you know how many quote-unquote good people I've convicted for murder?"

The question sat with the boy as they pulled up to the music hall. Spracklin grabbed a flashlight from the glove compartment, got out of the car and patted his side to reassure himself his sidearm was in the holster. He strode across the street. Jackson walked abreast of him.

The building was dark and the doors locked – obviously there weren't any shows on a Monday night. They skirted the building to the empty parking lot. They continued around and tried to find an open entrance. They came to the side exit that Spracklin had escaped through two nights earlier. It was locked. Spracklin pulled out a key ring with a selection of picks. He squatted down, careful not to lower his knees on to the wet ground, and began to work the locks.

"Shouldn't we get a warrant, sir?" said Jackson.

"We have reason to believe there's immediate danger."

"Who's in danger?"

"My daughter."

Jackson shuffled again. Spracklin knew the kid didn't know what he was talking about. Before the boy could ask anything else, the lock sprang and Spracklin was pushing into the narrow passage to the main hall.

The beams of the street lights invaded the hall from the high windows. Even the murals looked dull in the weak light. What had seemed like a vast barn a few nights earlier had nooks and crannies where Fox could be hiding. There was the bar, the stage, all the tables and overhead projectors, the bathrooms, a few other doors. Looking up, Spracklin saw a depression in the ceiling and a window in it. It was a lighting booth facing the stage. There must be a catwalk leading up to it. Fox could be anywhere in this building. Or he could be miles away.

Spracklin took out his revolver, flicked off the safety. He gestured to Jackson to get his gun out. The young man just shrugged. He was a cadet. He carried no weapon.

Spracklin crept forward, ducked down to check under the tables. Nothing. Jackson was still behind him, providing an extra set of eyes if nothing else. Spracklin stepped to his right, all the while sweeping the room with his pistol. He thought he heard noises, but couldn't tell if they were real, sounds from the street or just his imagination.

"If you were Fox," he whispered, "where would you hide?"

Jackson took a minute to survey the hall. "Near an exit."

Spracklin nodded. In addition to the door they'd just entered, there was the main entrance and another fire exit. There might be other doors off of side rooms. The stage was straight ahead. Spracklin focused on two doors – one he knew led to the washrooms, he assumed the other was a closet or a staffroom. A staffroom would probably have a window. He crossed the hall. There was a sign on the door that read

Vague-rants Only

Spracklin swung the door open. He waved the gun across the little room. He was about to check behind the desk, when he heard a creak from above them. It was a slow, shrill groan, the sound of two pieces of metal grating because someone had stepped on one. Spracklin moved out into the hall. He glanced at Jackson, who nodded and they both looked at the ceiling. They could only see darkness in the window of the lighting booth. Spracklin nudged Jackson ahead of him and they moved slowly toward the stage. Spracklin kept watching the catwalk. Whoever was up there had a clear view of him.

They moved behind the curtain so they couldn't be seen from the lighting booth. Spracklin trained his gun on the junk scattered in its dim corners: speakers, amplifiers, a microphone and huge props that looked like they came from a cartoon. He checked behind the piano, behind a great red and white toadstool and a paper-maché donkey. Nothing.

Their eyes had adjusted to the darkness and Spracklin could make out metal ladders at either side of the stage. Spracklin shuffled to the nearest ladder. He trained the gun up into the darkness but could see no one. He listened and heard nothing. There were two ladders. If Fox was up there, he and Jackson had him cornered. Now they had to go get him. Was Marie up there with Fox? Spracklin faced Jackson, tapped his own chest and pointed to the far ladder, then tapped Jackson and pointed to the close one. Jackson nodded and was about to go when Spracklin grabbed his shoulder.

"I think there's a horseshoe of catwalks up there that links the two ladders and the lighting room. I'm going to sweep around. I just want you at the top of the ladder to make sure no one gets out."

The young man nodded. The Lieutenant placed his gun in the cadet's hand, and whispered: "If you need to use this, I'll claim it."

Jackson shook his head and pushed the gun back. Spracklin stood firm. He didn't want a cadet going up that ladder unarmed. He crossed the stage to the far ladder before Jackson could protest further. He looked over to Jackson but could see nothing. He assumed the boy was already ascending into the darkness.

Spracklin felt for each rung as he pulled himself higher. They'd heard something up here. It could be Worthington. He felt his chest tighten as he went into the dark unarmed against a madman.

He stopped at the top and brushed the air with his right hand until he could feel the wall. He crouched down, and flicked on the flashlight. All he could see was a metal catwalk stretching out for about ten yards. He wheeled around. There was a little room – a nook off the catwalk. Someone had used it to store the props used on the stage below. He could see a huge horse's head, a car with a smiling face, and a massive unicorn. Then he noticed something more – a mattress with a tangle of sheets on it, burned out candles all around. There were a few clothes piled on the far side of the mattress.

Spracklin stepped into the room and shone the light about. With his shoe, he nudged the sheets but there was nothing in them. He looked at the clothes – men's clothes, blue jeans and T-shirts, a flannel shirt. Then he heard a crashing sound.

Spracklin tore off down the metal pathway. He could hear the thumps and thuds of a struggle. He rounded the corner. The projection booth was empty. He dashed past two massive spot lights and the graffiti-covered back wall and wheeled around the final corner. His flashlight beam caught two men wrestling near the top of the far ladder.

Jackson was facing Fox, had his right arm wrapped around the dealer and was pushing him against the wall. Jackson had dropped Spracklin's gun and was

209

now trying to stop Fox from reaching it. Fox was being overpowered but was attacking the cadet's back with a knife. Jackson used his left arm to deflect the stabs, but a few seemed to be reaching their mark.

"Drop it, Fox," Spracklin yelled as he ran up to them. He kept the light in Fox's eyes so he wouldn't be able to see the Lieutenant was unarmed.

"Shoot and your friend dies."

Spracklin could see Jackson's strength was ebbing, and it wouldn't be long until Fox realized Spracklin had no gun.

"Just put the knife down. You'll never get out of here." Spracklin moved forward until his feet straddled the pistol on the wire grating. Fox was moving back toward the ladder with Jackson. In the beam of the flashlight, Spracklin could clearly see Fox's face. It was older, more weathered than in the mugshots. He had crow's feet, accentuated by his angry squint.

"Drop the knife, Fox."

"You drop the gun."

"Building's surrounded."

"Bullshit."

Fox was finding it difficult to move now because he had to support Jackson's weight. He tried to stab the boy once more in the back, but Jackson deflected it. Fox pushed the young cop toward Spracklin. The Lieutenant broke his fall, bent and picked up the pistol. He rushed to the top of the ladder and shot three times. It was too late. Fox was already across the stage. He heard a fire door slam shut as Spracklin took off his tie and pressed it against the base of Jackson's back. He could feel the warm blood ooze between his fingers.

He lifted Tommy Jackson into a fireman's carry, moved down the ladder with him, then laid him on the stage. He rolled the cadet on his side and checked the wounds. Through the torn uniform, he could see five gashes. It looked like four of them might have hit the bone at the top of the pelvis but one looked deep.

"Hang on Tommy," he said. The boy was still conscious. Spracklin dashed into the office, and picked up the phone. He dialed and waited, cursing the night shift personnel. Finally, someone picked up and Spracklin spat out a Code Nine Nine Nine and read off the address. Then he ordered all patrols to scan the area for Fox.

Spracklin ran to the stage again to apply pressure to Jackson's wounds and pray that he would not be responsible for the death of another fine young officer.

Tuesday, June 4, 1968

CHAPTER 45

Spracklin held the yellow ribbon up so Ed Burwell could slip under and enter Vague Dimensions.

"Thanks," said Burwell. He held open the inner door and Spracklin walked through. They wandered in and stood in the middle of the music hall. Both Spracklin and the hall had changed in twelve hours. Spracklin had slept, showered, shaved, and dressed in a grey flannel suit. A rolled up newspaper was tucked under his arm.

"Bet it seems empty in the daylight," said Burwell, trying again to make conversation.

Spracklin surveyed the scene. Merrill Flanagan and some men from Park Station were searching the hall, which seemed bleached in the daylight. One man was on the stage and yelling up the ladder to others who were on the catwalk. They'd placed flood lights up there and the beams projected from the windows facing the stage. The presence of the police officers drained the vibrancy from the giant murals.

Flanagan walked over, wearing rubber gloves and holding two evidence bags, one with a hypodermic needle, the other a hash pipe. He paused in front of Spracklin, but said nothing.

"He's okay," Spracklin said.

"He'll make it?"

"Yeah, yeah. Tommy'll be out of action for a month or two. But he was able to deflect the knife thrusts. No damage to internal organs. He's resting."

Flanagan nodded and placed the bags down. "Tough kid," he said.

"Damn tough."

Over Flanagan's shoulder, Spracklin could see Agent MacLean come to the door of the office and look out. He'd obviously heard them talking.

"The Feds interviewing the owner?" asked Spracklin.

Flanagan turned and looked at MacLean, who began walking toward them. "Yeah, they've had him in there for about ninety minutes."

MacLean nodded a hello and waited for the conversation to resume. It didn't. He coughed and said, "How's your cadet doing, Jimmy?"

Spracklin looked at him. Flanagan responded, "Jimmy was just saying the kid will be fine. He's stable."

"Good, good." Spracklin waited for MacLean to ask what a cadet was doing in that situation. It turned out that not even MacLean was stupid enough to push that button.

"So has the owner said anything?" asked Flanagan.

"Tony Weinacht?" answered MacLean. "No, he's just an honest businessman who wanted to open a place where kids could play their music."

Flanagan nodded and in a mimicking voice said, "Fox? No, no, don't know a Fox."

"Exactly." MacLean laughed. Looking at Spracklin, he added, "Care to join us?"

Spracklin looked at the open door, then back at MacLean. "You want me to join you in the interview?" That prick, he thought. Trying to get in good with the locals after he grabbed our case.

"Can't hurt," said the Fed. "Maybe we can do a good cop bad cop thing."

"Good cop bad cop."

"Sure."

Spracklin smiled. "I'm the good cop."

"If you like." MacLean started to laugh.

"And you're the bad cop."

"Why not?"

"Should work," said Spracklin. "Christ knows you're the worst fucking cop I've ever met."

MacLean and the others chuckled. The FBI agent raised his arm to slap Spracklin's shoulder. Then he saw Spracklin's cold stare. One by one, the others stopped laughing and studied Spracklin. The Lieutenant removed the newspaper from under his arm and unfolded it. He could have given it to MacLean but he held it open so everyone could read it. It was that day's New York Times, opened to Page A29. The story at the top of the page was a follow-on article about the artist Andy Warhol being shot. Spracklin gestured to the story below. "Matt Findlay in the Mayor's office vets the national press each morning," said Spracklin. "He alerted the Chief about this. Bud called me this morning." As

Flanagan and MacLean read it, he added, "I picked up a copy of the Times at a hotel on the way over here. Cost me ninety-five cents."

> *FBI Probes*
> *S.F. Death*
>
> *San Francisco – The Federal Bureau of Investigation has been called in to find the murderer of Federal Agent Elizabeth Watkins after the lead suspect eluded local police Friday and Monday.*
>
> *Sources familiar with the matter said the San Francisco Police Department has twice been within reach of the lead suspect in the case but he managed to escape them. His evasion on Friday may have resulted in the death of Agent Watkins, who was on an undercover detail in the city's Haight-Ashbury district. . . .*

"Holy shit," said MacLean. "Look Jimmy, it must have been someone in Washington who leaked that. . ."

Spracklin didn't have to say anything. The men present knew that MacLean and his team had gone out of their way to discredit the Bureau of Inspectors with the eastern press. MacLean, who had a penchant for mentioning what he'd read in the *New York Times*, had obviously leaked it. Anyone else would have leaked to a local paper. The Lieutenant folded the paper again and tucked it under his arm. He knew MacLean would continue to deny his involvement, and the SFPD people would all know he was lying.

Spracklin walked into the office, a bleak room with nothing on the wall and a bare lightbulb hanging from the ceiling. Behind a wooden desk with initials scratched on the surface sat the silver-haired German he had seen a few nights before. Tony Weinacht had been full of life on Saturday night, but now he looked pale and weak as he puffed nervously on a cigarette. Several butts floated in a half-full Coke bottle in front of him.

"As I have told these men repeatedly," he was saying to one of the Feds, "I don't know Andy Fox. I don't know why this man was in my club." He spoke perfect English with a thin German accent, so it sounded like he said "*vy ziss man vas in my club*".

"We're not here to fuck around, Tony," said an FBI agent standing in his shirt sleeves next to him. "We want Fox."

"I don't know him. We have thousands, tens of thousands, of kids who come here to listen to music. I don't know them all."

"Did John Blakely ever come here," asked MacLean from the side of the room. It was as if he was trying to help Spracklin.

"I don't know who that was."

"I thought you were into the arts. There's an international market for his work.

213

You must have known him."

"As I said," said Weinacht, taking a drag of the cigarette. "We get a lot of people in here."

One of the FBI agents turned to Spracklin and nodded, as if to invite him to interrogate the witness. Spracklin looked down at Tony Weinacht, who tapped his cigarette against the mouth of the bottle. Weinacht looked up, and Spracklin held his gaze. He was trying to think of one question, that one question that would slice through the denials and show the Feds the value of local knowledge.

"Jasmine was playing here Saturday night, wasn't she?"

Weinacht stopped tapping the cigarette for a beat, then put it in his mouth. "Yeah, so?"

"You know her."

"Yes, yes, she plays in my hall sometimes. A very talented girl."

"And her housemate Raven came here with her," said Spracklin. The German again paused a second before answering. He didn't know who this new cop was, but he was wondering how much the guy knew. "A lot of kids come in here," he said. "We have young people, they come into my club from all over the world. I want a place where they can play their music—"

"Raven came in here. You knew she was here with Jasmine. Are you going to deny that?"

Weinacht took another drag on his cigarette. "Raven, yes, she was in here."

The accent reminded Spracklin of the Germans he'd taken prisoner as an MP a quarter century earlier. He thought of the monsters he'd guarded and interrogated in Nuremburg. "When?"

"I saw her Saturday night, Raven. We hoped she'd play the piano, but she disappeared half way through the night."

Spracklin wondered if Weinacht had seen him leaving with Raven, but the German gave no indication he had. "Did you know that the woman you knew as Raven was the federal agent murdered yesterday?"

"I know it now and—"

"And did you mention to these investigators that she was here Saturday night?" The G-men stirred. They were coming to life now he was making some headway.

Weinacht fished in his pack for another cigarette and fumbled as he tried to light it off his last one. "No, I . . . They were aggressive."

"Aggressive." Spracklin sat on the corner of the desk. "They're going to get a lot more aggressive unless you tell us the truth about Andy Fox and his relationship with Elizabeth Watkins. We've found paraphernalia that we believe has traces of narcotics on your premises. Your establishment is closed until we conduct tests—"

"You can't do that."

"—And further searches." Weinacht glared. "I damn well can. This is a crime scene."

"I'll go bust. I have debts to pay."

"Not my problem."

"But I pay taxes here. You can't put me out of business for no reason."

"We've got very good reasons." From the corner of his eye, Spracklin noticed a uniformed officer come to the door of the office. He signaled to both Spracklin and Flanagan. "But if you want to tell us what you know about Andy Fox and why he was in your hall, we could listen."

"You can't put me out of business. I employ people. I provide a place . . ." Weinacht continued to protest but Spracklin wasn't listening. He noticed that the uniform, who looked familiar, was holding something out for him with gloved hands.

He and Flanagan stepped out of the office, and glanced at what appeared to be a swath of denim. "Inspector Spracklin," said the constable. The inspector looked at him and recognized the young man who had shown up the other day when they'd found Derek. "I'm Lance Schmidt, and I've been searching the catwalk."

"Yes," said Spracklin again, looking at the garment.

"We've found some items that will need testing, but I came down to get you after we found this." He held up the denim. "Smell it, sir."

Spracklin bent and sniffed. Almonds, the distinct smell of almonds. "On Sunday, you said you suspected the dead hippie was poisoned because you could smell almonds," said Schmidt. "I thought of it as soon as I smelled this. Maybe we can hang those poisonings you're investigating on Fox if we can establish this is his."

Spracklin nodded and sniffed the garment again. There was definitely a scent of almond. They would need it tested but it was strong evidence.

"And we should be able to find someone who's seen the owner of this jacket," said Schmidt, opening up the jean jacket so they could all see the willow tree embroidered on the back of it. "I mean it's pretty distinctive."

Spracklin continued to nod as he looked at the unique willow tree stitched into the back of the small jean jacket. He was mesmerized by the feathery branches and clusters of leaves that seemed to wave when the jacket moved. The smell. That goddamned smell of the almondy poison was suddenly enough to drive

215

him insane. People were talking but he couldn't hear them. He examined the jacket. There were splatter marks on the left sleeve. It looked like blood. He held it up and studied it more closely. The fine details of the willow had definitely been produced by the tender hands of his beloved Marie. Could the red marks be blood splatters? Was she the cause of these blood splatters as well? Those questions and the smell of almonds made his gut churn with anxiety.

CHAPTER 46

Jethro disregarded Fox's warning that they needed clear heads. The giant was slumped on the mattress in the back of the van, his back leaning against the wall lined with shag carpet. He continued to sprinkle sinsemilla into the rolling paper. His left hand folded the baggie and tucked it into his breast pocket, then the right hand rolled the twisted joint.

"This shit's getting serious, man," Fox said. "We can't be stoned now."

Jethro just put the joint in his mouth and lit the end. He took a long haul, held it and continued to gaze at his friend as he exhaled through his nose.

"Jesus man, you know the next twelve hours will make or break us," Fox hissed at him. He was slouched by the back door and he was tempted to just throw it open and leave Jethro there.

Jethro took the joint from his mouth. He said, "Yerright."

"About what?"

"Next twelve hours will make or break us." Jethro shifted. "That's why she's a bad idea."

Fox started to wonder if he could get by without Jethro, but it didn't take long to realize he had to have Jethro. The Mantis, Derek, Raven, Reg – those losses were replaceable. Jethro was not. Fox had to have him on board.

"Listen," he said. "We need her for the drop. We got shit on her and I know we can trust her—"

"If we could trust her," Jethro said, "she woulda told us her old man's a cop."

He took another long drag on the joint, hard enough that you could see it burning down.

"It's, like . . . She has problems with the dude," Fox said. "She loves him and she hates him. It's the way you get to her – say things that bring him to mind. But trust me. She'll be fine with the drop. If not . . ."

Jethro stamped out the joint and exhaled again. He nodded, "If not . . ."

Fox eyed his partner, who was staring past him with a glassy look in his eyes. Fox was starting to understand that the game was changing for Jethro. The goal was no longer to run an operation that sold drugs, to beat the authorities, to make money. Jethro was reaching a point where the operation was just a vehicle that let him do what he loved most. The goal was to keep killing people.

CHAPTER 47

Sitting in his home office, Spracklin poured another splash of scotch into his glass. The sympathy card in front of him had a heading and single sentence. It had been fifteen minutes since he'd written them. His mind was filled with images of the embroidered coat, the splatter marks on the sleeve, the smell of almonds.

What could it mean? All his professional instincts told him Marie had been involved with murder. She was hanging out with a murderer. Could Fox have stolen the coat? It was a possibility, but Spracklin would never accept such a theory if it applied to someone he didn't know. That was the problem: he did know Marie. He couldn't believe she could poison someone. He had to prove it. He had to save that girl he loved so dearly, and do it without betraying his values, his department and himself.

Spracklin hoped another sip of scotch would clear his mind. He looked again at the card.

> Dear Dr. and Mrs. Watkins,
>
> I am a San Francisco police officer who had the pleasure, the honor, of working with your daughter, however briefly.

Spracklin's eyes blurred as he gazed at the open card. It was surrounded by the ephemera of the investigation – his notebook, photos of the house on Masonic and the stiff in the freezer, the dossier on Andrew Fox, the copy of the New York Times with the report on Elizabeth's death, the list of suspects (with Raven and Derek scratched out) in the Blakely murder. His list of suspects was now a mess as so many of them had died in the few days he'd been researching the case.

Reg MacIntosh	Mediocre artist – Jealousy
TOO STUPID	
~~Derek Hodgson~~	~~Teased about being soldier~~
~~TOO HONORABLE???~~	
Jasmine (Eleanor Jones)	Rape victim?
TOO INDECISIVE	
Rupert Hill	Vendetta against family.

<label>219</label>

> *POSSIBLE*
> *Gloria (Vanhusen)*   *Loud mouth ~~(But harmless?)~~*
> *POSSIBLE*
> *~~Raven (ELIZABETH WATKINS)Don't know enough yet.~~*
> *~~FED~~*
> *Andy Fox*   *Drug dealer. Did Blakely owe him money?*
> *TOO PASSIVE A MURDER*
> *~~The Mantis (Daniel Lake) ????????????????????????????????????~~*
> *TOO DEAD*

He focused on the card again and forced his pen to write the next sentence.

Elizabeth was a young woman of unique spirit, a vibrant girl who was full of life.

It should have been so easy because Agent Watkins was such an exceptional young woman – not unlike Marie. She had Marie's strength and determination. He thought again of the little girl he took to the shooting range all those years ago. Did she have the determination to kill someone? If she didn't have a gun, would she poison a person? Could the splatter marks have been blood? He remembered the pool of blood by the potter's wheel in the house on Masonic. Could Marie have been involved in that? He'd sent the coat to the state crime lab for tests. Benzedrine and Ouchterlony tests could tell whether the marks were blood, and whether the blood was human. He was sure the splatters were too small to get a reading on the blood type.

Outside he could hear Valerie marshalling the boys into the kitchen for dinner. He didn't want to eat with his wife. She refused to understand he had a responsibility to the victims and their families. A boy who fought for his country in Vietnam, and an artist with an international reputation.

"An international reputation." He said it out loud. He sipped his scotch, and pondered what he'd just said. MacLean had said it. When they were interrogating Weinacht, he'd mentioned there was international demand for Blakely's art. International? He looked at the Blakely file again, and confirmed what he remembered – Blakely's recent exhibition had been his first. And it had been local. But MacLean had talked about an international demand for Blakely's paintings. Then as Spracklin thought about it, he remembered MacLean saying he was familiar with Blakely's "exhibitions". Plural. But Blakely had only had one that Spracklin knew of.

Seconds later he was on the phone to the FBI field office and got through to MacLean.

"I know you're busy preparing for tonight," said Spracklin. The operation at the airport was important and he understood the agent didn't want to be disturbed. "But I need to ask you something about Blakely."

"I only know what I read."

"You said there was an international demand for his paintings and that there was more than one exhibition."

"Yeah, there was the one here last month, and the one coming up in London."

"What?"

"I assumed you knew. I mean it was in the *New York Times* last weekend. There's a bunch of American artists exhibiting in London this summer and Blakely's one of them."

Spracklin began going through things in his head. "Do you still have the paper?"

He heard MacLean flipping through papers. "Sure. I usually take a week to read the Sunday Times and then buy the next issue on the coming Monday." There was a pause in the search. "Yeah Jimmy, there's an exhibit of his work at Reinhold's Gallery in September. R-E-I-N-H-O-L-D. The paper's here if you want it."

Spracklin wrote down the gallery name, thanked him and hung up. He rubbed his eyes, took a sip of scotch. Blakely's work would be shown in London. There was no notice of it, no record in any of the evidence they had collected. Spracklin thought about it and nodded his head. It began to make sense. He flipped through the file and started to make assumptions.

He checked his watch. It was 4 p.m. – midnight in London. He had a contact, Chief Inspector Scott Avery, at Scotland Yard. It was too late to call him, but he'd get to him as soon as London was awake.

CHAPTER 48

Spracklin crouched and pointed the camera at the pile of sawdust in the corner. The camera and kitbag weighed on him, and he wobbled as he flashed the photo. He waited for the dead bulb to cool, then popped it out and placed another in the flash. He photographed the stubs of sawed planks that had been left behind from dozens of frames. He needed evidence in court – even circumstantial evidence – that there had been thirty, forty, fifty canvases painted by John Blakely.

The basement of 1340 Masonic was not as eerie as it had been four nights earlier. The lights were on now, and he could hear guitar playing upstairs. The freezer was open and unplugged and foul water had collected in the bottom of it. Across the hall, he could still see the blood stain on the concrete by the makeshift potter's wheel.

His knees creaked as he stood again. He felt re-energized and was putting the hell of the last few days behind him. A copy of the *Sunday New York Times* was folded in his camera bag. After he'd picked it up from MacLean, he'd read the article several times. He'd underlined the words "John Blakely".

The main story in the arts section was titled

> *The American Invasion*
>
> *Four years after the Beatles landed in New York, U.S. pop culture is swarming the British capital.*

The story was about the wave of young Americans flooding into London that year. A major retrospective by Roy Lichtenstein had been held at the Tate Modern in February, and young American actors like Dustin Hoffman and Warren Beatty were the toast of London. Rock groups like The Doors, The Grateful Dead and Jefferson Airplane would all play concerts in the city that autumn. And near the end of the article it mentioned that smaller galleries were hosting shows by up-and-coming American artists. They included "San Francisco hyper-realist John Blakely" who would hold a show at Reinhold's Gallery in September.

Spracklin shuffled to the top of the stairs. Several hippies he didn't know were milling about in the back parlor. They glanced at him then turned away, going back to making plans for the celebration of the solstice on Hippie Hill in three weeks. Word had got out there was space at the house, and a few drifters had decided to move in. He could hear the familiar guitar upstairs. He continued upstairs to John Blakely's room.

It was no longer Blakely's room. There was a new pillow and sleeping bag on Blakely's mattress, and two other bedrolls were stuffed into a corner. Someone had put up a fluorescent poster over part of Blakely's murals. In another corner, Spracklin could see the canvas of the dead flowers in a vase on its side. And slouched against the wall facing it was Jasmine, plucking her guitar. She gave no indication she'd noticed him. She sat there in a blue cotton night gown and strummed. He walked to the canvas as she began to sing.

> *January in Oregon, a sunny, salty day*
> *Noon up on a sandstone cliff, admiring foamy spray*
> *My second tin of Schlitz Bull, chased with airy brine*
> *How can I take this with me, this perfect place in time?*

She stopped playing when Spracklin took the canvas from the wall and turned it right-side up. He stepped back and looked again at the unfinished painting. The vase and drooping flowers took up the bottom third of the canvas. The empty space above that, where the live flowers should have been, seemed to symbolize John Blakely's life. It ought to have looked vibrant, but there was dreary void. Spracklin reached into his kitbag and took out another flashbulb.

"Souvenir?" Jasmine asked as Spracklin pointed the camera.

The camera exploded with light and he lowered his arms as his eyes again adjusted to the dimness of the room. "Evidence."

"Evidence of what, man? Like, that he did painting?"

He turned to face her, the poor girl burned out in her early twenties. "That's it exactly, actually."

He placed the cap on his camera and snapped shut his kitbag. "You once told me he was always painting."

"Right on. Dude was obsessed."

"So where are the paintings now?" She shrugged, started to play her guitar again, working into a song.

It was a question Spracklin should have asked himself days ago. Now he wondered if he was placing too much emphasis on it. Was he focusing on the missing paintings because he wanted to pin two murders on someone other than his daughter? He'd neglected to call in Burwell to help him with this part of the investigation – was that because Burwell would bring the discussion back to the owner of the denim jacket? Spracklin had gone over it again and again in his mind and he'd concluded: if he found the person with John Blakely's paintings, he'd find the murderer.

But still there were doubts.

"Jasmine," he said above the sound of the guitar. She looked up. "Have you seen anyone wearing a jean jacket with a willow tree embroidered on the back?"

She continued to play as she looked at him. Finally, she said, "Must be a big jacket if it's got an elm tree on it."

Spracklin turned away and shook his head. He usually put great stock in the testimony of the last person to see a victim alive. But Jasmine was useless. Utterly useless. He picked up the canvas, which was light if bulky, and she began to sing as he left the room.

> On blackened turf, 'neath mildrew sky
> By crumbling brick, they've crawled to die.
> A hot wind carrying sand and rust
> Blows carrion flesh to streams of dust

The canvas banged around as Spracklin carried it down the winding staircase and out on to the battered deck. It was dark now, and a fog had rolled in from the north – it was one of those fabled San Francisco summers. Spracklin had come to believe cops were at their most dangerous when they were certain they were right, but he felt sure he now knew who killed John Blakely and Derek Hodgson.

He put the canvas in the back seat of the Monaco. Before getting into the car, he took one final look at the house. He could hear Jasmine finishing up her song on the second floor.

> A child is born, too weak to cope
> Yet bears the weight of our great hope
> The strength to suckle one small boy
> And fill the craters of Hanoi
> And East Berlin and Central Prague
> Till roses fill each burnt-out crag
> A child is born, so carry on
> So carry on, so carry on

Yes, he thought. Carry on. He was worn out. He'd seen young people die. His daughter was with a violent drug dealer. His wife was estranged from him, maybe to an irreparable degree. But he would carry on.

CHAPTER 49

Spracklin was driving south through the fog on the 101, just turning off for the airport when he felt a smile cross his face. It was almost midnight and for the first time in hours he was thinking about something other than the Blakely case. The radio was on, and he was listening to Bobby Kennedy deliver a victory speech after trouncing McCarthy. Kennedy would be going to Chicago with all of California's delegates. He had the inside track for the presidency.

Spracklin had been working flat out for hours at the Hall of Justice. First he'd called Sherman Corbett, his favorite prosecuting attorney. Corbett was a veteran, a pro, and Spracklin liked him because he had excellent judgment. Corbett had been a prosecutor since the Depression, and had resisted the temptation of private practice because he felt it was his duty to prosecute criminals. He was measured, would assess what evidence was needed to bring a case to court and refuse to proceed before he had that evidence. The only problem with calling him in the evening was his wife was a crank. She was annoyed by these calls and Spracklin had to explain the case to her before she'd hand the phone to her husband.

Once Corbett was on the line, they discussed the case and Corbett saw the strengths. He agreed with Spracklin that they would find the murderer once they found the paintings.

Spracklin had carefully typed up an affidavit for a search warrant, making sure all the information was germane and understandable. He had to go through a relatively new judge named Veronica Mendes, a woman he didn't know. He called her to tell her he was certain he would have all the information that night that he needed for a search warrant. As a courtesy, he was letting her know he would probably call her in a few hours.

Then, shortly after 11:30, he called Scott Avery at home in London. He told him about the upcoming art exhibition at the Reinhold's Gallery. He needed to get the answer to one question and he needed it quickly: who was the middleman in America shipping over the paintings by John Blakely? Avery was on it and would likely have the answer by the time Spracklin called in a couple of hours. He could feel the excitement building in his chest. He was closing in on Blakely's killer.

At about 11:40, Spracklin got back in the Monaco and drove south to join the others at the airport. He wanted to be there when they captured Fox's mule. He flicked on the radio in time to hear the returns and Bobby's speech. His former boss had won 46 percent to McCarthy's 42 percent. Bobby would be the Democratic candidate.

Kennedy seemed weary and happy. The sound of his voice was enough to take Spracklin back seven years. He, Val and the kids set out for Washington to join the young president and his younger attorney general as they rallied the nation to a sense of duty. Maybe they would now join a new Kennedy administration. Maybe it would be good to get away from homicide, to let their boys see the East Coast. A job in Justice, a house in Bethesda, maybe even Georgetown, dinner with the family every night.

As the lights from the airport appeared through the fog, Spracklin listened to the candidate wrap up his speech. He expected to hear the standard RFK closer. Bobby always said that rather than looking at things as they are and asking why, he preferred to see things that hadn't happened and ask why not. But on this night he chose a simpler option. He simply thanked his supporters and said, "And on to Chicago, and let's win there." Spracklin broke into a grin.

Inside the airport, everything was calm. No one would have known three law enforcement agencies were conducting an operation in the arrivals lounge. He saw on the monitor the plane had landed and passengers were probably moving toward the customs hall. There were agents and officers he recognized in the crowd. Ed Burwell was at a Hertz counter talking to Merrill Flanagan. On an orange bench by the customs area, J.P. MacLean was chatting with some sidekick. Otherwise, it was just another night at SFO. About thirty tired and bored people, half white, half Oriental, waited for family, friends, business contacts and one drug smuggler. They didn't know that inside the restricted area, customs agents with eight detection dogs were going through every piece of luggage, emptying each one, measuring suitcase walls to make sure there were no hidden compartments. Most of these people would be waiting a while.

Burwell nodded his heavy head at Spracklin. The Lieutenant had called him earlier to relate the developments in the Blakely case. They both understood Spracklin was informing Burwell of developments, not asking him to help. The Sergeant seemed resentful. Spracklin didn't care. He needed to clear that case and Burwell had nothing to offer. Spracklin would soon start looking for a way to transfer him to another department.

"Nothing yet?" Spracklin asked him. He knew it was a stupid question. If they'd caught the mule, these guys wouldn't be standing around.

Burwell looked away and Flanagan shook his head. The only person who seemed interested in chatting was MacLean. The agent stood up and wandered over to the car rental counter.

"Lieutenant," he said.

Spracklin nodded.

"The flight is at the gate, passengers just beginning to disembark." He clearly wanted to make conversation. Spracklin remembered the drill from his days with Justice – always get on the good side of the locals.

"We gotta talk," said MacLean. "You know the Watkins case is tied in to the dead artist you're working on. We're going to have to work together on making cases."

Spracklin knew he couldn't raise his voice. He looked around the half-empty reception area and said. "So after you bust him, I write up the reports?"

"Look Jimmy, I respect your work – always have. But the murder of a federal agent is a federal case. Don't blame me – blame the Constitution."

Spracklin wanted to argue, but MacLean had helped him earlier in the day. MacLean had been too stupid to understand the importance of the Times article. But without MacLean, Spracklin would not have had the key clue. He said nothing and after a few moments MacLean skulked off to join his men.

Flanagan grimaced at Spracklin, obviously wanting him to be friendlier. Flanagan wanted this bust badly and didn't want any inter-squad rivalry disrupting things. He went over to chat with the agent, to make nice with the Feds. Spracklin's eye followed him and noticed the pilots and cabin crew were leaving customs, carrying their compact shoulder bags. Spracklin assumed that the customs agents had waved them through first as they concentrated on the intense search of the passengers.

Spracklin was always amazed at how refreshed the airplane crew looked at the end of a long flight. The pilots were erect as soldiers, the stewardesses had a spring in their step. They looked as if they'd just applied their heavy dollops of makeup.

One stewardess held Spracklin's attention. She was a trim young woman with her red hair in a bun. She was walking briskly with her head down, but what really stood out was the glint of a tiny metallic stud in her nose. It was rare to see someone with jewelry in their nose, even on Haight Street. But he'd seen it before. He was certain. As she reached the doorway, Spracklin remembered. The first night he went to the house on Masonic, a girl with a stud in her nose had been lounging on the sofa.

Spracklin lifted himself from the car rental desk and began to walk toward the door. It was a thin lead but it made sense. Fox needed someone making regular trips to the Far East. Spracklin's mind was working through the logic of it all when the first woman shrieked. "Sweet Jesus, no," he heard a voice scream as he walked abreast of the customs exit. The stewardess was now out in the night air, and he had to follow. Another woman behind him wailed in anguish.

He tried to concentrate on the girl. Fox needed a hippie, someone in his circle, who could travel regularly to Asia without raising suspicion. This girl would be the perfect candidate. For her, it meant she made great money and hung out on Haight Ashbury with minimal risk.

Spracklin stepped up his pace and tried to ignore the drama that seemed to be unfolding around him. People were turning to each other, trading news. People who had seemed to be strangers a moment ago were now embracing, trying to offer mutual strength. "Not again," a black soldier howled. Spracklin knew it was bad. Something must have happened to Bobby. But he had to focus on the girl.

He peered through the dirty glass door and saw the stewardess standing on the curb. The girl raised her arm and a burgundy Pontiac Parisienne pulled up. Spracklin pushed the door open so he could get a better look. His right hand was in his jacket, on the hand of his sidearm. If Fox was picking up the girl, he'd be there to arrest him.

The stewardess pulled the heavy door open and slid into the bench seat beside the driver. Spracklin came outside hunched over to get a view of the only other person in the car. He took his hand off his handgun. He paused long enough to commit the license plate to memory and ran across the road to the Monaco.

He would have to follow the car on his own. He knew it would lead him to Fox. The drug dealer had not been driving the car. The driver was Marie.

CHAPTER 50

The sight of a presidential candidate bleeding to death on a hotel kitchen floor broke the tension between them. Fox and Jethro were in a little den of a place off the Haight that Bogdan Polgar had lined up for them. The black-and-white TV was on with the sound down. Fox had caught sight of one of those news bulletin signs and they both turned to the TV. There was a grainy image of Bobby Kennedy lying on the floor surrounded by people. They were loosening his tie. He was staring at the ceiling.

"A mob hit," Fox said.

Jethro nodded. "Payback for his time as AG." They were sitting on the sofa and had the scales on the coffee table. Neither of them had the expertise to test the purity of the stuff, but they'd weigh it once it arrived. They'd pay the girl and be out of that house in a matter of minutes.

Fox walked over and adjusted the rabbit-ears, trying to get a better picture on the TV. "So when they get here, you leave her alone," he said.

"You said we needed her for the pickup. The pickup will be over."

Fox waited a moment before speaking. "Don't touch her."

"Her old man is—"

"I'm her old man now. Don't touch her."

Jethro would see. She was running errands. In the next day or two, she would help sell the shit. They'd test her. Then he'd get out of her whether she'd killed Blakely. She could be an asset.

"I don't trust her."

Fox wheeled around, dropping the antennae to the floor. "I do and that's what matters. Why don't you head up to the Drug Store Café? It's better if you're not here when they get back. We'll be there in half an hour."

"You're going to sell the shit yourself?"

Jethro looked at him. The big guy understood that they had to move the shit fast. But Fox also didn't want to get sloppy. They heard the key in the lock on the front door. Fox gestured to the back door and his partner nodded once and left by the rear.

231

CHAPTER 51

Jimmy Spracklin needed all his powers of self-control as he followed the Pontiac Parisienne north on the 101. He kept his eyes two cars ahead, and tried to think through the problem. He had to be calm or everything he loved would be torn to pieces. He left the radio off. He had to think about the task at hand.

He couldn't radio for assistance. His daughter was transporting imported narcotics. She was at the very least an accomplice. She may be an accomplice to murder. He had to bust Fox and get Marie the hell out of there before any other cops arrived. It would cost him everything if things went wrong, but he had to protect Marie.

She drove calmly, at about 55, through the light traffic. Her tail lights glowed red in the light fog as she came to the end of the 101. Spracklin slowed, followed her across Market, down a block and pulled over as she turned left. She was heading back up Haight Street. He waited a second then followed her.

The Parisienne proceeded slowly up the great hill. In the tenements and houses on either side, he could see the flickering of television light in darkened rooms. Several groups of black people were on their stoops, leaning in to transistor radios. Spracklin flicked on the radio.

A reporter was racing through a description of the bedlam at the Ambassador Hotel in Los Angeles. Robert Kennedy had been exiting through the kitchen of the hotel when a man moved in front of him and shot him twice in the head. The man was in custody. Kennedy had been taken to the hospital. Spracklin switched off the radio. He would mourn his mentor later.

Marie pulled suddenly into Lyon Street, giving Spracklin no choice but to drive on along Haight. Glancing over, he saw the Parisienne pull up to the curb. Spracklin parked by the sidewalk on Haight. He jumped from the car, walked to the corner, peered around the wall of a corner store.

Marie and the stewardess had left the car and were walking to a small modern house on the east side of the street. The stewardess was carrying her hand-luggage. The streetlight provided just enough light through the fog for Spracklin to study the building – probably two bedrooms upstairs, three communal spaces downstairs. It was an infill construction, built between two older residences. The girls entered without knocking. There were lights on in the front room, but the blinds were down so Spracklin could see no one.

The Lieutenant slipped his hand in his jacket and placed it on the grip of his handgun. He flicked off the safety and looked again at the building. He expected Fox to be there, possibly Jethro. Maybe there would be more armed men with them, but he doubted it. Fox's ranks had been thinned out. There would also be two women – one of them his daughter.

He walked across the foggy street and paused by the downstairs window. He could hear voices inside, a man's voice and at least one woman. Withdrawing his revolver from its holster, he moved to the door, turned the knob and slowly pushed it open.

He peered through the crack, making sure there was no one in the hall. He was at a huge disadvantage. If he did see anyone, his first task would be to make sure it wasn't Marie, then to defend himself. They would have time to fire first. The hall was empty. He stepped inside and closed the door. To his right was a stairway, and he could hear someone walking around upstairs. The steps were light, probably one of the women. Beyond the stairs was the door to the living room, and straight ahead the kitchen. He raised the gun and stepped to the living room door.

Andy Fox and the stewardess were seated on a sofa against the far wall. On the coffee table before them, the girl's shoulder bag was open. Fox had tossed clothes and makeup kits on to the matching chair. The black and white television was on, but the antenna had been knocked over, and there was nothing on the screen but a salt-and-pepper distortion. Fox was using his knife to cut through the bottom of the bag – obviously a false bottom. He finished and placed the knife down on the table. The knife looked like a switchblade to Spracklin, the blade about six inches long. It could have been the knife that had killed Elizabeth Watkins.

"Oh baby," said Fox as he reached into the bottom and pulled out three plastic bags, each about the size of a cassette tape. "You are the best, Sarah – the best." He looked in and smiled, suggesting there were more pouches inside, as Sarah looked at the doorway and screamed.

"Don't move, Fox," said Spracklin as he stepped into the room. The drug dealer's right hand was inches from the knife, and they both knew Spracklin would kill him if he tried to grab it. "With the back of your hand, flick the knife on to the floor." Fox hesitated for a second, then did as he was told.

Holding the gun on Fox, Spracklin told Sarah to move to the far corner and place her hands on the wall. She wouldn't have had a weapon on the plane, and he was willing to bet she didn't have one now. Then he told Fox to turn, spread eagle and place his hands on the wall.

"How'd you find me, Jimmy?" Fox said as the Lieutenant began to frisk him. Spracklin held the gun in the small of Fox's back as he checked around the ankles. Fox glanced over his shoulder and asked, "Your little girl tell you where we were and when the plane came in?"

Fox was talking. Spracklin wanted to keep him talking. "Discipline and hard work," he said. He patted around Fox's belt and chest.

"That doesn't tell me anything."

"You and I have something in common, Andy. We both run disciplined organizations." He stepped back and let Fox turn around. The drug dealer was displaying the same arrogance as the night before on the catwalk at Vague Dimensions. Spracklin knew he had to be careful. This was not a beaten man. Spracklin retreated to the doorway so he could see the whole room. "I was at the airport. I recognized the stewardess – she was at the house on Masonic on Friday. The rest was easy."

Fox smiled and nodded.

"I'm a lot like you, Andy," he said. Fox raised his eyebrows asking him to explain further. "You run a tight ship, Raven. You suspected her so you finished her off. And then there was The Mantis. He ran out on you and you went all the way to Fresno to take care of him."

Fox broke into a laugh, which could barely be heard because of the sound of the stewardess crying in the corner. "So is this where we engage in conversation and I confess to everything?"

"It would be nice."

"Sure we killed Raven – she was a narc. ..." Fox kept on talking, but Spracklin didn't hear him. By his left ear, he heard the unmistakable sound of a gun being cocked. He felt the cold steel nozzle against his temple.

"... doesn't really matter now," Fox said.

Spracklin looked over and saw a Colt Python pointing directly at his head. Holding the gun was a burly man – about six-five, probably 240 pounds – with straggly blond hair falling to his shoulders. Jethro, Fox's muscle. The giant stared over the barrel of the handgun at the detective.

"Drop the gun, Jimmy, and kick it over there," said Fox, gesturing to the doorway.

Spracklin forced himself to remain calm and assess the situation. He was sure Marie was in the house. If he could play for time, Marie might sneak out and go for help. He stooped and dropped his gun on the floor. With the outside of his foot, he kicked it so it slid past Jethro's feet. He expected Fox to retrieve it, but instead Fox picked up his knife. He stood smiling in front of the Lieutenant.

Spracklin instinctively raised his hands, but felt an iron grip on his left wrist. Jethro had grabbed it and quickly twisted it behind Spracklin's back. Spracklin struggled, but couldn't match Jethro's strength. In a second, both his hands were pinned behind his back and he was defenseless as he faced Fox with his knife.

"Sarah, you should leave," said Fox. The girl had been looking for her chance to flee, and she bolted.

"Now," said Fox. "How did you know where we were?"

Information. Fox wanted information. He was worried about snitches in his organization. He wouldn't kill Spracklin until he had what he needed.

"I told you, good police work."

Fox looked past Spracklin to Jethro and gave a slight nod. Jethro swung Spracklin around and slammed him into the wall. Before Spracklin could gain his balance, Jethro hammered him with a right to his gut. As the air flew from his chest, his knees buckled. Jethro's follow-up left with the pistol butt grazed his head.

Spracklin gasped, trying to draw air into his lungs as Jethro straddled him.

"Who told you?" asked Fox.

"We just found out."

Jethro pistol-whipped his face three times. The blows knocked Spracklin's head from side to side. The pain shot through his skull and he struggled to retain his composure.

"Who. Told. You?"

"Raven."

"Bullshit. We made sure she only knew about a phony drop. The Feds' response blew her cover."

Spracklin got his forearm in front of his face to protect against the next blows, so the big man stood erect and kicked him twice in the chest.

Spracklin again struggled for breath. He knew the struggle had lasted long enough that Marie must have had time to get out of the house. She must have. He knew he was going to die but at least Marie would be all right. He was about to say it was Reg MacIntosh when Jethro stepped back. Spracklin pushed himself up and looked at them. The pain made it difficult to speak or move.

"All right," he mumbled. He could barely move his jaw. "All right."

Fox squatted beside him and pricked his throat with the point of the blade. "I don't want any bullshit."

"No, no," muttered Spracklin. He breathed heavily and felt the pain of Fox pressing the knife deeper into his flesh.

"It was . . . He told us in jail, under—"

He never got the name out because of a deafening explosion. It was a gun shot. Spracklin tensed, knowing that Jethro had shot him. But there was no pain. Only the thud of the big body hitting the floor.

With his ears ringing, Spracklin thought he heard Fox say the word, "Honey?" Lowering his arms, Spracklin looked up and saw Jethro lying beside him. The Colt Python was on the floor. The left side of Jethro's head was missing, and blood and brain were spilling down the dead thug's face. Spracklin shot a quick glance at the door. Marie was standing with both hands clasped on his Smith and Wesson revolver, which was still smoking. She was pointing it at the big man, making sure Jethro was dead.

"Honey," said Fox again, rising to face her. Spracklin suppressed the pain in his ribs and twisted on to his forearms and knees to get Jethro's gun. In a second, he had it. He rolled on his back and trained the weapon on Fox, who was now moving at him with the knife. Spracklin cocked the gun and Fox stopped.

Marie pointed the Smith and Wesson at Spracklin, then at Fox. The gun was trembling. "Get back, Andy." She was trying to speak with a steady voice.

"He wants to—"

"I said, Get back," she screamed.

Fox stepped back. He held his gaze on Spracklin, the knife ready.

Marie was shaking. She turned the gun on her father now. "Both of you," she said. "Put your weapons down." Tears were beginning to flow down her cheeks.

Fox held fast to the knife. Spracklin kept his gun trained on the dealer. With his left hand, he pushed himself up, struggling to stand.

"He's going to kill us," said Fox. Spracklin knew that was a mistake. Marie would know he could never hurt her.

"Put the knife down, Andy," she said. "Put it down."

"Marie, sweetheart," said Spracklin. Sweetheart had always been his pet name for her.

"Put it down, Daddy."

She had the gun trained right at his head. He was looking into her eyes and she was returning his gaze. Her expression dissolved to one of pleading. They both knew she could not shoot him. Spracklin kept his gun on Fox. He knew how dangerous the man was with a knife in his hand.

Marie jerked the gun back. She put the nozzle in her mouth and winced, the gun was burning her lip. She took it from her mouth, placed it under her chin.

"No," screamed Spracklin and Fox simultaneously.

"Put them down," said Marie, with the handgun pointing at her own head. Her voice was firm now. She seemed prepared to die rather than be disobeyed.

"Don't do it, Marie," said Fox. "Baby, don't hurt yourself."

"You were going to kill my father."

"It was self-defense. He'll kill us just like he did your friend who went to Nam."

She pressed the barrel, cooler now, deep into her mouth. "Put. It. Down."

Fox looked at her longingly. It was almost as if he forgot there was a policeman ten feet away pointing a gun at him. He bent down and placed the knife on the table. "Honey, just don't hurt yourself."

Spracklin held his gun firm and glanced back and forth between them. He didn't like his chances if they disarmed him.

Marie removed the barrel from her mouth and pressed it to her temple. "Drop your gun, Daddy," she said.

"I can't do that, Sweetheart." She knew he was a police officer. He could never surrender his gun in this situation.

"I don't know if I can live in your world, or in Andy's world. And I can't live if you two kill each other. Put the gun down."

"Baby, pull the gun back," said Fox.

Spracklin studied both of them. Fox hadn't shown any emotion that his partner had just been killed, but he'd surrendered his knife because Marie had asked him. He loved her. And she loved him. Spracklin had to understand that she loved Fox, and that she had the potential to kill herself within seconds. Spracklin slowly bent his knees and lowered the gun to the floor, placing it so he could grab it instantly with his right hand.

He stood and, like Fox, raised his hands.

They stood there, the three of them, glancing back and forth, suspicious of each other.

"Now you put your gun down, Marie," said Fox.

"Just lower it, move it away from your head," said Spracklin. Fox's knife was on the table, elevated. Fox would be able to grab it before Spracklin could grab the gun from the floor.

"Hold on to your gun, honey," said Fox. "And I can tie him up and we can get out of here."

"You killed that girl, Raven," she said. Fox started to respond but she cut him off. "I heard you. You admitted killing her."

She put the barrel in her mouth once more. She was crying again.

"Marie, my sweet Marie, just lower the gun and we can discuss this," said Spracklin. He didn't need to accuse Fox now. She was beginning to understand his capacity for evil. He just had to get the gun away from her head.

She pushed the nozzle further into her mouth, not sure what else to do.

"Marie, don't hurt yourself," said Spracklin. "I'm struggling to go on without Mr. Kennedy. I can't lose you too."

She pulled the gun out. "Mr. Kennedy?"

"Mr. Kennedy was shot tonight, Sweetheart. He's probably—"

"It's a trick, Marie. Don't listen to him."

She pulled the gun an inch from her mouth. "Mr. Kennedy?"

"He was shot after winning the primary." Spracklin gestured to the television and the aerial lying on the floor. "He's probably going to die. It's on all the TV stations. Check if you don't believe me."

Marie's face melted into a look of horror. She lowered the gun and reached for the television aerial. It was enough. As Fox grabbed the knife from the table, Spracklin swept up Jethro's pistol, praying it was loaded. Fox dove at him with the knife poised to strike just as Spracklin squeezed the trigger. The report was deafening. The bullet caught Fox in the right shoulder. He spun in mid-air. The knife flew from his hand and struck the far wall. He landed on his back.

Marie dropped the gun and ran to the fallen man, who lay grimacing beside Jethro. Spracklin struggled to stand and picked up his weapon. He rubbed his hands all over the revolver to make sure only his fingerprints would be on it.

Marie was holding Fox's hand and crying. Fox was on his back, his left hand cover the wound, blood oozing out between his fingers. Spracklin doubted the wound was fatal. The Lieutenant was beginning to pat him down when he heard the front door fly open and someone holler, "Police."

"It's Lieutenant James Spracklin in the living room on your right," he responded. "I've got two suspects down and...their hostage."

Two uniformed men edged into the room, their weapons drawn. They studied Spracklin, and one seemed to recognized him. They glanced at the powder on the table, and the two bleeding men on the floor. "We got calls. Neighbors heard gunshots."

Spracklin stood and nodded. "There was a struggle, a fight." He motioned to Jethro. "I shot him during the struggle. He pointed to Fox. "This one I shot with his own pistol. Don't touch that knife over there – it was used to murder a federal agent."

The officers looked puzzled, possibly because one officer shot two men with two guns, possibly because of the girl crying over the wounded hippie.

"Call an ambulance," Spracklin said. He crouched again and continued to frisk Fox. Spracklin didn't believe the guy's only weapon was his knife. "This man needs medical attention."

Then he stood and looked down at Fox, who lay bleeding on the floor, accepting the pain. Fox gazed up at him and smiled. "You killed Jethro but I'm going to make it," he said. He closed his eyes.

Spracklin gently put a hand on Marie's shoulder. She stood, wrapped her arms around her father and sobbed. He held her tight. He squeezed her and patted her back. Fox was going to go along with the story that he, Spracklin, was the one who shot Jethro. The drug dealer did love her.

CHAPTER 52

Spracklin had draped his jacket over Marie's shoulders and poured them both a shot of scotch from the bottle in the desk drawer. He knew they had to get things straight before the empty office started filling up, which could be any minute. The clock on his office wall read 2:15. Burwell, Flanagan and the Feds would go to the house on Lyon. The Feds would stay there but Burwell and Flanagan would come looking for him.

Spracklin was typing on three-ply forms, scrambling to create a statement from Marie before the others arrived. He was almost finished when her feeble voice broke the silence. "Got another shot?"

Spracklin finished the sentence he was working on. It was enough. He looked over and was shocked. He studied his daughter as she clutched the coat and held out her paper cup. There was a darkness under her heavy eyes, a line at the corner of her mouth when she grinned. She was asking for another shot of scotch. She'd killed a man that night to save his life. It had been a year since they'd sat together. In that time his little girl had become a woman. He wanted to rush to her and hold her, but he had business to attend to.

He produced the bottle from the desk drawer and splashed some scotch into her cup. He slid the triplicate form over to her, and handed her a pen.

"It's your statement," he said. "You describe how you were at the house through the evening upstairs. Sometime after midnight, you heard a fight downstairs and then a gunshot. You came to investigate and found Jethro on the floor, and me with a gun. Fox took you hostage, holding a knife to your throat. When he was distracted by a car outside, possibly the squad car, you wiggled free and I shot him in the shoulder."

She took another sip of scotch.

"I can't let you go to prison, Marie." He had to reach her. "Whatever mistakes I've made in the past, we can discuss them. We'll discuss your mistakes as well. But we have to act quickly to keep you out of jail. If we don't work together, we both go to prison."

She looked up.

241

"I'm falsifying evidence in a homicide. I get caught and my career is finished. Everything your mother and I have worked for is crushed. I'll go to prison." She looked away from him. "And I'd do it in a second. I wouldn't regret it for an instant. I love you so much I'd sacrifice my world for you."

She turned back to him and held his gaze. It was not as loving or as appreciative as he'd been hoping for. But it was good enough. She picked up the pen and signed the bottom of the sheet.

Spracklin nodded. He took the forms, tossed away the two sheets of carbon paper and put her statement in a file.

"Now I need to know some things." He spoke softly, but she shrank back in the chair, as if he were bawling her out. She was in no state for an interrogation. "You need to be strong, Marie. I need information. How much did you do for Fox?"

"Nothing. I, we . . ." She had trouble speaking.

"I understand. You were lovers. In the loft at Vague Dimensions." Now she looked shocked, wondering how he knew. "I'm not asking about your personal life. I need to know if you helped him with any of his criminal tasks."

"No."

"But you picked up his mule at the airport tonight."

She took a deep breath. "He told me – he said he needed a favor – he wanted me to go to the airport to pick up Sarah." She placed her cup on the desk. "I had no idea what she was carrying. I only saw it after, after things went down tonight."

He crumpled the paper cups and placed them in the ashtray. "Your jean jacket," he said, "the one with the tree on it."

"I lost that when they closed down Vague Dimensions."

"We have it now. There's red stuff splattered on the left sleeve."

"It's dye. Made from beetroots. I was making twine belts and wanted to die them red. It splattered."

He nodded. He put the paper cups in the ashtray and lit them with his lighter. "That jacket is gone for good. Don't ask about it. And don't admit it was ever yours."

He lit a cigarette off the burning cups and glanced up to make sure she understood.

"You worked at Vague Dimensions?" She nodded. "And Tony Weinacht gave you the job?"

"Yeah."

"And he owns Tableaux and Trinkets in North Point?"

"Yeah, of course. He says he wants to be a multimedia cultural entrepreneur."

"Did you wear the jean jacket anywhere in his gallery."

"Yes. It's where I was working on a tapestry, and my belts. He was going to display it for me at his gallery."

"Where were you working?"

"In his basement."

"Where they also make jewelry – or trinkets as the name says."

"Yes. Have you been there?"

Outside the office, the lights came on, and Burwell and Flanagan strode into the room. There were two uniformed officers with them.

"No."

"Then how did you know?"

"It just all made sense."

Burwell opened the office door and came in. Flanagan knocked and entered as well.

"You okay?" Flanagan asked.

Spracklin shrugged. "Marie," he said. "Sergeant Burwell and Lieutenant Flanagan. Gents, my daughter." They looked at her, unsure what to do. "Marie has been traumatized this evening. She heard the shots when I neutralized the threat from one man, she was held hostage and witnessed me disarming another. I've taken her statement. She won't be answering any more questions."

There was a finality in Spracklin's voice. He knew they didn't like it, but no one outranked him. And he was the one who'd apprehended Fox and his shipment. He would be a hard man to try to overrule that night. They looked at each other and were distracted only by the sound of the elevator in the hallway.

A moment later, Valerie walked around the corner. Her cheeks were awash with tears as she stood and looked at her daughter. She could only speak one word, "Baby."

Marie smiled. She stood and ran to her mother's embrace. The men in the office watched as the two women cried in each other's arms.

With a cigarette dangling from his lips, Spracklin managed a smile too. He had returned Marie to her mother.

"Pretty good night's work, huh Jimmy?" said Flanagan.

"It's not over yet." He took a drag on his cigarette and looked at the clock. It was 2:30.

"We're writing reports now?" asked Burwell.

Spracklin shook his head. He looked again at his wife and daughter embracing in the middle of his department. He blew out a stream of smoke and said, "Sometime in the next half hour, my phone's going to ring. They're going to give me one name. We're going to get a search warrant approved and we're going to search Tableaux and Trinkets gallery. All before sunrise."

"Why?"

"Because its owner, Tony Weinacht, murdered John Blakely and Derek Hodgson."

CHAPTER 53

It was convenient that Anton Sebastian Weinacht lived in the upstairs portion of the Tableaux and Trinkets gallery on Filbert Street in North Beach. It meant that Spracklin only needed a search warrant for the one building, which Judge Veronica Mendes gruffly signed at three-thirty that morning. Minutes later, Spracklin, Burwell and Flanagan were driving through the fog to exercise the warrant.

"The big mistake I made was not needling Jackson more about his report," Spracklin said as he drove. Flanagan was beside him.

"What report?" asked Burwell from the back seat. He had said little all evening, still stewing that Spracklin had proceeded alone.

"It's in the file," said Spracklin as they stopped at a red light. "Jackson interviewed Weinacht last week but thought his name was Vinott – V-I-N-O-T-T. I think it was because of the guy's accent. I should have made sure that he'd checked the spelling."

The streets of the city were empty, but in the cream-colored tenements of Grant Street, they could see the flickering lights of television sets. People were watching the news, trying to come to terms with the second assassination in six weeks. Spracklin had turned the radio on long enough to know that Kennedy was in critical condition, Ethel was with him and Ted was en route.

"If I'd known that Tony Weinacht owned the gallery with a jewelry shop, and was always hanging around the Haight, I think I would have pieced it together quicker."

The car turned on to Filbert Street. Spracklin parked and cut the engine. They looked across the street, and through the fog they could just make out the unlit sign. Four uniforms in a squad car were already parked at the far end of the street. In between them, Spracklin could barely read the sign above the dark windows.

TABLEAUX AND TRINKETS
Fine Art and Jewelry

"I think we should nail the prick just for putting that faggy X on Tableau," said Burwell.

245

Flanagan chuckled. "We'll run it by the prosecutor," said Spracklin. He threw his right arm across the seat and turned to look back at Burwell. He didn't let on how much it hurt his ribs to turn. "But we're not going in there like we're here to nail anyone, right?"

Burwell glowered in the darkness of the back seat. "Then why the fuck are we here?"

"To get a confession. We have to close the net on him."

"We've got enough to bust him."

"Almost. We need a confession." He let the importance of the statement set in. "All I want you to do is go into his office—"

"I know. Jesus Christ. Find files on Blakely and shipping receipts."

"Well make sure you do. You've been bitching about being left behind. Start to act like a goddamned investigator."

Burwell pulled up the door handle and stepped out of the car. Spracklin looked at Flanagan, who nodded his support. They got out and Spracklin, clutching his file on Blakely, strained to stand erect. At the far end of the street, four patrolmen and a German shepherd began to move toward the gallery.

Standing by the door, Spracklin knew he had to clear the case that night. He breathed deep and let the light drizzle fall on his forehead. The floodlights illuminating Coit Tower sent a satanic glow through the fog and Spracklin felt as if he were standing in the midst of a shower of dull light that had no source. Marie and Valerie were reunited. Bobby Kennedy was dying. Fox was in custody, his henchman dead. Spracklin now knew he had to carry on and close this case. He thought of the words, *carry on.* Jasmine had ended her song with the words. He was carrying on.

The light upstairs flicked on after the first knock, and moments later they heard someone at the door. The man behind the door spoke with a German accent.

"I made a payment yesterday," he said.

Spracklin and Flanagan looked at each other. Flanagan was about to yell that it was the police, but Spracklin held up a hand to stop him. "What?" he called.

"I told you I made a payment. Bogdan knows I can't pay more for another week."

Spracklin nodded.

"Anton Weinacht, this is the police," he said. "We have a warrant to search these premises."

The door opened, and a disheveled Tony Weinacht looked out at them. As they'd arranged, Spracklin stepped into the gallery and thrust the papers at the owner.

As he explained the finer points of the warrant, the policemen filed in behind him. The gallery was a wide, spare room, with a high ceiling. On the walls were large canvasses of winter landscapes with muddy roads. There were showcases in the middle of the room displaying knickknacks and items of jewelry. Marie had told them that Weinacht's office was at the rear on the left, and the entrance to the basement and the upper floor were in a passage on the right. Burwell and the patrolman with the German shepherd went directly to the office.

"Why are you in my gallery?" asked Weinacht.

"We had some things to follow up on," said Spracklin. "When we interviewed you the other day, you didn't mention that you owned this gallery as well as Vague Dimensions."

Weinacht wasn't sure what the Lieutenant was after. "It didn't seem relevant."

"Is Fox here?"

"No."

"Has he ever been here?"

"Why are you coming here at four in the morning to ask me these—"

They were interrupted by the sound of the dog barking in the office. Spracklin motioned for Weinacht to turn around and go to the office, and Weinacht led him into a cluttered room with a large desk and three metal filing cabinets. Burwell was seated behind the desk rifling through papers in the drawers. The detector dog was barking at the lower drawer of the left-hand cabinet.

"It's locked, sir," said the patrolman.

"Open it," Spracklin told Weinacht.

"But I can't."

"We have a warrant. We'll break it open if we have to."

Weinacht let out a long sigh, and picked through a pencil holder for some keys. He fumbled with them but soon opened the cabinet drawer. Inside Spracklin saw a stack of random papers, a handgun and an assortment of junk. Amid the jumble of knickknacks and office supplies was a small vial half full of white powder.

"Don't touch that," said Spracklin, as he put on rubber gloves. "But tell me what that is."

Weinacht said nothing. The Lieutenant placed the vial in a plastic bag and began to read Weinacht his Miranda rights.

"Bingo," said Burwell, interrupting Spracklin. As the Lieutenant finished, Burwell pulled a folder from the drawer. It was labeled "John Blakely". Weinacht gazed at it as Spracklin finished reading his rights. Spracklin could see a flicker of anxiety in the gallery owner's eyes.

"Yes, John Blakely," said Weinacht. "Yes, I handled him and sold his paintings. A tremendous talent."

Spracklin didn't mention Weinacht had denied knowing Blakely a day before. Not yet. He wanted the guy to talk. The Lieutenant placed the file on the desk and began to flip through the pages. Just like the papers in Blakely's closet, there were letters written on multi-colored paper. And each letter was uniform in color – if the first page was lime green, each page that followed was lime green. Spracklin looked for an orange sheet and found only one. He pulled it out and inspected it.

"Mr. Weinacht," he said. "It seems all these letters were signed by John Blakely."

"Yes, we had an active correspondence. He liked to tell me the philosophy behind his work."

"My point is these letters" – he flipped through the papers – "were all signed. But this one, this letter on orange paper, ends mid-sentence."

He held up the orange sheet so they could both read it. The final two sentences read:

> *I won't waste my time on frivolous optimism. I believe*

"No punctuation at the end. No signature."

"So what?" Weinacht showed his disgust by pronouncing the word Vatt.

"Did Blakely ship any paintings to you before he died?"

"Nothing."

"And did you represent him in talks with others?"

"What the hell does this have to do with anything at four in the morning?"

"Just answer the question."

"I organized one show of John Blakely's work. We corresponded. That is it. Now you're trying to ruin me."

His voice tapered off as Spracklin held up the copy of the New York Times with the words "John Blakely" underlined in red. They could hear the other policemen rooting through the building.

"He has a show coming up in London," said Spracklin.

"That – it has nothing to do with me."

"I'm afraid it does."

Spracklin was about to go on when one of the patrolmen came in. "Sir," he said.

248

"Like you said, there's a workroom downstairs – looks like they make jewelry."

The Lieutenant nodded. "And."

"There's a shelf, jars of chemicals. One of 'em is labelled silver cyanide."

"I know nothing of that," yelled Weinacht. He started to shake.

"You're sure?" Spracklin's voice was soft and controlled.

"Of course. Why wouldn't I be sure?"

"If we find your fingerprints on that vial, it will look suspicious. My contact at Scotland Yard visited the Reinhold Gallery in London an hour ago."

Weinacht stood twitching. He was trying to respond but couldn't. Above them, two of the patrolmen were shouting to one another.

"Nigel Reinhold showed the Chief Inspector in London the agreement you signed to ship thirty-four paintings by John Blakely. He's sending the agreement to me. Air mail. You signed it on May 30 – four days after John Blakely died."

Weinacht's shaking grew worse and he had to sit on the edge of the desk. Merrill Flanagan and a patrolmen burst through the door. They were about to speak but Burwell motioned for them to be quiet.

"Here's what I think happened, Tony," said Spracklin. He was standing beside Weinacht so his lips were inches from the trembling man's ear. "You told me you had debts to pay off, but I doubt a bank would back your businesses. And when we knocked earlier, you thought we were Polgar's thugs. So who lent you the money? Was it Bogdan Polgar?"

Weinacht fidgeted, and nodded. "He learned I was looking to open the club. He offered finance."

"Sure he did. But you didn't know his terms. And the kids aren't pouring into The Haight like they did last year. He was squeezing you for the money. And the best cash cow you had was John Blakely. Every couple of days Derek the soldier would show up with another canvas from Blakely. Nigel Reinhold said he expects you personally can pocket two thousand for each Blakely canvas they sell in London – enough to get Polgar off your back.

"But you had to get rid of Blakely. You couldn't afford to split the proceeds with him. And if he was dead, his paintings would be more valuable. So you made a gift. You mixed some cyanide from your jewelry shop with heroin and you gave it to him. You'd seen his tracks. You knew he'd take it. But you wanted it to look like a suicide. You needed a suicide note."

Spracklin took the orange sheet in his left hand, and drew a clear-plastic folder from his own file on the Blakely case. In it was the orange sheet they'd found in the pocket of Blakely's jacket, the supposed suicide note. "It seems to me, Tony, that these are the same letter. Same color paper. The first one has an incomplete last sentence. And this one –" he shook the evidence folder "– starts midway through a sentence."

He made a display of reading the note.

> *there's a night of eternal blackness, endless in both time and space and whatever other dimension Man may discover. All of which of course is impossible as black does not exist in nature. That's where I'm at. That's what I'm exploring.*
>
> *Yours with respect.*
> *John.*

Weinacht looked at the page through deadened eyes, and Spracklin could tell he wasn't reading. He was staring ahead and Spracklin just happened to be holding the page in front of him.

"You had your brainwave, Tony. You went through his letters and you found something that might serve as an artist's suicide note."

"We both know that's nonsense," said Weinacht without conviction.

"Tony, you know we have you," said Spracklin. He was acting like he was the suspect's friend. "You know I have enough to charge you, to take it to court. Make it easy on yourself." He paused to let it sink in. "Just tell me one thing, Tony. When you met with Blakely to give him the tainted heroin – was it at his house?"

He let the question hang in the air. The policemen were all staring at Weinacht, not daring to hope he was cracking. "Here," mumbled Weinacht. It was a single word that told Spracklin he'd broken the art dealer.

"When you met with him here, you found a moment to slip the orange paper into his jean jacket pocket. You buttoned it up and he didn't even know he had it."

"Yes, while he was in the toilet." Spracklin put the papers down and fished out his cigarettes. Weinacht accepted one. "Just before I gave him the vial."

"What did you tell him? Why did you make the gift?" Spracklin lit their cigarettes. Weinacht's trembled as Spracklin lit it.

"We'd just had a successful sale. It had produced enough cash for one payment to Polgar. But his thugs were hassling me every day, every night. Phone calls at 3 a.m. You're right: when you knocked just now, I thought it was Polgar's people."

The art dealer settled into the chair behind his desk. He took the cigarette from his mouth and stared at Spracklin. "Art dealers from around the world were contacting me. They wanted to display Haight-Ashbury art, especially this Blakely fellow. I had a trove of his work in my loft. If he were gone, I could sell the paintings, pay off Polgar and be clear of him. I could start over."

He was relaxing now that he had unburdened himself of his secret. Spracklin had seen this strange form of release many times before. Criminals relax after a confession. "Last Monday, Blakely came by, delivering a painting personally. He was excited. He was entering a new phase of his work. Decomposition. He was going to paint dead things, especially plants. He wanted me to do an exhibition on it. I agreed and told him to keep the paintings coming and we would display them all over the world."

He took another drag and butted the cigarette out on the wood panel of his desk. He studied the burned wood and concluded, "Then I told John Blakely, the most brilliant artist I've ever met, that he deserved a bonus for his inspired work. And I gave him heroin. He had no way of knowing it contained cyanide from my jewelry shop."

"And the soldier, Derek."

"He kept coming around. He was a bad junkie. He knew I had the paintings because he'd delivered them. He kept asking for them back. I think he wanted to sell them. He was desperate. He could have ruined everything. So on Sunday I met him on Haight Street – I didn't want him near my studio – and gave him the heroin near the park. From what I understand, he used it before he went three blocks."

None of the officers moved. None wanted to interrupt Spracklin's work.

"Tony, you've done the right thing telling us this. You've saved yourself a lot of pain, and pain for the families of these young men. Just to make sure, we should go over to the Hall of Justice, and we'll have you sign a statement."

"A confession. Of course." He searched his desk and took out a pack of cigarettes. "But I want the confession to include one undeniable truth." He paused to make sure he had Spracklin's attention. "That all I ever wanted to do was to give these kids a few places to create their art."

Spracklin looked at him and nodded. "It's part of the story. Yes, yes, we'll include that." He motioned Weinacht to the door, then said, "But before we go, we'll need to get the shipping manifest for the paintings."

Weinacht gave a slight smile and shook his head. Spracklin was surprised – he'd been so cooperative until then.

"They're upstairs, Jimmy," said Flanagan. "We came in to tell you but we didn't want to interrupt. He hasn't shipped them yet. They're in a loft upstairs."

Spracklin realized he was about to witness something important about the victim. He told Burwell to take Weinacht to the Hall of Justice and get his statement. And then he followed Flanagan and one of the patrolmen along the worn wooden floors and up two flights of back stairs. On the top floor they entered a high ceilinged store room with wooden shutters covering all the windows. The floor was broad rough-hewn planks and the walls were exposed brick. Two industrial lamps hung from the ceiling and shone on several rows of canvases wrapped in brown paper. The paper was torn off the canvas nearest the door and Spracklin stooped to study it.

It was about four feet by three feet. It depicted a cat sleeping peacefully on a stove. The colors were subtle, almost greyish, and the brush strokes were fine. It looked like a blurred photo. At the bottom was the signature:

John Blakely
18/4/68

Spracklin pulled the wrapping off another and found a painting of a cat giving birth to a puppy. The detail was revolting. It was exact. It was brilliant. There were five rows of about a dozen paintings each. There were more than Weinacht had promised to ship to England. The stash was probably worth a hundred thousand dollars to Weinacht. Maybe more.

Spracklin reached for another canvas and lifted it. He ignored the pain in his ribs and tore the brown paper off. Ants carrying off a butterfly wing. The next showed a kitten with deer antlers. Then a lamb ripping the flesh from a disemboweled lion. Spracklin felt tears seep down his cheeks. He had to see every instance of Blakely's brilliance. He had to understand the artist who spent days in a Victorian flophouse on Haight Street pouring his soul on to a stretched canvas. He found a painting of a shark's mouth with torn flesh trapped between the teeth. Blowfish in a bathtub. A Siamese cat with a blue jay in its mouth – the cat's eyes were the same hue as the bird's feathers. He stopped when he found a picture of withering chrysanthemums decomposing on the top of a compost heap. It had been painted on May 24 – days before the artist died.

Spracklin felt a deep sadness. Blakely should still be at his easel but Tony Weinacht had decided his death was less painful than the torture threatened by Bogdan Polgar. Just as he'd decided the world would be better without Derek Hodgson. And Andy Fox had decided the fate of Elizabeth Watkins and The Mantis. Just as two men had chosen to point guns at Martin Luther King and Robert Kennedy and pull the triggers.

Spracklin stood straight and looked at the paintings. He would see they were returned to Blakely's family. He knew Flanagan and the patrolman were staring at him with his wet cheeks. Flanagan stepped forward and placed a hand on his shoulder.

"It's been a rough day, Jimmy."

"A rough day, yes."

"Let me go and wrap up the paperwork on this."

"No, no."

"Go home to your family, Jimmy. Your daughter's home. They need you."

Wearily, Spracklin nodded. He reached up and patted Flanagan's hand. "I'll go home to them soon, Merrill. Right now I have to close the case. It's what we do. We close."

He turned to his friend and smiled. He stepped out of Flanagan's grasp and left the room. He strode down the stairs, out of the gallery and into the fog of San Francisco.

ACKNOWLEDGEMENTS

I began this book about two decades ago, shelving it several times to work on other projects and raise a family. During that time, many friends and colleagues offered advice and support on completing the manuscript. So, let me begin by apologizing to anyone who I have left of this list. There are so many people I want to thank and hope they know how much I appreciate their help.

The team at New England Publishing Associates has been invaluable. My original agent Elizabeth Frost-Knappman schooled me in crime writing in one short lesson. Her successor Roger Williams became my agent and then publisher. Many thanks to Roger and his team at Poplar Press for taking a chance on *The Haight*. I'd also like to thank my new agent, Andy Ross, for representing me. Denna Jiang of JXD Design & Art Studio produced a magnificent cover for the book, and Mike Hayes, Benjamin Sullivan and the team at Charcoal Marketing helped immeasurably with social media and IT.

Here are just a few of the people whose advice helped to shape this project: Stephen Bagworth, Rose Behar, Pamela Callow, Stephen Patrick Clare, Stannous Flouride, Ron Mitchell, John Morris, Tom and Sue Omstead, Don Sedgwick, and Dennis Turner. A huge thanks to all of them.

My business-obsessed children Cat and Scott deserve my thanks for putting up with parents who are strangely afflicted with a love of books. And finally, to my unfailing editor and love Carol, thank you for putting up with my moods, eccentricities and typos for all these years.